This is a continuation from Alwa

C000095308

The author worked for many years during the Cold
War in both America and the Soviet Union.

Dedicated to Northumbrian Beaches

CONTENTS

Always Never, George, I Spy would not have
been possible without
Sara Banerji, author and lecturer at Oxford University Department for continuing education.
And thanks to M J Porter, author, for the ebook and print copy..

CHAPTER ONE

Within Deep Earth Humanity, Mason, Barbara and Miss Moneylegs, the three survivors of the missing four from Earth Crust Humanity, failed to have any understanding as to why the shut down following the Whale Anomaly continued with even greater intensity. Perhaps an hour had passed since the Whale Anomaly had sucked out the Earth atmosphere for the precious CO_2 (Carbon dioxide) gases on which the shoal had gorged itself. They were gone; Earth Crust Humanity in a few moments had suffocated to death. The Whale Anomaly again searching the Universe for carbon gases.

Here, in Deep Earth, the three were surrounded by a deafening banging of? They didn't know, except it all started as the atmosphere disappeared, as the last of the green babies arrived into their new world, the green babies now a record of Earth Crust Humanity, the selfish, self-interested Earth Crust Humanity.

Clanging banging, banging clanging, underneath the symphony of noise a new hiss hissing sound. Air escaping? Did anyone know what was happening? Tony Computron, back with the three, at last opened his mind and as all Deep Earth Humanity communicated without speaking, told them Earth Crust was on the brink of a nuclear war. Those underground establishments that had existed since the start of the nuclear age continued to function, fully self-sufficient with independent supplies of breathable air, food, resources, generator's to support life for a few years. With no one to blame for mass ex-

1

tinction, the military were able to take the world; a handful of the nuclear club members about to conquer Mother Earth for themselves.

The Computron continued,

'There existed many thousands of survivors in their protected underground little towns, the problem being they were unable to communicate. With the Whale Anomaly, the shoal of hundreds feeding on carbon gases, the little ineffective communication satellites had disappeared with the frantic activity of sucking out those last life giving drops of carbon gases. So the military might of the world couldn't communicate with themselves or their old enemies. It would only take one press of one button to destroy everything and nothing.'

Amazed stupidity, explained the expression of Mason and Barbara, two old spies and Miss Moneylegs, the television presenter, even Bruce the dog, now adopted, looked puzzled. With nuclear weapons, the fear had always been that a nuclear war would wipe out humankind, now there was in effect no humankind only privileged bunkered military mankind. One didn't need to be very intellectual to think that surely the priority must be to create Earth Crust Humanity again, no power more important than everything.

At this point Miss Moneylegs decided her time would be best spent looking through the Ewewatch Library records, the all-telling records of everything that had happened on Earth Crust since the beginning. Since the death of George, the third old spy, she'd created a picture of his enormous intellect and now needed to understand why he'd been made out to be a mad scientist. Why had his ability never been recognized, why had his ideas, his experiments not entered mainstream academia?

She decided to pick up his life, when entering University in 1952. There she found him in the autumn of that year walking through an avenue of conker trees in Cambridge. His University scarf so long it could only be two or three joined together, with a young lady attached to each arm, George – female friends? No it must be another George. Miss Moneylegs was convinced that somehow a system failure had located the wrong George, so she commenced a new search.

That hiss hissing sound created a greater volume of noise than only a few minutes ago. Barbara turned to the Computron to enquire what the noise level meant. Tony Computron,

'You'd better sit down.' Bruce the dog acted immediately to the command to 'sit'. 'Prepare yourself for information you will not understand. ('Just like waiting for bad news from the doctor,' thought Mason.) That noise is the accumulated sound of the Founding-Protectors.'

At which profound moment Miss Moneylegs burst into the area shouting (over-excitement as there is no need to talk),

"I've found George in Cambridge toasting crumpets with crumpets."

That annoyed the Computron,

'Obviously you toast a crumpet with a crumpet; otherwise he'd be toasting bread or something else. Obviously a toasted crumpet is a crumpet.'

At which moment the Computron wanted to get back on the life and death subject, however Miss Moneylegs continued,

"Tony (Computron) don't you understand that at that time 'crumpet' had been in common usage to describe an attractive female, so George was toasting crumpets with attractive female students."

Tony felt that Miss Moneylegs thought him ignorant, he left. 'Oh no! Not another Computron strike,' thought Barbara. Excitement of the finding of George started to decline so Miss Moneylegs enquired what she'd missed.

The reply came from Barbara "The Founding Protectors make the hiss, hissing sound."

Miss Moneylegs felt a spider moment coming on as her legs turned to jelly. Her mind went numb. Mason caught her as she fell. George would not have been impressed by her fragility, but then the ego of those in the broadcasting world is fragile. Tony Computron returned thinking, 'well, perhaps I did misunderstand 'crumpet' however I didn't pass out; these Earth Crust human bodies are so frail. It's easy to overload their primitive brain.'

Deep Earth water passed over Miss Moneylegs. She regained some composure.

'Why does she still put red stiff on her lips?' the Computron thought. Now back as the font of all knowledge (except crumpets) his information about The Founding Protectors continued.

'In your astrophysics you call them 'Neutrinos' they pass through solids, they can go in the Earth one side and come out the other side. Your scientists calculate millions of neutrinos pass through your body, through me, every second. They've existed forever, your scientists' state they existed from the very instant of the BIG BANG. Your scientists had little knowledge of why they existed, why they exist. So you're privileged to hear them. I have not heard them before; none of the Elders have heard them before. It is only from the Library records that we as Deep Earth Humanity know a hiss hissing sound is made.'

'We're all privileged to hear a sound from the very beginning of time, The Founding Protectors are active.'

"Why now?" Miss Moneylegs, now recovered, asked the same question that both Mason and Barbara wanted an answer to.

The Computron continued,

'Deep Earth Humanity is trying to understand, is it the possible nuclear battle? Is it the stars jumping? Is it something to create a breathable atmosphere? Is it a response to the souls of all those suffocated together in the same moments? Is it something we are not yet aware off? We are trying to protect ourselves.'

Barbara questioned if the scientific world here had ever interacted with them. Then one of those Tony Computron silences. If he knew he wasn't telling. Mason held out two arms,

"So millions are passing through me, so I am as nothing to them, no barrier to their onward journey, no solid is a barrier to their outward progress. They must have a purpose. What is their source of propulsion?"

Miss Moneylegs started to feel uncomfortable, starting to scratch, thinking of midges during Scottish holidays. It must be time for her to go back to George with his crumpets. Bruce the Dog wondered if he could smell these neutrinos so decided to join Miss Moneylegs, having a good sniff en route. In their own ways they both wondered what George would make of the goings on of the Founding Protectors, of neutrinos?

To humans a dog responds to commands. 'They forget I have a brain,' thought Bruce. 'I can communicate if only those now dead humans would listen; down here they know that I think. That Computron knows that I have a worry about a nuclear war on Earth Crust, even I, a dog, understand it's pointless. Go on Founding Protectors sort them out,' he barked. Miss Moneylegs jumped at the noise.

"What are you barking at Bruce?"

"The stupidity of a nuclear war," he replied.

Miss Moneylegs froze on the spot. Which of the two was more amazed at the conversation was difficult to judge. Bruce stood still. They just looked at each other, until a passing child of Deep Earth Humanity remarked,

"Have you seen a ghost or are you learning to communicate together?"

In fact the three were communicating, a child of Deep Earth Humanity, an adult of Earth Crust Humanity and a dog. So the three sat down to have a talk on one of those many 'park bench' type seats, except this one was made of the useless item to Deep Earth Humanity called gold. In fact many things down here were made from this very abundant, cheap material of no value to anyone.

Out of the mouths of babes (the child),

"Are you afraid now that you can hear the Founding Protectors?"

A double yes from Bruce and Miss Moneylegs. The child continued,

"You shouldn't be, the Founding Protectors are here to protect Deep Earth Humanity."

With a hint of anger, Miss Moneylegs stated, "They should have protected Earth Crust Humanity."

"Why?" the child asked, "The Founding Protectors decided the Whale Anomaly was more important."

Bruce, "That's straight talking!"

The child continued, "I think Earth Crust Humanity only existed to produce CO2 gases to feed the Whale Anomaly. Why else would they continue to produce CO2 gases? I think their brains were adjusted so they couldn't understand the danger. CO2 gases were positive in their thought, nothing to worry about."

Miss Moneylegs, "Why don't the Founding Protectors stop asteroids hitting the Earth?"

"Why should they?" replied the child. "Are you saying Earth has a right of way as it travels through the Universe and anything else should get out of the way? Perhaps it is the Founding Protectors that keep the Earth just the correct distance from the Sun? Perhaps they provide what you call 'gravity'. Life is everywhere. You are blind to most things."

"You win," indicated Miss Moneylegs. "What is your name?"

"Call me Esamia."

"Do you remember George?" asked Miss Moneylegs.

"Yes," said Esamia, "he would have been a great 'Elder' here. He was so young when he died."

Bruce agreed.

"We're going to look back on his life," continued Miss Moneylegs, "would you like to join us?"

"No," replied Esamia, "the world of Earth Crust Humanity no longer exists."

At that point friends of Esamia arrived and she went on her way with them. Instantly, the Earth shook, everyone froze on the spot, within the same movement racing off to the nearest Ewewatch screen.

Miss Moneylegs knew instantly that on Earth Crust this would feel like an earthquake, a seismic event, feeling it so strongly down here meant a major event. Had one of the asteroids smashed into Earth? Bruce got to Esamia ahead of Miss Moneylegs. The children's faces were expressionless. They were looking at an enormous gapping deep scar, mile upon mile long, thousands of feet deep. Whatever had been there, no longer existed. They all waited to see where it had been. Which country on Earth Crust?

Barbara had gone over to the Library expecting to join Bruce and Miss Moneylegs. Finding them not in residence, she picked up the historical view of George herself, without any doubt it was George with three young female students. It fell to them to toast the crumpets whilst George went on and on about the evil of nuclear weapons. The three hung on every word he spoke, George pontificating, held court, all three girls obviously crazily in love with George. 'Oh! George,' thought Barbara, 'how did you go from this to be called a mad scientist?' She continued to view.

Somewhat nostalgic, Barbara thought back to her early 1950's. The Coronation of Queen Elizabeth II provided her first view of television, a small black and white picture in a very large brown box (television set). Then off to the local celebrations, like all other children she went in fancy dress. Children's races, egg and spoon, three-legged, the sack race. We were all given a Coronation Crown Coin in a presentation box. Why is childhood such a happy time of memories? It was only seven years since the end of World War II, life never easy. They conquered Mount Everest for the first time that year. She tried to recall if that 1953 Football Cup Final resulted in Blackpool and Stanley Matthews being the winners. She could consult the Library, not that important.

She had a faint memory of Ration Books, certainly you couldn't just go to the shop and buy sweets, and you needed a ration token and money. Did she remember sweets coming off ration and then having to go back onto ration because such demand had built up? School a long walk, yes walk, no family car. Mothers always there at the end of the day to collect the children. Autumn days remembered as foggy, the sun a soft pale yellow ball as fog started to lift! Oh yes! No central heating, cold mornings to get dressed, ice on the inside of windows. Those thoughts made Barbara think of the abuse of children, the abuse of materiality, the abuse of having too much. Abuse created within a consumer society, the 'I MUST HAVE' syndrome.

Miss Moneylegs, the expressionless children, with Bruce, all focused on the big screen. Where had the devastation taken place?

Barbara followed George through his three years of University, the ever-coming and going of female friends, his countless debates expressing his views with the most intellectually gifted 'Dons' of his College, the University in general. A debating society did not exist without the presence of George. Even before the end of his second year, George had received a position within the Foreign Office as long as he obtained a First. George a natural leader; a 'prima donna'.

Only Miss Moneylegs with Bruce continued to look at the screens, the bored children had left. The explosions had been a series of un-manned (no one being left to man them) nuclear power stations going active. Un-manned (no politically incorrect, should be un-personed). Why had none of those clever engineers thought of such an event? Part of Japan no longer there!

'Why call it Japan?' thought Bruce, 'bet the first humans who lived there never called it Japan or Nippon. Perhaps the first inhabitants called it simply home,' he thought. 'Then again did they have a word 'Home' or just grunt?'

Bruce, now perplexed thought 'why did those humans need such names, I know where I am by smell, how difficult life will be if the sensation of smelling no longer exists. How would they know danger if they can't smell it? How would they know fear if they can't smell it? How would they know time had come for sexual activity if they couldn't smell?'

He thought that they must have had the ability to smell things in their beginning. How can you live without the sensation of smell? Miss Moneylegs brought Bruce back to reality saying,

"Time to go back to the Library. Back to see what young George had been up to."

Barbara quickly brought them up to date to now show George entering the Foreign Office. Well, not yet entering. He was walking down from Leicester Square Underground station heading towards Big Ben. He looked every inch the gentleman; bowler hat, umbrella, black gloves, smart and conservative City suit, tall, lean and handsome. He walked, everyone walked, a few cars, many black cabs, an abundance of red London buses. Everyone walked, the traffic didn't move, a good old-fashioned traffic jam. George would have walked anyway, 'good for the constitution.'

Miss Moneylegs said it first but they'd all noticed, "People aren't eating in the street or walking along with plastic coffee cups."

The going to work commuters weren't fat. No one looked hungry. No one looked over-weight. Then she realized that there were no fast food establishments, Whitehall without polystyrene cups, burger boxes, and chocolate-bar wrappings. 'When did the human brain decide it needed to feed as it walked? Could it be when it was told to stop smoking as it walked?'

George didn't carry a cigarette, many others did. Even ladies were smoking. They were obviously ladies, as they didn't wear trousers. Coats, scarves, handbags, heels, smartly dressed but these were still the days of before 'You've never had it so good', pride in appearance Barbara reminded herself.

George progressed down Whitehall, a solitary policeman standing outside Number 10 Downing Street. No gates, no railings, no police with machine guns. 'How had it all gone so badly wrong? Must be CO2 emissions affecting the mind?'

More earth tremors as more Nuclear Power Stations exploded into nothing good.

Miss Moneylegs exploded, "Where were the coloured people?

Did George work in a world of only white people?"

She looked again and again, walking down Whitehall (irony, yes white people, Whitehall) she could see a coloured bus driver, perhaps two at least three bus conductors, that amounted to a sum total of no more than four out of a mass of many thousand. 'That must be a waft of pipe tobacco, so George when you were a twenties year old, many smokers, next to none-coloured people,' she thought, not racist, just a fact of that time. What would the BEEP make of this, no need of political correct-ness? (The BEEP is the fondly used name of the B.B.C., British Broadcasting Corporation.)

Hardened as a reporter a tear came to her eye as she thought of her struggles to become a reporter when preference always went to a member of the so-called ethnic minorities. 'Colour of skin, not ability the deciding factor. Again thinking it must be problematic when a simple walk down any high street had such a different appearance to George's younger time. Then again, I must ask Barbara and Mason, they grew up during such population changes. A London of only white faces. Unthinkable to Miss Moneylegs.'

Then a Big Ben filled the screen, another minor tilt, yes Big Ben tilts, not as much as the Tower of Pisa. The iconic London landmark is not as secure as the world might believe with its poor Victorian foundations. Victorian builders cutting corners to save money. Perhaps they didn't expect it to stand upright forever, or a Victorian conspiracy to build the Leaning Tower of Big Ben. In political terms, leaning to the right (Conservative) or left (Labour socialism), or a lesson not to take the center ground.

In deep thought Miss Moneylegs wondered what happened to the politicians of conviction, replaced by career seekers. Did these career seekers go into politics for politics? Did they go into politics to create a web of contact for after political life? Then a black thought. 'So we pay them so that they can create a future for themselves? Keep your names clean, don't offend the PARTY, get a seat in the House of Lords, that fatuitous pretense of Democratic institutions. The House of Lords shouts, 'don't reform me come and join me', vested interests keep me alive even if some of the occupants are half dead.'

George now entered that venerable institution, the Foreign and Commonwealth Office. Salute from the doorman, into cathedral like 'hush', up the sweeping staircase, paintings of the great and good. Row upon row of fine large wooden doors, into one and closing, then the sound of 'Good Morning.' A little line of female staff to relieve him of his outside clothes and bring him up to date on happenings.

The Foreign and Commonwealth, the hub of the Empire, a career progression institution, a, 'yes Sir! No Sir!' progression if possible to a nice Ambassadorship to sunny and warmer climes. Paris highly sought after except for the French, Canberra, Australia, ideal for cricket enthusiasts, a South Pacific Island ideal for the none decision maker. What about Washington? What about Moscow? What about Berlin, best left to the friends in the Intelligence Service (MI6). Before the British Empire began to breakup there were many attractive overseas postings. Main form of communication by cable and landline telephone, everything of importance arriving in the Diplomatic Bag. In high profile locations like Hong Kong, the Diplomatic Bag would arrive by aeroplane. Always hand carried by a Foreign and Commonwealth Security agent from London to final destination. Not just simple hand carry, no with lock and chain around the wrist of the carrying agent. Never to leave the agent's side regardless of the length of the journey. Two seats together in First Class for the agent; one for him, one for the bags, sleeping not allowed, special meals, no alcohol.

George looked at his in-tray, dull boring routine, one of the girls giggled. As he had done every day the in-tray switched to the out-tray, mundane routine out of the way. Not in the in-tray, rather leaning against it one of those inter-department brown envelopes. Had he transgressed again? This time it contained an invitation, therefore an instruction, to attend a week long development course in Snowdonia. Plenty of advance notice,

Monday next, so who originally chosen had dropped out? A few days' notice is not the way of the Foreign and Commonwealth Office. They say a week is a long time in politics. The FCO does not do politics, so a month is quick time, three months a good norm, best of all kicked into touch (Rugby not soccer) for the next season, so George dispatched an assistant to accept, get all the details, most importantly the 'expenses advance'. A distraught assistant returned with travel vouchers, not liked by George, no flexibility; all hotel expenses already paid by FCO finance, the only flexibility a *te deum* (daily allowance) of £1 per day. A quick glance at the travel voucher confirmed his expectation of First Class travel. Who else would be in the compartment? Not a quick journey, London to North Wales, check that a dining car existed. Good, meals and drinks.

The invitation contained details of clothing to be taken, primarily that suitable for outside activities of a strenuous nature. Trekking and climbing concluded George. Dinner dress would be informal. Also attached a list of the twelve selected participants, detailing status, time with the Civil Service, yes Civil Service, not just Foreign and Commonwealth Office. George knew none of the others, still Monday next gave him time to make enquiry, start with the two females. Two females would be the 'token' to demonstrate that woman could make progress through the ranks of the male dominated Civil Service. One of the unexpected benefits of the National Health Service continued to be the high proportion of female employees, it only a normal progression for some to attain solid middle ranking positions, like say a Hospital Matron or a G.P. (Doctor).

In many of the larger Embassies a doctor would be included in the staffing levels, ideal if a female doctor had married into the Foreign and Commonwealth Office male Embassy staff, two for the price of one, so to speak. The late 1950's starting the unexplored road to equal opportunity, though at the time considered more of a 'sop' to the idea rather than an endorsement of the principal. Most women only having a vote since the 1920's.

George dismissed the two, whoever they will be as little

competition to be the 'top dog' of the group. George expected to be 'top dog,' the leader, the center of attraction. In his mind not self-importance, just how it would be, for most of his life being described as a born leader. A born leader with intelligence, which could be dangerous one of his uncle's exclaimed in a temper having been trounced at chess by an eleven year old George. To make matters worse George only played chess on sufferance, not his idea of sport, as no sport was with the exception of shooting and fencing, benefits of a good public school. Rugby just acceptable for the good of the house team, George fast enough to keep clean as a wing.

Miss Moneylegs wondered what George had done wrong to end up in the backwoods. Could it have been because he'd been to Cambridge? He was too young to be associated with the Cambridge Four (the Soviet Spy Ring). Perhaps everyone from Cambridge had been tainted by the scandal. Perhaps there had been yet another Spy ring that the Security Services still kept secret.

CHAPTER TWO

Mason found himself with the scientists that made up George's old team monitoring the Whale Anomaly as they progressed back into the farther parts of space, already within the extremities of the Milky Way. Those clever scientists had been humbled by the event, urgently needing a greater understanding of 'from where to where'. Tony Computron joined them. Even the Computron missed George. What would George make of the hissing hissing sound of the Founding Protectors?

As if from nowhere Mason said,

"What do you think of the 'Big Bang Theory?'"

(Mason later insisted his question had been for Tony Computron). Silence descended, everyone in the complex instantly ceased their assignment. As one they all looked at Mason. Poor Mason, what had he done? The Computron sighed in disbelief at the question. Mason with Tony Computron found themselves in the middle of everyone. Only one started to communicate, the Senior Elder present began,

"The Big Bang Theory (not a theory) itself based on accumulated Earth Crust Humanity knowledge, any scientific data came from a very small area of research."

"The theory begins at some 14 billion years ago, before that your scientists referred to Planck Time, that is the time before which your scientists could not explain any form of existence. So the name Planck Time is only an explanation of Earth Crust limited knowledge, with greater knowledge there would be no need for an expression called Planck Time. So you say the Universe became created some 14 billion years ago, your scientist's also say that the Universe consists of three septillion stars. Now you cannot even agree what a septillion is, some say 10 to the power of 24, some like the British say 10 to the power of 42. Whichever figure you take, the quantity of stars coming into existence in some 14 billion years is a mind numbing number."

"So before Planck Time, Earth Crust Humanity has no description or knowledge for what existed, so in the shortest space of time there existed no existence, nothing, a void, at the termination of the shortest space of time there became one existence expanding into something called the Universe (The Big Bang Theory). In less time than the blink of an eye nothing then everything began. Will it end with a Big Bang? If so, when?"

The Elder Elder continued,

"When George still lived our scientists gave him some of our theories, to recall they were,

IF THE BELIEF IS OF ONE UNIVERSE, THEN WE ARE NOT AWARE OF A BEGINNING OR AN END. WHEREVER IT BEGINS, WHEREVER IT ENDS. EARTH AS WE CALL IT IS NOT IN THE MIDDLE. IT IS OF NO CONSEQUENCE. IT IS A MINOR PLANET AROUND A MINOR SUN (STAR)."

"IF THE BELIEF IS OF MORE THAN ONE UNIVERSE, TO US THAT IS INTELLIGENT LOGIC. WHY SHOULD THERE ONLY BE ONE UNIVERSE? IT IS ONLY OUR FEEBLE MINDS THAT RESTRICT THAT COMPREHENSION. IF MORE THAN ONE UNIVERSE EXISTS, THEN LOGICALLY AN 'EXISTENCE' COULD TRAVEL BETWEEN THEM. IF MORE THAN ONE UNIVERSE, WHY NOT MANY?"

"IF YOU BELIEVE THAT THE UNIVERSE HAS MANY DIMENSIONS, HOW MANY DIMENSIONS? OUR LIMITED THINKING POWERS FAIL TO SUGGEST OTHER DIMENSIONS. IT IS ALMOST IMPOSSIBLE TO COMPREHEND THAT MASON, IN YOUR SPACE, OTHER DIMENSIONS COULD EXIST. HOW COULD YOU NOT FEEL SOMETHING, NOT TOUCH, NOT HAVE AN INNER FEEL-

ING OF ANOTHER PRESENCE?"

"IF YOU BELIEVE IN THE BIG BANG THEORY, WHY NOT MANY BIG BANGS? MANY BIG BANGS TOGETHER, BIG BANGS IN SEQUENCE PRODUCING DIFFERENT RESULTS. IF YOU LIKE, DIFFERENT TYPES OF UNIVERSUMS. IF A SEQUENCE OF BIG BANGS, WHERE DID THEY BEGIN? ARE THEY STILL CONTINUING? IF A SEQUENCE, WHERE IS THIS UNIVERSE IN SUCH A SEQUENCE?"

"ANOTHER THEORY WORTHY OF INTELLECTUAL THOUGHT IS THE BUSH. IN THIS THOUGHT, MANY UNIVERSES INTERTWINE WITH ONE ANOTHER. NO PHYSICAL BOUNDARY, LIKE A BUSH WHERE BRANCHES TOUCH, INTERWINE AND CROSSOVER. THE PRESENCE IS ALL COMPOUNDING – NO TOP, NO BOTTOM, NO SIDES. WITHIN OUR UNIVERSE WE AS YET CANNOT DETERMINE IF INTERTWINING EXISTS. AT THIS TIME THE THEORY STANDS."

"ANOTHER THEORY IS CALLED 'ICEBERG', MASON, YOU UNDERSTAND THAT ONLY ONE SEVENTH OF AN ICEBERG IS ABOVE THE SURFACE, AND THE OTHER SIX-SEVENTHS ARE SUBMERGED. SOME OF OUR SCIENTISTS THEORISE THAT SOME UNIVERSES ARE ONLY BLACK MATTER, THAT THESE BLACK MATTER UNIVERSES IN A SIMILAR WAY SUPPORT UNIVERSES LIKE OUR OWN, AND THAT BLACK IS HEAVIER, EXISTING BELOW THE WHITE MATTER."

"Somehow your Earth Crust Humanity spent time resolving their own man made problems not thinking of the bigger picture. Take rubbish disposal, different coloured waste bins to make recycling easier, most of that rubbish completely unnecessary, like food packaging. A created industry to make particular food look more appealing. Pretend it is a health issue. It never was. They should have gone back to the old ways, pick it up, help yourself, then into the shopping basket when paid for. So they got rid of shopping bags, replacing them with plastic bags, then introduce a charge for plastic bags to pay for the disposal. What madness! Whatever happened to the 'just in case' bag carried in pockets or handbags. Of course, they didn't have adverts on. Plastic bags, adverts, the ultimate in consumerism, and the consumer paying the establishment to carry a bag with the establishments name on. Similarly the thrust to have the 'right brand', never mind the quality, never mind the price as long as the name is right. Then a separate industry to copy 'Brand names' to pretend they are the real genuine item. Madness."

Ian from the Secret Service MI5 (British) remained alive proving he must be the ultimate survivor. Within the last few hours before the Whale Anomaly arrived to deprive Earth of an atmosphere, Ian had arrived at the underground base near Corsham in the Cotswolds, codenamed Burlington. No last minute decision or instruction, just a long-standing date in his diary to give an after dinner speech at the annual dinner of the underground establishment. So he could be seen in dinner suite, bow tie, best-blacked shoes as Humanity on Earth Crust ceased to exist. An underground base closing itself down to the outside world in a slick, well-rehearsed routine. For perhaps forty minutes, everyone carried out the original functions, and then reality set in. Family, friends, all gone. Would down here survive? It fell to Ian to address the assembled staff, dinner suited! Giving information no one wanted to know. There started a terrible hiss hissing sound surrounding everyone. Where had that come from? No doubt some design fault now that all systems faced the ultimate test.

Behind Ian the huge electronic world map showing all other known underground bases, some in very strange locations, like under Central Park in New York, under 'Disney' in Orlando. Ian stated,

"All satellite communications have been knocked out, we're unable to communicate with the outside world." (Someone said he looked like our own James Bond. He most obviously shaken, but would he be stirred?) "Underground cable networks need activation immediately."

Easier said than done. Were underground cables still intact?

The Corsham site with the code name Burlington existed as a thirty-five acre subterranean city, initially for the Cold War, some one hundred feet below ground with sixty kilometers of roadways, enough area for four thousand people to live for three months. Diesel for generators stored in a diesel lake, abundant fresh water, the second largest telephone exchange in the country. During the Cold War refinements, new technology, a reduction in personnel, a change of time frame from underground for three months to five years. Fewer people, huge increase in food supplies, eventually growing fresh produce. This would be the base of Government if London had to be evacuated, with all the necessary support staff. An underground railway station with connection to main Great Western Railway lines, special engines, special carriages to be used to see what, if anything, remained after a nuclear war.

Burlington existed as the hub, hundreds of smaller bunkers around the country, all connected by underground cable to Burlington. Did no one notice all this activity, in the 1950's and 1960's, none as blind as those who do not want to see? What excuses had been given? Where did all the money come from? Who controlled the bunker system? Who decided who could be saved in the carnage? Which government ministers could be sacrificed? What about the opposition leader? Is that why many Royal homes are in the Cotswold Greater area? Oxford and Cambridge Dons were safe; they had their own bunkers within each city. Who decided which specialization should be saved? Sciences, obviously, yes! Arts mainly, no! Do you tell loved ones 'you're dead, I am saved?' No keep it a secret, Official Secrets Act, so they believe it is wrong to tell, to say, self-preservation at the ultimate. Is it at that time that under Moscow another underground Moscow has been built? Where would the American president be, with the Vice-President or separate?

Having listened to the Elder Elder, Mason felt pain in his brain from attempting to comprehend. Pain in his ear from the hiss hissing sound of the Founding Protectors reached a higher pitch of ear splitting insanity. Mason thought 'have I lost my mind? Why on Earth do the Founding Protectors attempt to protect? If they just pass through me and this place we call Earth, then if Earth is here or not makes no known difference to their existence?'

Mason felt a need to go again to that part of Deep Earth Humanity where all that had existed remained in this huge interdependent world of animals, insects, birds and all the rest. His first visit had a menacing feeling of fear, on his various returns his communication skills improved; he didn't feel at home, he felt comfortable.

Arriving in expectation that change would have taken place with the disappearance of Earth Crust Humanity appeared wrong. Without the destroyers of so many species he almost expected to see 'dancing in the streets'. No. All continued as before. Earth Crust Humanity had just come and gone, a momentary inconvenience of the self-first. So intelligent, and so much cleverer than everything else that they destroyed themselves. He reminded himself this world of all living things did not exist in 'pretty, pretty, pretend, it does not happen, life, death, eat be eaten, everywhere.' To Mason it now appeared farcical that Earth Crust Humanity couldn't understand, couldn't communicate with all that was here. Did they actually understand what had happened above their heads? Could he say their enemy had been destroyed? Had they encountered the Whale Anomaly in past times?

A lamb came to rescue his mind,

"Of course we understand the events that have taken place. That your type of so-called Humanity no longer lives on the surface. Your time on the surface will soon be forgotten. Your Humanity did not exist for very long, just a momentary blink of the eye."

CHAPTER THREE

George arrived in good time for the train, found his way to the First Class carriage. He counted three First Class, four standard (second class), whatever the politically correct terminology. Each First Class carriage had separate compartments with six seats in each. He expected to find the others on the same journey. Were they late?

The compartment entered onto a long corridor that ran the length of the carriage, then joined the next carriage. On the train First Class would be at the back, then the dining car, then the standard class carriages. Then the tender and steam engine. The second-class food and drink counter next to the First Class Dining kitchen. Such were the ways of steam travel.

As the train pulled out he found himself in an empty compartment, five reserved seats but no passengers. Where were the others? Obviously he had the correct day, the correct time, his reserved seat ticket matched his reserved seat. 'Why am I alone? Everyone must be together in the next compartment.' His compartment had been the first in the first of the First Class Carriages, so on the platform he'd walked past the Guards Van, then an open door into the carriage, past the toilet compartment, then immediately into the compartment. He arose to get to the compartment door.

The train lurched over badly positioned points, George catapulted forwards, smashing his head into the door, fell backwards, passed out with blood shooting out of his mouth, as if he had pyloric stenosis.

His vision blurred, gradually lifting himself onto a seat. Pain in the head intensified, he felt weak. George passed out again. Green lights, his mind kept seeing green lights, all the signals must be green, and the engine had green lights to keep going. His mind reported going faster. How fast can it go? The carriage was shaking from side to side.

'Those green lights are all over me. Am I a green man? Am I dying, entering another world of green? Faster, faster, is there a more explosive word instead of faster? The engine is flying. Am I flying? Faster than the speed of light. Is that what is beyond the speed of light, the colour green? Why do I call it 'green'? It isn't green in reality. It is what I've been taught to call it. Can anyone tell me what the colour really is, or is it only an imperfection within the human eye?'

'When will the engine stop? I can't breathe. Is this the end or a new beginning? Another Foreign Office in a foreign place. Blood in the mouth, choking, thinking too young to die, green or not. Then .... I'm rising. I'm floating. I'm going to heaven. Those green lights are pulling me back. Green lights please let me go. I want to go to heaven. Green lights let me go, let me go. Where are they coming from? Let me go.'

George thought they were saying, 'no! Not yet, no! Not yet'. He knew green lights couldn't speak. Then .... a silence. The green lights had given up. Now it is one light, one colour blue. Silly thought. 'What do you get when you mix green and blue, yellow-yellow-yellow? Yes, he entered, entered, ENTERED yellow, yellow the colour of the sun. New birth, new life, every sunrise. Why do we call it 'the Sun'? Why not 'our star', something more dramatic would be appropriate. 'Always' that's not very dramatic, factual though, ALWAYS there, without ALWAYS, no way would Humanity live.'

How long can Humanity survive if the Sun disappeared? Nothing can replace it, so the Sun fades gradually. Goodbye Earth. Where will Humanity be then, poor thing?

George could see a face above him, the mouth constantly

moving. George heard not a thing.

The mouth continued, a man's face, then another face look-ing, another man, mouth, lips moving, George could hear only silence. 'What do they expect me to do, I can't lip read? Who is most stupid? The two men who believe I can hear them, some-how incapable of seeing that is useless, or myself for failing to stop the pointless communication.'

Now a female face. Instantly George aroused a glow, more interesting, can I touch, concentrate. He touched her white coat, a breast under there, memory lane. One of the two men, 'he's not brain dead.' She came closer, pulled his right eyelids apart, shone a white light into his eye, and then pulled his left eyelids, the same white light. His arms went for her waist pull-ing her on top of him. She had green eyes, very red lipstick lips. The two men pulled her away, she laughing, they angry.

"Plenty of life in him," she laughed again.

George sat bolt upright. Equipment went everywhere.

One of the men, "Grace you're a miracle worker." George fully sensed, now talking directly to her.

"Where am I? Who are you?"

"We thought you were dead," she replied.

"I must catch the next train to Wales," George whispered, just an excuse to get closer to her body. He knew his normal voice would have been possible.

Whispering again to her, "Can I leave?"

She was aristocratic, elegant even in her white Doctors coat, articulate in her response,

"No! No! No! You are still in emergency care. When the am-bulance arrived, medical staff thought you were dead. Everyone had feared to touch your body with the strange green-ness, the immediate thought that your body should be sent for isolation in the mortuary. Then the admission doctor thought that we three, specialists in tropical medicine, should take an immedi-ate look to see if the staff here needed to be placed in isolation. In an instant you were not dead, the green-ness went away. You may remember you went for my breast, that will be recorded as a brain fever," again laughing. "So you're unable to leave until the fever is regulated."

George protested, "I need to get to a meeting in Wales, urgently."

She again, sternness, no laughter, "Alive here in hospital, or dead en route to Wales. No self-inflicted arrogance, George!" She'd said his name.

George wanted to sleep. Grace and the two men kept him awake going through a routine of test upon test upon test. What tropical disease were they hoping to find? Perhaps a new disease that they could name after themselves. What about "Choakaberrigreenmalitus," for short, "Gracedisease?" When they'd finished, George fell asleep. He kept dreaming of Grace in green stuff.

When he woke up, she instantly appeared. The two men had gone. Grace started speaking,

"The Foreign Office want you at the meeting in Wales. They're providing a car and driver and have also requested that the hospital send a member of staff to monitor you during the journey, to stay with the group in Wales, then if necessary, to get you back home." He noticed she had no white coat on, instead a well-tailored jacket and skirt.

"George I am the short straw, I'm going to be your doctor for the trip to Wales."

He could see the tailored suit exaggerated a small feminine waist and then his mind went 34, 21, and 33. George was always good at figures.

Grace, "I'll be gone for ten minutes while you dress. Your suitcase is here, dress for comfort, not style. Oh yes! You'll have to be in a wheelchair to get to your car."

George needed help to dress. Each time his head went forward, he felt light-headed. Still, it happened to be a male attendant, so it provided little embarrassment when it proved impossible to get his legs into underpants and tuck in that part of the male anatomy that somehow combines pleasure with! Strange how in later life the need for pleasure is replaced by a constant need to urinate. Would it wear out more slowly if never used for pleasure? Sad malfunction of the male anatomy. Which came first? The need for pleasure or the need to urinate? Which had become an after-thought? Fairly basic design fault. However, would it pass health and safety laws?

Wheel-chaired, clothed, ready, Grace reappeared again in her white doctor's coat, stethoscope swinging uninterrupted by the area of uneven hillocks, her chest. Orderly pushing the wheelchair, another carrying two suitcases, both identical brown leather. Grace leading the way.

With Miss Moneylegs watching all these events, Tony Computron with Bruce the Dog, joined her. Tony Computron felt competitive.

"When did your women and men get overweight? Look at Grace the doctor, like most women of the day, she has a figure not layer upon layer of fatness. Glad they went away with the Whale Anomaly."

"You mean suffocated," retorted Miss Moneylegs.

CHAPTER FOUR

The Foreign Office hadn't sent a car. It had sent an ambulance, somewhat longer than normal. Still an ambulance is an ambulance, big or small. Two uniformed men stubbed out their cigarettes as the wheelchair arrived. The hospital staff went to place George in the ambulance only to receive instructions not to.

One driver took hold firmly of the wheelchair. The other opened one back door. George was pushed in, Doctor Grace close behind. George was placed on a bed, the chair removed, the entry doors banged shut. George could see this looked unlike any ambulance he'd ever seen.

Doctor Grace, "this is more like a travelling hotel."

From the driver and passenger seat the two men turned around, addressing Grace. They said in turn,

"I'm Syd G, G is for grey hair."

Then the other, "I'm Syd B, B is for black hair."

That ended any introductions. Off moved the ambulance. She was now busy looking at all the equipment. Everything was here. 'Is George actually royalty?' she thought. Methodically she went through cabinet after cabinet, drawer after drawer, marveling at what she found. Within each cabinet or draw a list of contents with an instruction to sign for all items used. Behind the driver a private toilet, to the side a dressing table, everywhere so brightly lit. Then behind the co-driver another fitting looking like a toilet, this had a sliding door at about waist height. Locked from her side, she opened to see Syd working in the smallest of kitchens.

"Would you like some tea?" he asked, so matter of fact that it had to be normal to say, "Yes please." Then she asked, "Are we totally self-contained?" Matter of fact again, "We can survive in here for twenty-four hours and 1500 miles." She had to ask, "Where is your toilet?" "Under the passenger seat which also re-clines so that we can take it in turns to rest, nod off, not sleep. If we decide it's safe sometimes we stretch our legs, on our official work, police will close off laybys, where, if necessary, we can be replaced by other SYD's. She did laugh, his official face gave way to a grin as he handed her tea on a silver tray.

"This George must be important," he commented. "It's not usual for us to be taken out of the Royal Motor Pool for such a journey."

"Yes," she said, "I've also been wondering about George." Then stuttering, "You do know his name?"

"Don't worry Doctor, we've been briefed on the usual need to know basis. As far as we're aware, George is George, a high flyer at the Foreign and Commonwealth Office. Here, his file says very little, but you're welcome to read."

A brief file indeed, little other than name, age, and basic em-ployment history with notes on his University career. Oh yes, his blood group as well. File handed back, she sat back in an arm-chair to drink tea.

There were two armchairs, real armchairs on a swivel, if swiv-eled to look at the inside of the outside. Then a working table dropped into place. Playing further, the armchairs reclined al-most to make a flat bed. 'How the other half live?' she thought, 'this must be a Rolls Royce Tank.' Her conclusion was spot on, only the name of the manufacturer incorrect. So who did make such a fabulous vehicle? As she handed her silver tray back, Syd gave her a menu.

"If you want anything, just ask. Sorry, nothing special, only basics on this trip."

One basic caught her attention, smoked salmon with champagne. 'Very, very basic, would George choose to have that?'

At which moment George stirred, rose to sit in the other armchair, stating he felt hungry.

"Not yet," came a medical response, "blood pressure and pulse first."

Then she gave him the menu.

"You choose. Looks a bit fancy for a sick man. Perhaps they could make thin chicken soup."

Again, she thought, 'my tea failed to slop or spill. There is no rocking motion. How is that possible? We're certainly moving.'

Sudden excitement, the ambulance bell shouting out, 'keep out of my way, emergency.'

On an intercom that she'd not previously found, a Syd said,

"Traffic hold up. We don't stop. These vehicles will get out of the way to let us through."

George said, "Mashed potatoes, cold beef with salad, with tea. What will you have Doctor?"

She replied, "Why not call me Grace? My real name is Grace. May I order smoked salmon and champagne."

Syd had food prepared as if expecting the order. George told him to dispense with the fancy.

"Just use everyday crocks and cutlery."

Grace asked George, "Did you know about this type of transport?"

To which he replied, "We have lots of special transport like this within the Civil Service. Make it look ordinary then no-one asks questions."

Grace thought he'd now started to be official not the pathetic lump of flesh she helped revive nearly a day before. She took the bull by the horns.

"Look George, twenty four hours ago you were dead to the world. Don't talk to me in that official tone. Yesterday you were touching my breast. Have you forgotten your misdemeanour so quickly?"

George mumbled what might have been an apology, and then stumbled out the words,

"I'm not used to treating women as equals. The Foreign and Commonwealth Office is very 'man' centered."

Miss Moneylegs, still watching, could not believe that this arrogant man could possibly by the George she knew. Old age might have mellowed him. This person is almost unpleasant. Does he not understand how long it takes to train, the years at University, the slog of being a 'Houseman' for a year or two? An academic woman in a man's world. Then Tony Computron started,

'Be realistic. At this time women had only been voting for Parliamentary elections since 1928. Remember they had to be over twenty-one as well. With George born in 1934 he would have grown up with a mother only just starting to vote, and then probably voting as her husband told her to. Don't judge with today's values a matter from the past. George never spoke about his family, let's look back to when he would be four. Not long before the outbreak of World War II.'

Miss Moneylegs, using Ewewatch, found four year old George on a sunny summer day. He stood in the middle of a circle with six older girls holding hands to prevent him exiting the circle. They were singing 'whose a little mommies boy,' 'who's a baby bunting.' They continued to circle around him, perhaps like Red Indians encircling a wagon train! Then obviously the mother's voice, "Girls, where is George? He should be at the piano." Four girls ran away leaving two. Mother again, "Joy, Heather, what's happened?" George raced past mother and into the house. The girls, his obvious two older sisters responded, "We were playing 'Ring a ring a roses.'"

George joined in with the sound of piano playing. Mother returned into the house. The sisters found the friends all having a good laugh at George. Mother now stood at the side of the piano, whenever he looked at the keys; she hit his fingers with a cane.

Miss Moneylegs let out a gasp of disbelief. "That's illegal or cruel or both."

She went on a little further, George now seven, 1940, two

years into World War II. It was winter. Thick snow everywhere. George being bombarded with snowballs, somewhat lopsided, George on one side, his sisters and friends the opposition. In an instant, they had George captured. Off came everything below his waist; trousers, socks, wellingtons, underpants. He was left bare-bottomed, sitting in the snow. They were dancing around him waving clothes in the air, singing, 'Baby, baby punting, Mommies gone a hunting, to get a little rabbit skin to put the Baby Bunting in.' Then Mother's voice,

"George its piano time. Where are your clothes? You'll catch your death of cold."

The attackers had melted into the snowy background, no point in George telling on them, just get into the warm and play, pretend nothing had happened, build up more resentment. 'One day,' he thought, 'I'll get my own back.' Victorious girls re-appeared to plan the next humiliation for George.

Miss Moneylegs drew proceedings to an end, indicating she had seen enough. Tony Computron indicated dissent. He wanted to understand as to why the sisters disliked their brother. Miss Moneylegs said she'd seen enough leaving the Computron and Bruce continuing to look into the past.

Grace felt she'd established some form of understanding that she did not exist as a little meek do as you tell me stereotype, for a moment George actually looked embarrassed. George decided better to get her talking otherwise a long quiet journey ensued.

"Tell me about yourself," he asked.

Grace thought at least an effort (in different surroundings he would probably have started, come and look at my etchings) so I'll meet him half way.

"It would be best to start with my parents. My father was born in 1892 to a minor Italian Royal Family. He entered the Italian Civil Service Foreign Office. My mother arrived into the world in St Petersburg, Russia in 1898 also a member of the more distant relatives of the Russian Royal family, still a relative of the Tsarist autocracy. My mother's name is Anastasia. My father, I always called my father, 'Count'. The Count received a diplomatic posting to St Petersburg in 1913, a young handsome man of twenty-one posted as the Third Secretary to the Ambassador. He died in somewhat strange circumstances during World War II. As I was only six when he died, most of my memories are from photographs or stories my mother told me."

One of the Syd's said,

"We're being pulled over by a police car travelling at high speed from behind." He went on, "we've only just left the Greater London suburbs travelling up the A5."

Passenger Syd could be heard talking to pursuing police, agreeing to pull over at the upcoming layby. Then instructions to George and Grace.

"It may be a police car but in no circumstances are you to get out. As soon as I get out, the vehicle will be locked from the inside."

All very dramatic, thought Grace. This is an ordinary 'A' road almost into rural England, nothing happens here with all these vehicles passing on the other side of the road.

So Syd alighted from the ambulance, standing by the passenger side door. From the back of the police car a rain-coated-trilby hat-ed figure appeared carrying a brief case (so if it is a brief case for a man – is it a knickers case for a lady?). As he and Syd were behind the ambulance, unseen from the road, another car sped past, shooting with an automatic at the police-car. Syd the driver could be heard saying,

"That happened too easily. I have the registration. It was a Soviet Embassy Diplomatic car."

At the same moment the Soviet Embassy reported the theft of the very same vehicle. Syd in the driver's seat unlocked the central locking system. The other Syd opened the ambulance back door. The mackintosh/trilby man passed the bag to George saying,

"Your assessment required as soon as you arrive in Wales."

The police car, with no see-able damage, had already made a three point turn as Mackintosh/Trilby man climbed back into the back, then speeding off back to London. 'Why not chase the Soviet Car?' Grace thought. Perhaps two minutes for the whole incident to take place, for the ambulance to be off again at speed.

Grace looked at George and mumbled, "Not an every day journey then?" The remark went unanswered; George already reading papers from what she realized must be a Diplomatic Bag. Again she thought, 'Who are you George? What do you do?' She looked, George smiled. Passenger Syd said, "Stiff drink Miss? What would you like?" Without a thought Grace said, "Vodka."

Still watching, Barbara let out a very unlady-like whistle. Mason entered, looked at the screen then said,

"This noise of the Founding Protectors has set my nervous system on edge."

(If only he'd said my nervous system is reacting to the Founding Fathers). Tony Computron told Mason not to change the subject, 'You were Mackintosh/Trilby.' Mason and George had kept the little secret for too many years.

"Yes, it's me."

Many years later, after his retirement, Driver Syd having had a few too many drinks always referred to the incident as his alien encounter, always convinced that little green men kept the bullets away from the ambulance and police car, that the bullets rebounded back into the shooters in the Soviet Diplomatic Car.

Driver Syd had no idea of a Top Secret File 7447007 that remained open to the end of Earth Crust Time. The file recounts the incident, shows black and white pictures of the Soviet car parked at a nearby main-line railways station with bullet holes all along the passenger side of the vehicle. No hospital reported an admission with gunshot wounds, no blood in the car. Where had it been for the ten hours until being discovered during the night? Both policemen, Driver Syd, all reported the same green lights. In the fullness of time, many, many years later, the file ended up with Mason in his departmental responsibilities for looking into UFO's.

After all these years Tony Computron wondered, but not thought, if he should tell Mason the truth.

The ambulance proceeded with added urgency, standing rules required Passenger Syd to open-up the gun cabinet; keeping within easy reach automatic guns for both himself and Driver Syd. Grace felt the first 'vodka' did not hit the spot, so she asked Passenger Syd for another.

"No!" came the polite answer. "We all need to keep our wits about us. Would you like tea or coffee instead?"

She requested a strong, sweet tea. George, now deep in thought, read at an extraordinary fast speed. He didn't attempt to hide each paper as he read it so Grace, without even being nosy could read 'Top Secret' across each page as George read it. Soviets, Americans, Cuba, kept appearing.

Grace always remembered the date. It was the same day and month that her father, the Count, had been reported as dead. Even as a little girl she remembered how her mother wept and wept and wept for days on end. She could not be comforted. What would her mother think when she told her of the events of the day, the man George, who everyone at the hospital thought had died until she Grace, yes she Grace, yes Grace your daughter, had touched him? Then how George had grabbed at her. Then back looking at those top-secret papers, here she could see the internal workings of the Cold War. The Americans, the Soviets, pointing nuclear warheads with enough power to wipe each other and the rest of Humanity into everlasting oblivion. When a three-minute warning, what use would three minutes be? Would sound the end of all things. Such destructive power in the hands of so few, a finger on the trigger of eternity.

Syd Passenger somehow changed seats reverting to Syd the

Driver, they hadn't made a stop. Grace only knew of the change when he made apology for taking a corner to fast, resulting in the Top Secret Papers falling in disarray onto the floor. George so preoccupied made no movement; Grace did, starting to place them back in numerical sequence. So she started to read.

"They are very important," George spoke. She was startled and embarrassed. She knew what she'd just done by reading the papers could cause her great trouble if anyone found out. George again,

"Are you listening? Do you speak Russian?" A moment of hesitation,

"My mother brought me up to be fluent in Italian and Russian." Why did she say Italian and Russian, not answering the question directly as to Russian and Italian? He didn't ask her to translate or interpret, only the simple question, 'Do you speak Russian?'

She placed the papers in numerical sequence close to the desk George had used. Silence, more silence, George totally silent.

"Can I have something to eat please Syd? George, do you want a meal?" Again, "George do you want to eat or drink?" Silence. Wherever George had gone, food or drink was of no interest.

"Syd, have you two hot meals? Perhaps George will eat with a hot meal in front of him."

Syd replied they were going to have chicken and veg themselves in the front. "Is that okay for you?"

"Give George the breast, I'm easy."

The two Syd's burst into laughter, she blushed. 'Here I am again, George and breasts. Will I always associate the two together?'

Grace had consumed half her chicken, leg of course; more laughter from the front two when she noticed no eating from George. 'Right George,' she thought, 'the Doctor is going to feed you.'

Mashed potato on fork, "George open your mouth." George obeyed.

"Eat," said Grace. George obeyed. So it continued, did he

understand a grown man needed feeding? George thinking about major, massive World events, fed like a baby. Could George have placed himself in a trance? She had no idea, no medical experience like this. 'Do I 'compliment him when the plate is empty? No, I'll take it away without comment.'

Syd Passenger as she passed the empty plates back, "He is a queer one Miss, highly thought of for his analytical brain."

Grace answered, "Only twenty-four hours ago we thought his brain dead. Then a miracle type recovery."

CHAPTER FIVE

Without further incident, the group of four arrived at the country hotel somewhere at the base of Snowdon. Two of those who were there immediately took George into a private meeting. The Two Syds, Grace, were all taken to separate rooms to give detailed accounts of the journey. Their evidence taken under oath by the three most senior officers from the County Constabulary.

George slumped into a very deep easy chair, and then with Foreign Office training politeness asked the level of security status of the two. They called themselves Cedric and Herbert. George then passed firstly to Cedric the papers marked Top Secret that had been delivered to the ambulance. After that he passed his assessment. Quietly Cedric and Herbert read, as they read on their expressions changed to 'grim grey'. Quietly the three spoke concluding the 'assessment' should with urgent haste get back to London. They agreed the two Syds would return.

The police interviews concluded, the Syds were told to eat a hot meal, wash and shave, departing to London within the hour. George alone then prepared a further manuscript copy, this placed in the bag for London, the original placed into the hotel safe, the only key given by the manager not to George, not to Herbert, but to Cedric.

The interview with Grace went slowly. George interrupted the two,

"Why so long?"

The Chief Inspector with obvious irritation, "I have an interview to do, of the four who travelled in the ambulance three of you are subject to the Official Secrets Act, the Doctor is not. The Doctor is cooperating completely, as soon as I am finished, you will be informed."

George very matter of fact, "Then with more speed. I am waiting for my next medical examination."

Stalemate!! Looking at the Inspectors report at a later date it was noted that he failed to establish that Doctor Grace spoke Russian.

With a minder listening, the two Syds were told to advise their next of kin that their return home faced a delay. Their departure required a lengthy list of instructions from Cedric, prime instruction to stop for nothing. Their delivery a matter of National Security. They both thought the same, 'Not for the first time mate, these instructions go with the job.'

Grace still with the Chief Inspector waited in silence for the next question.

"Doctor, there are only two of us here. Tell me the truth."

Grace, tired, dirty, hungry started,

"Are you sure we are only two. If I have a split personality then we are three, if you have a split personality then we are four. What if we are here living in more than this dimension? What if another dimension exists and other things are also here with us. Do you not feel a presence? Don't you feel claustrophobic? What if someone has planted a listening device? This is an old building, have you checked for secret passages?" She now in full flow, he was unable to write fast enough.

"Just look at my watch, follow the swinging, you're feeling tired."

"Now Doctor, no funny tricks."

Then he had gone. He existed only under the control of Doctor Grace. She said to him, whispering into his hairy ear,

"When I say 'bandages' you will wake up. Write the words, 'she is bonkers' at the end of your report then say the interview is over."

Grace sat where she had before, said 'bandages', the Chief Inspector awoke, concluded the report by writing, 'she is bonkers' then indicated Grace could go. He went to the bar for a double brandy, helping himself, saying the heat had got to him, he felt faint. Certainly his face looked very red. Doctor Grace watched, also feeling faint with amusement.

George had his next medical check-up, then Cedric with George, invited her to have a hot meal with them. Herbert spoke,

"Arrangements have been made with your hospital to stay here to monitor George. Who do you need to inform of these new plans?'

"I live with my mother."

To avoid delay, Herbert took her to a telephone, listening to her conversation.

"Mother, this is Grace (mother's ears listened intently). The hospital needs me to live in with an important patient for a few days to provide on hand medical care. I will telephone each evening to make sure you're alright."

Both phones were placed back on their base at each end. Herbert commented that she had not received permission to make a daily phone call, then thought the mother would think it worrying if regular calls were not received.

Tony Computron, watching the screens, thought 'Doctor Grace you are very clever.'

Barbara, collecting the thought questioned, 'What do you mean?'

'Time will tell,' came back Tony's thought.

Barbara again, "We are here watching in real time events yet we are not watching for days."

Tony Computron, in his best headmaster type reply looked at Barbara thinking, 'You have hit the nail on the head. You Earth Crusters assume your time is real time. You have imposed a time constriction in your brain. To me and the rest of Deep

Earth Humanity watching events on Earth Crust is everything taking place in slow, slow, ... slow motion. Think of it in this way, your people invented super-fast computers, your brains created machines that think faster than you do. Complex calculations concluded in an instant. What prevented Earth Crust brains training to do the same? The obvious answer is you used the brain to store useless rubbish. If only your people had cleared out the rubbish.'

Back to the screens, the mother of Doctor Grace placed the empty milk bottles on the front door step. Wedged into the top of one bottle a note, 'milkman, one pint less, Grace is away.' To explain, milk, up to the most recent time came in glass bottles; each bottle contained a fluid pint of milk, sealed at the bottle top. Milk obviously comes from cows. A milkman delivering every day, except on Sundays, taking away the empties to reuse. Then, once a week, the milkman would also collect the money due. No supermarkets, no plastic bottles, a real person. Winter birds often pecking into the milk top for the cream.

Herbert took Doctor Grace into the bedroom showing her the medical equipment at her disposal, showing her a communicating door into the next bedroom that George would occupy. During the working day of the group her time would be free, if she went out of shouting range to seek permission, if she went any distance a starting pistol would be fired three times, that would be an emergency call. All her meals as and when she wanted them, as with the rest of the group a small tedium of £20.00 per day (please do not discuss with the group as their tedium had to confirm to Civil Service guidelines, therefore a much smaller amount). Herbert continued,

"I cannot over emphasize that George needs to be kept at your center of attention. If in your opinion he should be back in hospital, urgently inform either Cedric or myself. The local hospital, some twenty miles away, will provide back up. A member of their team will visit you tomorrow at 11.00am."

Not for the first time Grace thought, 'this George is somewhat special.' Then Herbert again,

"the group have a meeting tomorrow, including George, at 10am. It will last until lunch time."

The outsider to a group always feels uncomfortable, in this instance, all the group were strangers to each other, with the obvious exception of Cedric and Herbert. Night came, George, aware that Grace occupied the next room. It passed quietly, then breakfast. By 10.00am the group had been locked away into a library type room, Grace now off duty. She noticed that not only had the door to the library been clicked into locked status, that in addition Herbert pulled up a chair to sit on the public side of the locked room. Doctor Grace again thinking, ' just who are this lot?'

Within the locked library, Cedric started handing out nametags.

"These are your new names; note Christian names remain the same. You all have a new surname."

George had the name George 'Smile'. Other surnames included Cryer, Painter, and Brewer etc.; all so normal it might be abnormal. Cedric continued,

"You have all been selected to create a new section of the Security Service. You will be based in the Ministry of Defence, also at Corsham underground city in Wiltshire. The team will be split into two; half of you will be in Corsham, the other half in London. None of you are married, none of you have long term relationships."

A whistle from a man now named William Brewer followed by him saying,

"What don't you know?"

Cedric, "We should know everything about each one of you, even your shoe size."

Then Cedric delivered the punch line,

"Your section will be to think of the unthinkable and plan for it."

Real death like quiet. Cedric gave about a minute then said,

"Let me introduce you to your section leader, George Smile." George didn't move, all the room looked at him, the new appointment was news to George as to everyone else except Herbert and Cedric. How high do they go within the Security World to make such an announcement, to have total knowledge of the new group, everything about the new section known to these two? How many more in the loop?

Cedric again, "You have twenty minutes to decide if you wish to join this new section, then you will each be required to sign a new notice of compliance to the Official Secret Act in both your real name and your new name. If you decline the invitation to join there will no mention of such fact on your employment record. You will pack your belongings, a taxi will take you to the station, the train leaves at 12.45."

No one left, the atmosphere full of excitement, the words excitement with Civil Service rarely join together. Cedric brought the group back together with a further statement saying everyone now had a salary rise, their grading's all having moved up three stages.

Herbert opened the locked door, in marched the County Chief Constable, together with fourteen plain-clothes officers. Herbert also came in handing the door keys to a Detective Inspector. The Chief Constable stood next to Cedric, and then spoke.

"The Ambulance that left here did not get to London as expected. They have been located up a farm track on the Welsh border. The drivers, when found, were tied up in the back of the ambulance, the four tyres slashed until flat. The Civil Service bag with them, the contents removed."

George showed no emotion, his assessment taken. Each member of the group was taken by a police officer to their bedroom that the officer searched then took a statement under oath. One by one the fourteen returned to the meeting room, each wondering which of the group would be discovered as the culprit. When all had returned, the Chief Constable who never left the meeting room again started to speak.

"To avoid rumour amongst yourselves I have been authorized to tell you all what happened to the ambulance also to remind you this information falls within the Official Secrets Act."

"A few miles after the Welsh/English border the ambulance entered a series of continuous 'S' bends that went on for half a mile. At the sharpest of the bends, two cars were blocking the road, with a man administering medical aid to a body between the two cars. Both Syds had strong medical emergency professional training, overriding that however a standing instruction that one 'Syd' had to remain in the driving seat at all times. Such standing instructions related overall to the protection of passengers, with no passengers, both of them ran to the victim. In a moment they were pinned down by six garlic stinking thugs (male deodorant still a novelty not in general use). Blindfolded, tied, gagged they were bundled into the back of the ambulance which then drive off. In their minds both of them counted, as if in seconds, hoping to keep brains alert. Counting the outward journey one of them reached 980 and the other 1026, counting the last 200 interrupted by suspension breaking bouncing, obviously up an off road track with the last bounce somewhere the chassis cracked. Silence, more silence, they were alone. Six thugs in two cars now away. Well trussed neither found himself able to effect the untying which always appears so easy in film land. Both must have passed out. Quickly after discovery they realized they had been dead to the world for over two hours."

The Chief Constable concluded by saying the only items missing, the Civil Service briefcase contents, and the briefcase left behind.

Without exception all looked at George. Without hesitation George addressed the Chief Constable asking if all the hotel staff had given a statement. Only in the fullness of time did the police report that none of them had interviewed Doctor Grace. For a second time, in the fullness of time when the shit hit the fan.

George then stated, "time for a late lunch, and remember that no discussion should take place about the ambulance in public areas. We will meet back here in two hours."

George went directly to his bedroom meeting Grace along the corridor. She gave him another medical check up. George elected for room service, then for sleep.

George directed Grace to awake him twenty minutes before the hour. She stayed in his bedroom, sitting on a chair looking through the window up at 'Snowdon', then looking back at her handsome patient. If only he knew what she thought about him. If only she knew what dreams entered his mind about her. Does love at first sight happen in the real world? Well cinemagoers of the period would certainly think so.

Entrance to the farm track found a police car with a couple of Constables moving on those rubbernecks trying to see what had taken place. Instructions from London to the local police were precise, do not interview the two drivers, get new tyres fitted, and get the ambulance back to the outskirts of London where the Metropolitan Police would take over escort duty. The two Syd's had plenty of time to rehearse their story prior to the inevitable period of questioning. In fairness the story (the truth) they had to tell would be factual, their problem why they both left the ambulance in defiance of standing instructions. They both agreed to tell it as it happened, accept the reprimand, then move on.

All security staff were instructed from their beginning 'own up to any mistake at the earliest available opportunity', nothing annoyed the 'Top Brass' more than the waste of manpower, the waste of money of an internal investigation. Intolerable for outsiders to get involved. When absolutely the last option is necessary then appoint a retired section head of MI6 (The Intelligence Service) to investigate MI5 (The Security Service) and vice versa. At all costs keep outsiders 'out', if the Home Secretary pushed hard keep reminding that National Security is at stake. An MI5 file will exist on the Home Secretary as with all cabinet members, all members of Parliament, Lords and Commons. Most have a pressure point to be exploited. Money! Sexual anomalies! Extra marital affairs!

Doctor Grace woke George up with some thirty minutes to go until the next meeting. Retiring back into her own bedroom whilst he did what men have to do. A few minutes later, without thinking, she walked back into his room to see him standing tall, naked, and erect. Even for a Doctor much to admire. 'Homo erectus.'

CHAPTER SIX

I an from MI5 now in the underground bunker at Corsham received report after report that the underground telephone cables would not work. With all satellites gone in the Whale Anomaly there was no means of communication, satellite or ground cable, all failing to operate. Obviously the screen behind him with lights flashing at other bunkers around the country meant nothing. The logical assumption must be that they were stranded underground. That hiss hiss hissing deafening kept on and on and on, for some real ear pain problems caused nausea. Each team had gone to investigate their own area of responsibility within the bunker all reporting back that no structural or mechanical malfunctions existed. The only certainty, the never-ending noise. All, Ian included, were under no doubt that somewhere within the complex a major malfunction existed, the only question, would it be catastrophic or could they discover and rectify?

Earth Crust Humanity had no knowledge of the 'Founding Protectors', awareness did exist of particle physics and neutrinos, not yet the 'Founding Protectors'.

Ian concluded that somebody had missed the obvious and sent out the groups again for another search, unpopular no doubt but vital for continued existence without questions. If only they could contact another bunker to understand if the noise existed elsewhere? If the noise existed specific to Corsham or if the noise existed everywhere on what remained of

Earth Crust?

Deep Earth Humanity knew the answer. Mason, Barbara, Miss Moneylegs could end the problem in an instant. Tony Compu-tron could resolve it even more quickly. Even Bruce the Dog knew he could help. For the time being George would have to wait. They all consulted the Library records looking as to how the underground cables from Corsham could be brought back into usage.

CHAPTER SEVEN

George reassembled the group, again the entrance door locked with either Herbert or Cedric taking it in twenty-minute turns to sit outside. To the outside world the closed door had a sign reading 'Meditation Conference. Quiet please.' This then provided the excuse for Herbert and Cedric to sit at a desk pulled across the doorway. A major problem for the two appeared to be the length of time taken in completing The Times crossword. Such are the ways of the highly intellectual that in each twenty-minute spell the existing crossword clues were replaced by their own with different answers to the correct ones, still containing the same amount of letters. Not a project for the feeble minded.

Doctor Grace took the rare free time to telephone her mother, not the agreed time, just a surprise, also to say how much she missed the home cooking. Mother sounded somewhat cross as that infernal milkman had continued to deliver too much milk ignoring her note. Grace with great sympathy told her to leave him another note also telling the milkman not to leave any cream. Without Grace there her mother had already noted in her own mind 'no fresh cream Victoria sponge' as Grace was not home. Grace again,

"Is it Bridge as usual this evening (obviously a yes reply). Please don't mention my special missions, indicate the hospital has sent me away on a medical course. I will telephone again after Bridge."

Playing Bridge provided the mother of Grace with her social contacts. She had always played even before she married the Count, until very recent years her ability resulted in her playing for the County, serious, almost professional. Her regular group consisted of fifteen trusted friends, different nationalities with a common language 'Bridge'. The house she lived in was large enough to support a dining room in which could be set four tables of four. Hers was the main weekly venue. The group only changed on death or when these four foreign diplomats left the London posting. The current four were an American lady, a Russian man, a Swiss gentleman, and an Italian gentleman, United Nations united in Bridge. The serious format even required 'no' drinking before, only after. To that end a drinks cabinet marked 'Bridge only' existed in one corner of the dining room.

Custom provided for eight players to bring bottles one week, seven players the next, it was considered bad form for the hostess to provide a bottle as well. The none bottle group had responsibility for preparing, cleaning and washing up at the end. In addition the fifteen left an agreed weekly contribution to cover other expenses. As with Bridge itself, detailed, specific, rules on etiquette.

When a child Grace knew when the serious playing finished by the increase in excited chatter, when a diplomatic member of the group left, the late evening wondered on into party mode. Grace remembered that the Italian gentleman would be leaving his London posting, that this would be his last evening playing Bridge with the group. So a small party with a little parting gift, normally a nice set of playing cards with everyone leaving a message on their own particular card. Yes in this formalized gathering all had a specific card attached to their name, so Grace's mother always signed the Queen of Hearts, the diplomats could choose from the lower numbers of three or four on any suite. Most male diplomats over the years would choose from the black cards, whilst lady diplomats would choose the red. When Grace rang again in the late evening her mother as usual sounded happily tipsy, saying that Stephen Ward had brought one of those girls with him. They both left early, the girl Mandy.

George commenced the meeting with the statement that the stolen papers were his assessment on reports of the Soviet Union starting to build a massive missile site or sites on the island of Cuba. Stunned silence within the group.

George again, "this escalates the 'Cold War' into a heightened tension. I will state the obvious. Cuba is a communist state, ruled by Fidel Castro, with the strongest of links to Moscow. Cuba is some 100 miles from the American mainland. In our terms Birmingham having nuclear missiles pointing at London. America could calculate a nuclear war now would prevent the construction being completed. If nuclear warheads existed in Cuba forget about the three-minute warning, to the Southern states of America, three seconds would be realistic. Three seconds provides little time for counter strikes or intercepts. This information is a result of American spy-planes overflying Cuba. In my opinion this Soviet action in Cuba is a direct result of the invasion at the Bay of Pigs in Cuba on 17th April 1961. The Soviet Union does not want to loose all the advantages that communist Cuba provides both militarily and the effect on the American psyche. As Soviet military often remarks, 'if only Alaska had not been sold to the Americans during the years of the Tsar.' Imagine Communism in the North in Alaska, with also a Communist Cuba. America would have been in the middle of a Communist sandwich waiting to be devoured. 'Do as we Communists say or we will squeeze and squeeze and squeeze.' Sounds rather like the three little pigs."

George went on, "the information is up to date but limited. The observations have been made by an American spy plane at very high altitude, and some preliminary investigation into ships docking into Cuba over the last six months. It is a matter of the greatest American Intelligence concern that these events have been taking place under the very noses of American Intelligence or in reality the lack of intelligence. Further to remind you that the British Commonwealth of Countries has many members in the West Indies, therefore a commitment from all Commonwealth countries to protect each other. Rather than me talking please break up into groups of two people to think through the consequences of 'A Cuban Missile Crisis'. After an hour or so each group will share thoughts with the rest of us. This is not a game, our facts are limited. The consequences of giving bad advice to Government, enormous."

Grace continuing her telephone conversation asked if the Soviet Navel attaché came with Stephen Ward.

"No", mother replied, "they came separately only speaking together in very polite terms. I think they have had a fall out. You know my dear Grace, these naval attaches are really..."

At that instant the phone went dead, Grace in some anxiety continued pressing the phone to get a reconnection. It would not work. On the other end Grace's mother also pressed down her phone getting an immediate dial tone. A telephone fault at the other end, she thought, 'Grace will be back in touch when the fault is mended.' With the receiver back in place the phone started to ring.

"It's Stephen here, is Grace about?" Mother knew the voice of Stephen Ward only too well. He continued, "I am sending out invitations for my next exhibition, it will be limited invitations so didn't want to send one out if Grace is on duty."

Mother in reply, "She is away on hospital duty somewhere in Wales. I don't have a telephone number where she is. Anyway, I was just talking to her when the phone at her end went dead. I'll tell her you called."

Stephen gave a polite thank you and rang off.

Grace gave up on the telephone. She knew only too well what word her mother had been about to say when the phone went dead!

The meeting room door had thrust open with the obvious voice of a public school educated officer giving instructions to everyone to sit tight, they were the military acting on behalf of the Security Services. Pandemonium broke out. The lights went out, a voice shouting.

"There shoot."

Another shouting, "shoot to injure, she is wanted alive not dead. Shoot at the legs."

Another voice, "get the light back on," the same voice, "can anyone see her now?"

All she could think of, the 'D' words, duck, dive, decoy. She ran thinking duck, dive, duck, dive, and decoy. Then, out of breath, a bullet hit her left thigh; she dragged her left leg, the second bullet went into her right thigh. Then she hit the ground, put the pistol into her mouth, pulled the trigger. No last moments of thought, dead and gone. Getting to the body first the Cockney solider knew she was dead from the lack of much of the head, still he gave the corpse a kick just to make sure, then another kick to make extra sure.

CHAPTER EIGHT

G race and favour went through Barbara's mind as they watched Ewewatch, that which watched every part of Earth Crust.

Esamia had called back to see Bruce at the moment the Cockney solider kicked the body once, then twice. Looking at Bruce she stated the all too obvious.

"He'd not do that if his favourite dog had been shot."

Miss Moneylegs without thinking, then wished she had thought nothing at all, 'that happened in the 1960's in 2010 it would not have happened like that.' Bemused expression from Esamia obviously too polite to think that Miss Moneylegs had sounded stupid. Esamia continued with her thoughts.

"You Earth Crust people have always been without real morality, you are unkind! No, wicked to one another, you treat all living things with no respect. Your level of judgment is impossible to comprehend. Some of your greatest hero's are military. What do military do but kill each other. Name me any of your military hero's who have not killed. Somehow you make a distinction between murderous deaths in battle and a murderer. So much of the animal welfare is no more than maximizing profit before slaughter. Remember how Bruce had been badly treated," Bruce growled. "Take some of those pampered dogs, what happens if the pamperer dies before the dog. Will someone else pamper the dog or will it have a more normal existence? Is the owner or the dog at fault? How easy your morality that it has no second thoughts about squashing a spider, treading on an ant, swatting a fly. All actions you perform resulting in death; hook a fish, use a mousetrap, and shoot a pheasant. How many chickens die needlessly in factory farming, pecking each other to death demented by the overcrowding. Your superior beliefs in yourselves, that you have control over all living things, where are you now? Dead and gone. The creatures of the oceans remain. Even to the very last moment of Earth Crust Humanity military engagements took place. How many were murdered in that last minute before all your Humanity suffocated to death?"

Barbara looked at Esamia.

"Did you study Earth Crust Humanity at school?"

"Yes," she replied, "you were one of our sciences, if you like, as rabbits in a laboratory. At school we attempted to understand why so much of your life centered on self-destruction. To us you were involved in two interlinked self-destructive activities. Firstly those imposed upon the individual, religious mutilation, military, wars, need to work (with most working the same daylight hours), mass transportation, air pollution, centralized medical treatment. Then secondly, those activities that the individual imposes upon themselves, particularly people in the more affluent countries; overeating, sedentary life style (too much television viewing, not enough activity) mobile telephone communications."

"Our scientists studied this 1980's mobile phenomena exploding into the worldwide population and the effect it had. Would you walk around with a microwave oven on your head? We could see the results on health, day by day. Well it doesn't matter anymore. Our scientists' long-term projections were frightening. Then there existed the wave upon wave of radio waves hammering into Earth Crust human bodies. Oh yes! And the electric waves from overhead cables. Diesel fumes happily inhaled, sitting in traffic jams happily inhaling more fumes."

"We never understood why you sat in traffic jams but then insisted in exceeding your strange speed limits. So you had to be told how fast you could drive, your feeble brains not comprehending danger, we as small children played a game of guessing, watching vehicles on highways, motorways exceeding speed limits, getting as close as possible to the vehicle in front. Always more exciting in torrential rain and dense fog; the game guessing 'how many vehicles would crash into each other?' To us it was unbelievable that travelling at 100 miles per hour, drivers didn't understand they needed more than one car length in front to stop without hitting and being hit. A multi-car sandwich with real blood instead of jam or beetroot.' Esamia laughed at her own humour, expecting one of the Earth Crusters to enquire about the knowledge of jam and beetroot. Little did she realize they were concerned with her statements of the obvious facts from one so young.

Without hesitation, Esamia continued,

"Your religions talk about a creator of everything, that creator you are told sends a representative or a representative receives special power to explain to Earth Crust Humanity which religions should be followed. Why have Earth Crust Humanity ended up with many different religions? Why could those religions not find a commonality? You know only too well that Earth Crusters had many wars over which was the 'very best religion' to believe in. Think how wealthy the religions were, all the buildings, all the land. I can think of one that has its own bank. Yet poverty existed everywhere under the noses of the religious. Why were religious buildings not used to house and provide food to the homeless and to the poor? Most are empty for most of the week. Where is religion if the homeless have no help to seek a dry bed or a dry roof within the interiors of spaces within those vast religious buildings?"

"Or another way, religions did not trust the poor, the homeless with the fabric, bricks, the mortar of their religions."

All Barbara, Mason and Miss Moneylegs could do was nod their heads in total agreement.

Esamia left with another parting question,

"Is George in trouble yet, or are you still in the dark? You'll be surprised, George could have been a great leader within your Humanity or my Humanity." Off she skipped.

All the others returned to the Library screen with Bruce in attendance. 'Never feel hungry' he thought, 'I'm not losing weight.' Bruce had quickly learned to stay close to Mason or Miss Moneylegs. He felt Tony Computron got upset if he got too friendly with Barbara. 'Still I'm here, alive, everyone down here is very friendly, except for that Computron.'

The Computron knew what his thoughts were, giving Bruce a Computron stare.

CHAPTER NINE

G eorge arrived when the second kick of the Cockney sol-
dier landed full square into the chest,
"Grace!" shouted George.
No reply.

Again, screaming more than a shout, "Grace." In some sympathy the Cockney said,
"I think she's dead, Sir."

Esamia bobbed in again saying, "Is George in trouble yet?"

Hardly had the word 'Grace' left the lips of George than a
very angry official like figure looked at the Cockney demand-
ing knowledge of where the officer in charge could be found.
The Cockney soldier escorted the angry official away, leaving
George with the body. One good learning curve within the British Army had always been the ability to recognize authority
with respect. Another good lesson, learnt early in military life,
to stand close enough to a commanding officer to hear when the
Commanding Officer receives a bollocking, but far enough away
for the Commanding Officer not to believe you were eavesdropping.

Angry official to Commanding Officer,
"Who gave the order to move in?"
With the authority of arrogance this Commanding Officer

clearly, loudly, so anyone within shouting distance could hear demanded,

"Who the hell are you?"

Angry Official, "My name is Baxter, of the Security Service MI5, we have spoken by telephone many times over the last few days to coordinate the arrest."

Saluting him with a very stiff arm, Fortisque (the Commanding Officer) without apology replied,

"I gave the order. We had received a telephone call; my Sergeant took the call, to say you were delayed, that I should take control and not wait any longer. My Sergeant was told that the danger was immediately imminent, we therefore secured the outside then the Corporal used the main switch on the hotel electrical switchboard to put all into darkness. Within seconds the female fled the building with two of my men placing accurate shots to take out her legs. At no time in any of our conversations did you indicate she would be carrying a pistol."

(In the subsequent investigation no one involved at MI5 had any knowledge of a phone call or even making the phone call. The Sergeant gave information that the voice he heard had a cultured sound, sort of public school. He knew a female voice introduced the male voice that went on to say 'Baxter' of the Security Services.)

Fortisque continued, "the female obviously knew the game had come to an end. Instantly deciding not to be captured, to commit suicide instead. I repeat at no time did you Sir (Baxter) tell me that she would be carrying a weapon."

Through all this conversation, George remained by the body. Perhaps in all the talking had taken forty or fifty seconds. George gave another loud shout of 'Grace' only to be escorted away by the Cockney solider, who in any event wanted to report back to his mates the heated conversation that had taken place between Fortisque and Baxter.

To George, the Cockney kept saying, "Come on Sir. She's dead. Nothing to do here for you."

George still looked back to look at the skirt, the blouse,

that he knew only too well from the hospital journey to here. He thought Grace probably had no knowledge that he knew exactly her clothes from that journey, he noticed every day what clothes she had, he noticed the lipstick, he knew the smell of the perfume, still one last look, her legs exposed to the suspenders.

Baxter came close to the body, told Fortisque to over the legs, post a guard of four, place guards on every outside door, no one in, no one out. Then he stated that a clean up team had already left Northolt by helicopter. They had the responsibility to remove the body and leave the area as if nothing had taken place. Two Chief Inspectors from the local Constabulary would soon arrive.

"Let them into the hotel, the clean up team will deal with them so that a common story line will emerge."

Fortisque had heard of the miracles performed by the clean up team, officially Department 13. They made sure no damage would arise for either the Security Service (MI5) or the Intelligence Service (MI6). Department 13 existed as a common department to both services, consisting of professionals, each team always had a posting from the Services so as to learn the fine art of a clean up. Based at a hanger at Northolt Airfield, a team of six stood on duty every passing second. If one team went into action, another team would be on standby. If the existence of Department 13 had found its way into the public domain, no doubt there would have been an outcry on the waste of public money. If the public knew how often the department had to protect the reputation of the United Kingdom, even the most ardent protestor of public money would agree to its cost effectiveness. Within the department a fine reputation had long been established for returning a body to family members in beautiful condition, whatever might have been the cause of death? A beautiful body would be created but not so for enemies of the state, they went back in glorious blood and gore.

The hotel now cordoned off, the local Police Constable found himself knocking on village doors telling everyone to keep inside.

"A large quantity of old dynamite had been found in the hotel grounds. Experts were on the way to deal with the very real danger. Stay indoors."

Likewise the road through the village found itself closed. The local bus dropped off village passengers who were then escorted to their homes. Any villages returning home by car had to park outside the village and then be escorted home. Village children started to hope for the next day off school, proving the point that someone always benefits from every crisis. The dynamite discovery in a Welsh village had a listing on the National news, never quite making it onto the running list for broadcast. Most of the news having been taken up by an argument between two Cabinet Ministers on the benefits of the Eleven Plus examination. (Children took a National Examination at eleven to determine the type of their future education, Grammar or Secondary education. No child wanted to fail the 11+ as failure condemning the child to a second rate education. Parents would bribe children with money in an effort to maximize the child's effort. Strange to decide a person's future at the young age of 11. One of the high flyers at MI6 passed his 11+ then because of limited Grammar school places in his area had to attend an interview that he failed. The Headmaster who interviewed him happened to be a well-known supporter of Communism. That high flyer went on to a red brick university where he degreed in Russian (Slavonic languages). He now speaks Russian better than the average Russian. His time is spent in fighting the evils of Communism.)

Then a last minute story concerning the marriage of a well-known actor. Still the local radio did mention that the village road had a temporary diversion due to unexploded dynamite from a quarry.

Back in the hotel conference room, George filled in any missing details the group was not aware of. The two lady members offered to go into the bedroom Grace had used to clean up then pack the belongings up. George thanked them saying that Department 13 would sort all that out, as they would also contact the family.

George felt somber, the group was somber, no one particularly knew Grace, not even George, her friendly attitude missed by all, and even Herbert and Cedric appeared somber. The question for George or Herbert or Cedric, 'what to do during this time of a totally messed up programme?' Herbert made the suggestion,

"At some time we will be asked to recount the events of the last few days, in particular the last hour, let us come to some common set of facts."

Cedric received a telephone call that the group would leave during the evening with additional helicopters arriving from Northolt. Everyone would be moved to another location to prevent any possible encounters with the press.

"Pack, ensure nothing is left anywhere that could give any clue about the meeting."

One man and one woman were designated as ferrets to go everywhere making 110% sure nothing remained. Baxter made sure guards allowed no one, not even themselves, into the bedroom occupied by Grace, leave it all to Department 13.

George always remembered those few days in Wales.

However it happened the helicopters to evacuate the group arrived before the helicopter from Department 13 arrived. Cedric announced they were all being redeployed to the underground base at Corsham. Arrangements for the arrival would initially keep them separate from the operational staff,

"To remind you all this is not an invitation to see if you like working underground, you have already signed up for this."

"Are you saying we are in isolation?" asked one of the group.

"Well, yes," replied Cedric, "until Department 13 are finished. Anyway you all look exhausted, after a good night sleep, perhaps the clean up will be over. Sorry, the first night everyone is sharing, two to a room, you can choose your room mate."

The Department 13 helicopter made an enforced landing on route; nothing apparently serious, they arrived after the group had left by which time the guards had been changed several times. Baxter grew increasingly impatient at the lack of activity, time passing, the body getting colder, and the hotel staff at a loss as to what to do. To them it seemed unnecessary that they were locked up in small groups with a sentry on door duty. Prepared under guard, Baxter allowed hot drinks, sandwiches, for all.

Esamia reappeared this time with a selection of friends, as the members of Department 13 exited the helicopter. She pointed to one of the figures,

"Look I told you so."

George with the group arrived at the underground base, without further incident only to find themselves immediately taken for individual debriefing, exactly as Cedric had predicted. Tired, upset, somewhat hungry, ideal conditions for a debrief to get the real facts, (note facts not truth, the truth of the event not yet decided upon by senior Whitehall officials).

CHAPTER TEN

E samia with greater excitement, "look, look, the one on the left now. Look, there is Barbara."

Silence from the Earth Crusters. Off Esamia skipped again in absolute triumph. Why did she not mention those very faint green lights in the distance?

Barbara broke the silence, "So I nearly met George all those years ago."

Now Miss Moneylegs, her journalist nose twitching, she asked the question to Barbara (she in her mind totally sure of what the answer would be).

'Why did your helicopter make an unscheduled landing?'

Barbara replied, now in disbelief, at her own words,

"The two flight officers thought they could see green lights on the landing wheels. Green lights are not put on wheels. The flight officers inspected every inch of their flying machine without finding any malfunction."

Miss Moneylegs knew, and then thought, 'All those years ago, Deep Earth Humanity did not want you to meet George.' So her thought processes entered everyone's, with Tony Computron adding, 'just a coincidence'. Neither Mason, Barbara nor Miss Moneylegs were convinced with the reply. Even Bruce gave a bemused dog stare, then for no obvious reason, jumped up, placing his front paws on the Computron then starting to lick where a face should be (good story for the old tabloid, 'Dog kisses machine from 'The Outer Limits!'")

Barbara recounted to the others that she'd spent six months in Department 13 very early on in her secret life.

"I still remember as if it were yesterday some of the messed up human bodies that we dealt with. Department 13 is professional, always caring about the family waiting for the remains of the loved one killed in action somewhere in the World. I couldn't stand it as a permanent posting, constantly covering up the truth, constantly giving answers to relatives that I knew were untrue. An important task, however, not for me. I was a thinker not a doer."

Miss Moneylegs questioned, "Do you remember this clean up operation?"

"Well, what I've forgotten, I'll soon be able to recall. Sitting here looking at the screens, it is a very faint memory."

CHAPTER ELEVEN

I an at the same underground establishment, some 50 years after George, continued looking for a method to establish communication links in case any other underground bases had survived the Whale Anomaly. Obviously it was impossible to go overland; death would be almost instant and had asked all present to think outside the box for ideas. One of those all too young computer 'geeks' suggested, then gave all sorts of reasons, as to why his suggestions would be impossible.

'Yes,' thought Ian, 'a brilliant mind afraid of his own brilliance. Will these 'geeks' get so young that they will be too young to employ?'

So the 'geek' named 'Bi' – William shortened to Bill, shorted to 'Bi?', started.

"Somewhere near where the massive telephone exchange had been situated cables would have been put underground, probably placed inside culverts, or more likely pipes. That underground cabling would have needed access points for telephone engineers to make repairs, to lay new cables. My little group have looked for the old plans, we can't find them, so we all need to look in the old exchange area for covered over exits where the original cables would have entered into the exchange."

That received a round of applause; 'Bi' blushed deep red.

Photographs of the original exchange had been saved for posterity. Ian instructed that part of the area easily identified be drawn on the floor into three meter squares, five individuals given the task of crawling around the floor looking for evidence of 'new work'. Even the five wandered into each other's way and concerned onlookers dispersed. The search found nothing. There was general agreement however that the idea of 'Bi' should be pursued.

Ian asked the Librarian if she had any plans. Her reply only too obvious.

"They're kept securely in London. We do have a number, quite a lot really, of photograph albums, individual photographs. One of the activities here provided a well-supported photography club. All photographs had to be stored here. No one was allowed to take them when they left."

'Quite a lot really,' transpired into thousands, tables in the Library were loaded with photographs. Again groups were formed comprising the amateur photographers with the professional interpreters of satellite maps. Any photographs of the telephone exchange at any time were pulled out for very detailed examination. This took time, slow, laborious.

(In Deep Earth Tony Computron thought, 'how feeble this activity is. We Computrons could locate what they want in seconds'. 'Do it then,' thought Barbara. She knew 'no' to be the answer.)

Any photograph of help found itself scanned into the computer to produce 3D imaging. To the delight of 'Bi' and everyone else, the haystack produced a needle, pictures of workmen removing the old telephone exchange with a new one. Further changes had taken place as the current telephone exchange was definitely different from both of the other two and the workmen had performed a fantastic job in covering any ground cable access.

Painstakingly two access holes were detected with the resident builders setting about moving all surface material. (Yes in this underground city builders, plumbers, electricians, all on the staff register.) A time arrived when the builders advised Ian that they could now break through into what existed underneath. Work halted, Ian called a meeting of team leaders of the safety officers. Ian started the discussion with,

"We can't just break the floor. We have no knowledge of what is there, poisonous air, a water surge etc. etc. We need a well-planned opening up strategy."

(Tony Computron thought, 'what fools. Go for it. You're dead anyway, in the future.)

"A structure would be built over the work area and protective clothing. Other than the work team, everyone else was to stay away in the bunkers within the bunker."

A small hole was drilled downwards, ready to be capped instantly if necessary. Then a second, then a third and fourth. No escaping anything, liquid or gases. The first area eventually reached the size of a manhole cover, the second area producing the same, and all access now available to the underground.

At this point the Safety Officers took control, got into protective clothing and carrying seriously powerful torches and rope already well secured above ground. They would attempt to walk along the culvert for two minutes, then return. That proved a success. Next walk along for five minutes then return. They confirmed that the theory 'Bi' had was so far completely correct.

Safety Officers changed over, again in protective clothing. Now they proceed for thirty minutes then returned. All staff were informed to go back to normal duties, keeping away from the explorers. This time they would go for sixty minutes. They returned after forty minutes, having been head high, the piping suddenly went substantially smaller, little more than crawling room above the cables. Not enough space for those Safety Officers to proceed anymore. A new forward group of the smallest would have to be found. Volunteers to crawl into what?

In Deep Earth, Tony Computron decided enough was enough of these feeble activities (those still underground reported seeing green lights). The big communications screen instantly stopped flashing madly, something like green lightening flashed across, then a voice, a second voice. Cheering, loud cheering, communications from somewhere. They were not alone. Cheering behind the voices they heard. Everyone wanted to talk at once and it was therefore difficult for Ian to impose authority onto the deep emotions of others alive as well. Within moments the Communications team were in position. What were the green electrical discharges, almost like forked lightening? The Northern Lights dancing over the screen then gone. Screen was an understatement of the huge display board, as big as three double decker red London buses, as high as Big Ben. The entire world there.

Tony Computron, having interfered with Earth Crust Humanity found himself summoned to the Elders. He had interfered in the past, a golden rule that Deep Earth Humanity should not affect events on the surface sometimes relaxed, he thought, 'in trouble or not Senior Elders, get straight to the point.' They have not existed in Deep Earth for millions of years without enforcing decision making in the interests of all.

Tony Computron thought back to the nuclear missile launched from an Asian country, the collective mind power of all the Elders preventing the launch taking place. Even for the collective of Elder Elders that had been an enormous use of energy. As he waited, that even louder sound of the Founding Protectors made Tony and all of Deep Earth Humanity understand a prime, fundamental problem existed, someway Mother Earth remains in danger following the encounter with the Whale Anomaly.

Venerable Elder Elder informed Tony that the 'Golden Rule' needed to be amended. The Founding Protectors knew danger existed on Earth Crust with all those underground bunkers unable to communicate a pointless nuclear attack could easily happen. Deep Earth Humanity itself would be placed in danger. Two tasks were imminent; get communications working and make nuclear missiles, nuclear warheads, unusable. Then a third problem; those nuclear submarines armed to the teeth at large in the oceans. 'The seas,' Tony Computron thought, 'no small task then.' A reprimanding thought, 'any of those nuclear bombs would give Deep Earth Humanity concern.'

Computrons (of which there are many) took moments to effect the complete shutdown of all nuclear equipment. In Earth Crusters language rather like the finals at Oxford University giving science students a three-hour paper with one question. 'Write down the chemical formulas for oxygen,' then what to do with the remaining 2 hours 59 minutes and 59 seconds. Nuclear weapons useless everywhere, were they fit for purpose, no doubt, no! If they were somebody somewhere would have pulled the trigger.

Perhaps all participants knew the toys could not work. Where would any defence industry have been without nuclear? Where might the none working part be? Probably in the guidance systems. Nuclear submarines started to malfunction, would they float up, would they sink to the bottom? Submarines could be left on the shelf. Now onto communications, make usable, inbuilt Ewewatch, a control system for the Computrons to use. Miss Moneylegs would be the face of control, comfort in a human face for Earth Crusters. Bring the television studio back into use. Earth Crust engineers could not create any communications other than those through the decades out of date cables.

Then the voice, Miss Moneylegs,

"A temporary communications center is set up here. I can now communicate with all underground establishments worldwide. We will shortly supply each country with a listing of those establishments still operational within their own borders."

Tony Computron thought, 'what a waste. Nowhere for them to go outside limited supplies of everything, waiting for death. What will worry them most, 'who is in control? Where is control? Why are our communications controlled?'" The Computron could say all communications have been controlled for a long time. To the younger Elders this felt as a complete pointless exercise. Earth Crusters would all be dead in the

underground coffins soon enough. A very basic national, international communications system now in place.

CHAPTER TWELVE

With a regulated communications system in place, with nuclear warheads now lumps of useless material, the ear smashing noise of the Founding Protectors eased a little. Nuclear submarines had an even shorter life expectancy, six months if lucky, so why were the Founding Protectors remaining active? Elder Elders from everywhere started to arrive, 'Time to use those thinking hats.'

Mason had decided to return to animal world. He'd been deeply upset to see staff from Department 13, they might have been the very people who reconstructed his sister after her death in MI5 action when they were both in their twenties.

With the Elderorium of the Elders in progress, a consensus formed that the logical obvious concern of the Founding Protectors centered on the 'jumping stars.'

The Galaxy did not jump, but there existed a distortion, then normality. For this first instance George's team had described it as a wave or a wind, both words profoundly inadequate to describe such a movement. A movement of universal size. Now the effect of the disturbance existed as fact. What did not exist as fact was where the wind, the wave, came from? Where it would be going, and how it had started to exist. Would the Milky Way be affected?

The Elderorium of the Elders had no certainty that the wave/wind jumping stars represented the threat of the Founding Protectors concern. Logically it had to be. If the stars jumped what chance of Earth surviving? Earth as nothing compared to the smallest of stars. A deep thought came from an Elder, 'If the jumping stars event is caused by a 'Big Bang' somewhere out there, would the Founding Protectors be the same or different from our Big Bang Founding Protectors?' Silence, deep deep silence. Could the Founding Protectors have a concern with the impossible thought of their own end? Having existed from the very essence of time beginning. Having gone into, then gone out of any mass, any solid, any gas, and any special distortion. Is this their alarm sound, not knowing what happens to them next?

As if George had not died, the teams found new goals, new theories to understand, most of all what happens to Mother Earth? As parochial as ever, Miss Moneylegs enquired what could be done to help Earth Crust Humanity deal with this new catastrophic event? Her head ringing with severe reprimands from everywhere.

Tony Computron took sympathy with her view, asking her in turn,

'What do you feel can help Earth Crusters?'

'Tell them,' she thought.

The Computron, 'Why? They are already entombed in their graves. Nothing can be done to save them anyway. Not even we understand what will happen if the wind/wave hits Earth. I'm sure the Elders will help if anything can alleviate their plight. If we tell them their fate would be worse. At this moment they have some hope of a future.'

Elders were repetitive in the only question, 'When will the wind/wave arrive?'

No answer. The best answer, "not immediate."

Mason removed himself to animal world on one of those flying carpets that Mason, Barbara and George had christened 'the flying transport.' Not a bird, perhaps the original flying saucer, you sat on the body? In the middle and of course, you just thought of your destination and off you went. Mason had found solace in animal world before. The first visit he admitted to fright when encountering a very wild dog like animal with gigantic jaws. This time he returned having seen Department 13 at work. Always he'd had questions as to how Cynthia, his sister, had died on duty with MI5. They never gave any information. His one thought, 'why did she die so young?'

Mason's friends in animal world were kangabee, something from New Holland (Australia), in-between a kangaroo and a wallabee. Their only occupation, their only relaxation, playing cricket. Mason had even stood as the scorer, when would he be allowed to umpire? If only they could serve cucumber sandwiches, ginger beer on white linen tablecloths. A game in progress, no limit to the number of players, did a game ever end? Were enemies lurking in the bushes waiting for a tasty kangabee? Could that be the fate of bad players standing at third man or long on waiting to be gobbled up? Nearly a duck!!

Mason well knew animal kingdom did not exist as a well fed zoo, animal, reptile, insect life in the kill or be killed world. Anyway kangabee's play cricket. Mason thought back to happy cricket days. Test matches at Lords (London). County matched in Cheltenham Cricket festival week. The ever-present question, would Worcester be flooded at the start of the season? Here would have been ideal, except for fielding at third man. You would soon find out if you were unpopular.

Esamia returned with a lady who introduced herself.

"I'm a teacher of Earth Crust behaviour at the school Esamia attends (no wonder Little Miss Cheeky Esamia kept quiet for once). Could Miss Moneylegs come to the school and join in a discussion currently taking place?"

Miss Moneylegs puffed out her journalistic chest, joining in conversation (without speaking) with the teacher. Now the room in which the class was meeting did not exist in regimented rows of desks, more like round tables on which students could lean, height adjustable, then hanging from the roof some sort of multi sitting swings. The teacher occupied another single swing from which she could view from various heights what the students were doing. No hiding place at the back of the room, every student visible. A formal introduction from the teacher, no doubt out of politeness, all Deep Earth Humanity knew of Miss Moneylegs.

Introductions over, the teacher explained, 'the class is trying to understand why Earth Crust Humanity ate so much food. Let me explain further that these figures come from your specialists. They estimate that a male human eats ten times his body weight each year. So in general terms, Earth Crust humans consumed between half a ton and one ton of food each year. So a sixteen stone man living to seventy of your years would eat seventy tons of food in his lifetime. In our society that is a terrible misuse of resources. That is a terrible negative return as to input into the human body against the output of activity, that is a terrible laziness in not producing those resources that your body actually needed to continue to function. To us no active research has taken place by the food industry rather it continued to exploit a captive market. Giving someone seventy tons of food in their lifetime is a disproportionate use of scarce food resources. A very ineffective body you have/had.' 'Have' directed to Miss Moneylegs, Barbara, and Mason. 'Had' at Earth Crust Humanity now suffocated to death.

Miss Moneylegs replied that,

"In all her life she had never thought about food consumption in that way. Going on diets, eating less, yes that had been common, the thought of eating tons of food in a lifetime made her feel sick." She continued, "basic information was never taught, people spoke of food waste, not total food consumed."

The teacher interrupted saying,

"But how could your society go on and on eating without stopping to think? Let me give you some idea of what that might look like. Place ten London double decker buses side by side, yes 10, those buses would weigh about seventy tons."

All the children looked at Miss Moneylegs with the same thought, 'did Earth Crust Humanity ever think of serious matters?'

CHAPTER THIRTEEN

Within a few hours of the theft of the stolen report written by George with advice on the Cuban Missile Crisis to the British Foreign and Commonwealth Office, the foreign thieves received well-deserved thanks from their superior who in turn was passing on the thanks of the London Ambassador. British Security Service, MI5 now had operatives placed in and around any of the potential embassies that could have organized the theft.

All of the so-called Soviet Union satellite countries could be called upon by Moscow to undertake the assignment. All such Embassy staff understood the game, 'If Moscow asks, you say yes, knowing full well that Moscow will disown you if you're caught.' For the KGB a good source of willing participants had always been the East German Secret Police, the 'Stasi.' As the British Commonwealth began to break up in Africa, the 'Stasi' found particular influence in Ghana, where it ran a large network of informers, a 'Stasi' speciality.

This theft did not involve the 'Stasi'. The KGB didn't exist alone in the United Kingdom; there also existed the Russian Military spies, the G.R.U. Also the satellite countries of the Soviet Union had their own spy networks. The London Ambassador of that country arranged that his naval attaché would pass over the report to the third naval attaché at the Soviet Embassy. In Soviet terms, third naval attaché existed very low in the pecking order. The two naval men knew each other, had passed documents over to each other in the past. Both knew as soon as they left the home soil (an embassy is always accepted as being on homeland ground, not the ground of the host country, when of course in reality it is host country land) such are the niceties of the diplomatic world, they would be picked up by British MI5 agents. So in the strange world of spying the Soviet naval attaché would have a group of Brits following him, the same for the other Embassy man also being trailed. So the game for the naval attaches had to be loose those following you, if impossible abort returning back to base. It is fair to say most Soviet spies knew their way around the streets of London as well as a London taxi driver; they were equally at home using the underground. Buses were more difficult, not enough space to hide. The favourite game to loose the followers would be to get off the Tube at every stop, then pretend to get on the next tube, then alight (jump off) moments before the doors closed. Cat and mouse games for humans, time never a constraint. If necessary the game could be played all day. The Security Service, MI5, only has limited numbers of staff to use on such occasions. In reality unless a known drop was taking place following lower ranks of the Embassy staff could be viewed as a waste of resources. Then of course the double bluff allowing a drop to take place when a foreign agent reported to British Security what was taking place. So on it went, a never-ending web of intrigue. There have always been spies; there always will be spies. So the report of George ended up in the Soviet Embassy, Kensington Palace Gardens, on the desk of the 'resident' highest-ranking KGB officer in London.

Another Bridge evening had been going well for the mother of Grace. All her favourite friends had gathered, even Stephen Ward, this time with a beautiful, very young, blond, on best behaviour. Behind hands to the mouth the ladies were trying to decide if the very young blond had any undergarments under her glittering long pale blue low cut dress. A loud repeated knock at the door, Stephen jumped up to answer. Three men standing outside the door, two obvious uniformed police officers, and the third perhaps a detective asked the question,

"Is Countess Parmatti at home?"

Stephen went for the upper hand using deliberate brakes in the name to emphasize the incorrect pronunciation.

"Do you mean Countess Par-mat-ti?"

"Yes," replied the perhaps detective.

"One up to me," thought Stephen. Then in best British polite manners,

"Please step inside and wait in the hallway," the hallway somewhat larger than a police house. Even a uniformed officer could recognize items of opulence and wealth. A chandelier glistening with exquisite hand cut glass. A long, long sideboard, deep black encrusted with gold inlay. Such the wealth of even minor Italian royalty. On top of the sideboard, under glass, items from 'Faberge' at least two being the ornate 'Faberge' eggs, such the wealth of even minor Russian royalty.

The perhaps detective suggested the Countess should be seated as he had some bad news for the mother of Grace.

CHAPTER FOURTEEN

Debriefing continued at Corsham Underground Base with the exception of George. He went immediately to the secure Telex facility where the Senior Telex operator established a secure scrambling line into the Foreign Office Telex Machine room.

She typed at great speed the Cuban Assessment that George had previously sent by ambulance, that report then stolen. Having received the report, the Senior Civil Servant in the Foreign Office telephoned George on a very secure phone to read the report word by word back to George, then asking George to detail exactly those differences between the stolen report with the real report. George went precisely through those changes then again word for word the difference in his two conclusions.

The Senior Civil Servant then confirmed that George understood that the name of George would be on the report, that George accepted that he, George, had full responsibility for the conclusions, that the report and conclusions would be presented by the Foreign Secretary to a Full Cabinet Meeting the next morning. Another copy would go in advance to the Secretary of State for War, John Profumo.

The conclusions that George presented:-

1)   The information about the Soviet Union building several missile sites since May 1962 is now confirmed. The missiles are medium-range and intermediate-range ballistic

nuclear missiles (MRBMs and IRBMs).

2)   This deployment follows the American attempted overthrow of the Cuban Regime with the charismatic Fidel Castro on 17 April 1961, referred to as 'The Bay of Pigs'.

3)   The deployment follows the Americans placing nuclear missiles in Turkey and Italy aimed at Moscow.

4)   This now presents the most serious threat of a nuclear war since the beginning of the Cold War.

5)   Reality is that this country can do very little other than involve the United Nations supporting initiatives taken by doing so.

6)   Response is to place this country on a war footing without causing alarm to the population. (In the stolen copy it reads 'response is not to place this etc. etc.)

7)   Activate all underground establishments, all regional control centers. (In the stolen copy it reads 'do not activate any underground control centers).

8)   Advise all Military Commanding Officers in Caribbean Commonwealth countries to be on the highest state of readiness expecting a Soviet Attack. (In the stolen copy this is exactly the same).

9)   Advise all Military Commanding Officers in all Commonwealth Countries to be prepared for a Soviet Attack. (In the stolen copy this is exactly the same).

10)   All Military establishments in

Europe, particularly those on the Soviet Union borders to reduce the state of readiness 'to active only'. (In the stolen copy this is exactly the same).

11)
74966387252147339826385476 58 (in the stolen copy every fourth number had been changed.)

In final conclusion there is nothing that this country can do to prevent a nuclear encounter. The resolution only is in the hands of the Americans or the Soviets.

By the time the Cabinet in London had sat down to look at the report the KGB (Soviet Secret Service) were also looking at the report in central Moscow. The false report had arrived in the diplomatic bag on an Aeroflot scheduled flight from London, using a Tupolov 104 aeroplane. The Tupolov TV-104 was a twin-engine medium range narrow body turbojet, sometimes referred to as the World's first successful jet airliner. The TV104 was the sole jetliner operating in the world between 1956-1958. Normal configuration was for eighty passengers. Did it deploy a tail parachute to assist braking when landing?

The KGB with the GRU (Soviet Military Intelligence) prepared those reports for the 'Kremlin' to make a decision on making a first nuclear attack. (Similar meetings were being held by the American Intelligence Agencies advising the White House on making a first nuclear strike).

Soviet Intelligence Agencies looked for any clue in the 'George Report' that could throw light on the American thinking. All security agencies around the world knew of the close relationship between the American and British military. Would the Soviets find a clue?

CHAPTER FIFTEEN

ountess Parmatti, the mother of Grace, sat with that stiff upper lip that royalty inherits, the 'perhaps' detective asked if her friends could leave the hallway as the information could not be shared with anyone else. One uniformed officer ushered friends back in the 'Bridge Playing Room' then closed the door staying in the room to prevent eavesdropping, listening at the keyhole. So the 'perhaps' detective opened his mouth, words came as if in slow motion,

"A body recently discovered in Austria is that of your husband."

Countess Parmatti sat statuesque. Now obviously not a detective he continued,

"A government car will collect you at 10.00am in the morning to take you to meet the Home Secretary. The matter is highly secret. You must tell your friends the following, 'a large sum of money held in a Swiss bank account has been traced as belonging to your father. You are needed to provide further information.'"

With that the three returned to wherever they had come from, Countess Parmatti explained to her friends the money story. Bridge playing was quickly replaced by money talk, everybody speculating on amounts, on consequences, none more so than Stephen Ward. Even his very attractive blonde companion joined in the money guessing game. If only Grace could be contacted? This would happen when she had gone away, when no telephone number existed to contact her. Why had the thoughtless girl not telephoned this evening? If only the Countess knew!

Every single one of the Bridge friends offered to stay the night, alone the Countess wanted to be, alone she would be. When the last one left she switched off all lights except that on the upstairs landing, the other in the bedroom. On the landing she opened what everyone assumed were normal cupboard door. Inside a family chapel, perhaps ten feet deep by eight feet wide, at the very back an alter, in front of the altar a rail, in front of the rail, kneeling stools. Her Russian Orthodox faith always with her. On the altar a magnificent gold cross, some eighteen inches high, studded with rubies, on either side of the cross, an icon, one of Jesus, one of Mary. Both in traditional wood cases, gold, precious stones encrusted. Then at the side of one icon her marriage photographs. At the side of the other icon, Grace as a young girl. Around the room portraits of her family members. Inside this room of great material wealth, the family of the Countess at hand to talk to.

As she had done all her life, she prayed, then with a tear in her eyes, asked the Count where he had been found, then to Grace, where are you? I need you for tomorrow. Then she closed the door on her Russian life and when in bed turned to the poetry of Lermontov, reading the poem, 'Because."

'If I am sad it is because I am in love with you
and well I know the blight of rumour most untrue
Will not forbear to mark your blooming youth with sorrow
For every hour of joy. Fate will exact tomorrow
a toll of tears and pain that you alone must pay
So I am sad my dearest love.'

She never read the last few words since the Count disappeared, but over and over she repeated,

'So I am sad my dearest love'. She slid under the bedclothes, as always the landing light stayed on, without an alarm she woke at 6am. As normal the poetry of Lermontov still by her side. She prayed for strength for the day, that Grace would be safe.

Precisely at 10:00am a Government car pulled up outside her house. A young man knocked on the door, introduced himself then opened a rear door of the Rover, then instructed the driver to go. In fact, in reality, the Countess could have walked from St James's to the Home Office.

While the Countess would have been getting ready, the Inspector of Department 13 returned to Northolt with Grace. That gave enough time for the file on the events in Wales to get to the Home Secretary in advance of the Countess. So by the time the Countess arrived to meet the Home Secretary he had ample time to study that file, he already having studied in detail the file about the Count. In all his long years in politics, two major event files concerning one family had to be a new experience, preferably, not to be repeated.

The Countess, accompanied still by the young man, entered the Home Secretary's palatial office, he placing the 'Grace' file inside a drawer. Even now, not so young, the Countess could still turn the heads of the suited brigade, elegant, always elegant, the self-confidence of the privileged upbringing, the self respect to her body to keep it in proportion; still a trim waist so in an emergency she and Grace could exchange clothes.

A firm handshake from the Home Secretary, the young man pulling out a fine leather armchair, she sat. The young man sat at the Secretary table to take notes, a male private secretary taking notes in shorthand, not an insignificant appointment, recording for posterity word for word all that would be spoken, Opening the file, the Home Secretary with a word formed on his lips, heard a knock on the door that took the opening word away from his lip. The young man looked at him. He nodded. The young man arose, and then opened the door.

Esamia appeared yet again at another critical moment, repeating the question, 'Is George in trouble yet?' then continuing, 'Barbara can you come and answer some questions like Miss Moneylegs did? The subject is different.'

Miss Moneylegs looked at Barbara with a head shaking, saying 'no'. Bruce the Dog thought no would be best. Tony Computron encouraged Barbara leading with Esamia to the expectant class-room. Again, a warm welcome from the teacher, explaining 'we (the class) are trying to understand Earth Crust Humanity's apparent obsession with the motorcar, personal transport. How the need to 'own' exploded in the last seventy years of existence.'

A young boy started the questions,

"What is wrong with your brains that the people do not understand what a speed limit is? From our observations, it would appear that your brains see 'speed limit' then go faster over and above the limit."

Barbara; "I don't know the answer. It is criminal. It is unfortunate that the authorities did not prosecute offenders with any rigour, almost as if they were pleased to allow speeding for the extra revenue in fuel taxes. For a country, obviously the faster you go, the more taxes are paid as consumption increases."

The boy,

"So you're saying people like paying extra taxes?"

"Not really," Barbara replied.

The boy,

"That is one reason we are confused. If, say a country increases income taxes, people complain. But when the same people have the ability to pay reduced taxes by driving within the speed limits, they refuse the opportunity."

Next question, from a girl. Barbara had seen the girl with Esamia.

"Would you look at these pictures? It is the M25 motorway that goes around London in England. You will see the weather is bad. It is a winter's night about 10pm. Now watch", three cars flashed through the screen, the screen flashed speeds of 132 miles per hour, between the cars, no more than two car spaces apart. No police, yet the motorway cameras still show exactly that they are speeding.

"Now watch," the front car brakes, the second car smashes into the first, the third car smashes into the second. The second car is squashed, squeezed, pulped into less than 25% of the original size. The driver in the first car is uninjured. The driver in the second is dying, the passenger in the front is dead, there is/was a female passenger on the back seat, her dismembered remains were difficult to piece together (the jigsaw never completed). The driver in the third car lost a leg for life, his female passenger shot out through the windscreen, ended up in the central lane with multiple injuries. Thankfully, she ended up dead under the wheels of a 40-footer supermarket delivery lorry. Police arrived within six minutes, ambulances stuck in the accident tail back, took another 3 and a half minutes. It took the emergency services nearly two hours to remove the leg of driver number 3, by which time the driver in the second car had passed away. The thrill of exceeding the speed limit, replaced with the eternity of death. Life then death in the fast land.

"Barbara, the question for you please is why did Earth Crust Humanity not value the life given?"

"Difficult," started Barbara, "Earth Crust Humanity was a relatively new addition to the Earth. The brain, still developing, and then that incredible leap from horsepower to motor power. Free spirit not comprehending danger, self-interest more important that self-regulation. All aspects of life taken to excess, speed, drugs, sex, risk taking, money, self interest to gravitate to huge city communities, almost as if like ants. Really in conclusion, a complete lack of regulating self."

Definite applause when she finished. Barbara beamed. If Tony Computron had a chest he would have puffed it out. His Barbara was popular!

During the answer the pictures from 'Ewewatch' had continued showing how fragile the human body had been. One of the children,

"Can people clearing up the bits of Humanity body parts receive extra payment? Could they say they would not help anyone obviously causing an accident? And why were these 'people movers' cars not made more strongly?"

Barbara replied,

"These emergency people did not receive extra money. In fact they were lowly paid."

The child continued,

"These people do a terrible job. They should be very highly paid."

Then another child,

"Why were 'bank gamblers' paid so much? It wasn't even their own money! We could show you on 'Ewewatch' how they colluded together to make more of the worthless paper you called money. They used other people's money to make gigantic salaries. What did they contribute to society?"

Barbara simply replied, "Nothing. Back to self-interest with no regulation."

The teacher thanked Barbara again, more applause from the class, then escorted back by Esamia. Barbara thought of the little rhyme often whispered in the corridors of power, 'Bankers are wankers'. Barbara mused when, she first started in the Civil Service 'nice ladies might think it, not say it. As time progressed the words were spoken out loud and often.'

On the outside of the door, not moving in, a lady with an envelope. The young man took the note, asked the lady to wait, and handed the envelope to the Home Secretary who read it. Addressing the Countess, the Home Secretary apologized saying their meeting needed to be delayed, perhaps for thirty minutes as a very serious matter had arisen. He addressed the young man as Charles saying,

"Please escort the Countess to the anteroom and ask the staff member who had delivered the note (he absolutely famous for the inability to remember names) to sit with her and also to arrange tea and coffee."

In the anteroom the Countess flipped through the pages of Vogue, then The Lady, whilst sipping green tea with lemon. Yes, the Home Office management canteen could produce green tea with lemon.

Thirty minutes passed, nothing, another five minutes. Without listening, somehow hearing the names Profumo and Stephen Ward in the same sentence by a person in the office of the Home Secretary. Stephen Ward only yesterday at her Bridge party, John Profumo, a minister she had met several times at social gatherings, and Cliveden, a country house she had visited over the years.

Another five minutes, the constant conflict of state against individual. What could be more important for the Countess after all these years than to hear what had happened to her husband? Nothing more critical in her life, yet the State dictates her concerns have now become relegated to second or third place. Dealing with any State is a lottery. Will your number come up today to deal with your concerns? At least in those states where bribery is commonplace, once the bribe is paid, events happen more quickly.

Another five minutes, the minder produced another green tea with lemon and more magazines to read. They were getting older, still pictures of friends to look at. Now looking through the window. The Countess could see members of the Foreign and Commonwealth Office walking around at their own particular pace. If only that daughter Grace could be here, then there would be someone to share the concerns with. The sorrow of the unexpected news about the Count. Where could she be? Surely that special medical assignment had finished? When will she get back to home and normal hospital routine?

An hour now passed, minder, fidget, fidget even more. Eventually the young male secretary returned full of apology, not however as great as the apology from the Home Secretary.

Back into the fine leather armchair. Momentarily the Home Secretary opened the file, quickly realizing he had the wrong file, replaced and changed for the correct one. His mouth again formed to say the first word, then another knock on the door.

Charles looked to the Home Secretary in disbelief, he again received the nod. For the first time the Countess fidgeted, 'not pleased' written all over the elegant demeanour. Charles opened the door again, there yet again another unnamed staff member guilty of the first interruption.

Charles said, "Please come in."

Grace limped in looking like death warmed up so before the Countess could speak 'Grace' simply said,

"I'll explain at home."

Charles pulled up another fine leather chair so they were together. Grace held out her hand with broken fingernails, bruised knuckles. The Countess held it too tightly and Grace flinched in pain. The grip eased. Grace no longer found the hand painful.

At last, at last, the Home Secretary uttered his first word, and then forgot instantly to welcome Grace.

"Some seven weeks ago your husband's body was found lying in a deep grave in a lead lined coffin. It was found when construction work started in a small hamlet on the Austrian/Italian border. When I explain the events you will understand even after all these years, we know it is the Count. You will remember that your husband excelled in languages, accepted as fluent in Russian, German, English and of course, Italian. Your last time together in 1939, he had secret orders preventing him giving you information about where or what his posting would be. He had, in fact, joined the Officer Corp of the German Army working in a special group to turn dissenters into supporters of the German cause. Our Military Intelligence deliberately requested he undertake this difficult assignment in order to obtain whatever first hand information he could get. There then existed an elaborate system for information to get back to the British military. He did not exist in isolation. An elaborate support team existed as well. To identify members of the group, each member had a three-digit number engraved into one or more of their back teeth. Regarding the Count, his numbers were 278, which I understand Countess, is your birth day and month?"

She nodded.

"National Security prevents any further details entering the Public Domains."

Indignantly Grace snorted,

"We are family, not public."

Without answering the Home Secretary went on,

"The Count will receive a posthumous award for bravery (details still under discussion). You will receive all his back pay. Then you will receive his pension so that the cover story about 'money' has validity."

"Thank you," the Countess spoke then in a voice of sharpened steel, looking straight into the eyes,

"I demand to read the file about the Count."

The Home Secretary,

"It is impossible."

Countess, more ice cold steel,

"I demand to see the file."

Charles the Secretary moved his chair in discomfort. Silence, more silence, knife cutting silence. Then from nowhere, the Countess let go of the hand of Grace, stood up, placed her hands on the vast desk acting as a barrier to The Home Secretary, looked down onto his now flushed face. Calmly, with extended syllables,

"Stephen Ward – Jack Profumo,"

Flushed went to red,

"I also ask to see your file you had in the top left hand drawer when I came in."

"Please excuse me while I make a phone call," countered the Home Secretary.

"No!" she said.

"Phone call, yes, we will sit here and listen."

Charles the Secretary politely coughed,

"Sir, I believe a precedence exists provided the file is read with a member of Security Service sitting in, also no note taking is allowed."

Countess; "Such an arrangement is agreeable to Grace and myself?"

A good politician is aware when to accept the inevitable. Polite friendliness returned to the meeting. Charles, with his intervention would be propelled quicker up the ladder of Management. Of course, no precedence had existed. A small team of Civil Servants soon found (or invented) one. Charles would organize the time and place for file reading. The Countess gave Charles the look of steel.

"It will be within five working days."

Cornered, Charles replied, "Yes."

He escorted them back to the Government car, and then went with them back home. Politeness ruled the day, only small unimportant talk.

As the Countess, with Grace entered home, the phone was already ringing with the inquisitive wanting information on the money found belonging to the father of the Countess, who took the phone off the hook. She wanted to find out what had happened to Grace.

Grace, now in the kitchen, preparing green tea for the two of them, tea in a teapot, the everyday china, all on a tray, carrying all into the morning room. She sat down only to find mother standing over her looking at the injuries and bruises. Grace wanted to get a message to George. She started her explanation by saying George thought she had died.

"Who is George?"

Grace began to explain when George had gone to start the last meeting before the shooting activity began. She'd climbed the stairs, started to walk along a bedroom corridor. When passing a bedroom, she could hear the voice of George from the inside. Impossible, she'd thought she'd left him only a minute before at the conference room door. He had not passed her on the staircase. He had either climbed up the outside wall or flown (he couldn't be that athletic!).

So she knocked on the door; which opened. She entered, but there was no one to be seen only a recorder listening to talking from the Conference Room. It definitely was George talking. After that she only remembered a bang on the head, a sharp needle into the arm. Very, very vaguely, two figures, male and female. That is all she could remember. Vaguely she recognized the language they spoke, the next she remembered a medical person attempting to revive her. Events in-between she only knew following information from some people from the Security World called Department 13. Her clothes had been removed to leave her only in nothing, the female of the two attempted to escape dressed as Grace, even her hair the same colour, the same style. In the escape, the person when caught pulled out a gun blowing off her face, then fell face down, all that everyone could see had been a dead figure dressed as Grace. To everyone it had been a dead Grace.

The male figure escaped with the recordings that had been made. Upon investigation, it had been obvious that the meetings had been compromised. She explained for five hours, no one found her. It took that long for the delayed Department 13 to search the hotel, only then did they understand about the recordings. She had been found tied up, gagged, covered over by bed linen in the corner of the built-in wardrobe.

The Countess examined her precious daughter again, bruised, shaken, lump on the head, nothing broken. Grace concluded saying that she returned to Northolt in a helicopter and had then be brought to the Home Office by Government car.

"Right young lady, that's enough for one day. Go have a bath, then into bed. I will speak to the hospital."

"No need," Grace said, "some Government person spoke to the hospital Chief to say I had been taken ill on the assignment. A Government doctor will visit me mornings and afternoons to check me over."

At which point, Grace started to climb the stairs to do as told. Halfway up, a knock at the door. She turned to come down only to be told very curtly by the Countess to get into the bath.

"It is probably the doctor," Grace responded, "I'll have the bath when he has gone."

Like all naughty girls, Grace went upstairs, then leaned over the bannister rail to watch. The Countess opened the door. Grace recognized the driver who drove her from Northolt to the Home Office.

Barbara and Miss Moneylegs were now having private bets as to when Esamia would be back. Sure enough, here she appeared again. Usual question, "Is George in trouble yet?"

"Not that we're aware off."

With noticeable disappointment Esamia skipped off. With Miss Moneylegs thinking, 'wish those Founding Protectors would shut up. I can't concentrate.'

At the front door the driver asked,

"Is Miss Grace at home?"

"Who are you to ask?" questioned the Countess.

From upstairs, but not in the bathroom, Grace shouted,

"Mother it's the driver who brought me this morning."

So the Countess invited the driver in. The driver didn't move, but behind him, and to the right, a figure appeared. From the bannister rail a scream,

"It's George."

How quickly can you get from upstairs to downstairs? Very quickly when you slide down the bannister rail. Grace had done this all her life, always to be told, 'Grace that's not very lady-like.' Never mind, she made it down. There stood George, bunch of flowers in hand. The driver turned,

"Say 1 hour sir. I am waiting in the car."

"Welcome George," the Countess spoke, "What have you done to my daughter? Come in."

Grace, now hesitant. She wanted to throw her arms around George, hug him and kiss him. George stood still.

Grace took the initiative. Forgetting every ache and pain, hugged him. Would he respond? How would he respond?

Then the Countess like all mothers,

"Come out of the doorway. The neighbours will talk."

That there could not be any neighbour, the nearest house 100 meters across the road was immaterial. George returned the hug, their lips met for the very first time. A kiss.

Decorum restored, the Countess saying,

"For goodness sake, come in the pair of you."

Even for the Countess, now a day of emotional extremes, dead husband to Grace obviously in love. She would have to use her network of influential friends to see if this George could be suitable for her little girl. The Countess went off to make tea. Grace took George into the morning room to tell the story all over again. George questioned every detail (only at a later time did Grace get concerned). The tea came, went cold. The Countess came and went at least three times. She noticed they were clutching hands, their discussion so intense that holding hands was an outside representation of intense feelings.

Another knock at the front door. The Countess let in the driver who pleaded with George that they must go; already they were eighteen minutes late in leaving. Reluctant George held Grace saying,

"I'll be away for a week."

Grace froze. The Countess froze. Exactly the same words the Count had used when they last said goodbye.

George had gone, the driver left at speed far exceeding the speed limit. When the Countess passed the bathroom, Grace could be heard crying; crying for both the Count and for George. So the Countess went to the little church sanctuary on the landing to pray.

Within hours George had returned to 'Corsham'; all being re-interrogated for the slightest, minutest detail regarding the two who'd listened in. George recounted his meeting with Grace. It had not been a matter of chance that he went to see her, as pleasurable as it had been. Only official business had allowed him to make the visit. Then always the questions for a spy. Did I talk to her to protect her? Did I talk to her as required by the State? Why should the Security Service take it upon itself to interfere with the bond between Grace and myself?

In the mortuary at Northolt, painstaking reconstruction started on the body of the unknown woman. Another specialist team arrived at the Welsh hotel using technology breaking forensic science to obtain the least scrap of information. Of greatest concern, preventing the 'Corsham' underground establishment's existence getting into the hands of a Communist block country. Both people, the man and the woman, had arrived together about fifteen minutes after the ambulance. The under manager dealt with them. They asked for a twin or double with facilities, as quiet as possible. They changed rooms several times (different reasons given for unsuitability) then accepted the bedroom above the conference room. Their arrival had been by motorbike with a sidecar, in the sidecar, bags, the lady riding pillion passenger.

Payment had been made for a week, paid cash in advance. On their first evening, the lady had been ill, then eating meals in the bedroom. The man took the opportunity to mingle and talk in the bar. He appeared to speak with everyone at some time or another. He went for walks or further afield on the motorcycle. No interest whatsoever shown in the conference room.

With all good hotels the registration book (written in hand by the guest) contained space for amongst others, name, address, vehicle number. Each section completed in front of the Under Manager. Department 13 established the information to be completely untrue, no such address, no such vehicle of any sort with the given registration vehicle number. General agreement from the staff that the motorbike might be a Triumph.

Even if you are preparing to leave in a hurry, there is nearly always something forgotten. Dustbins had not been emptied yet this week; a wonderful source of every day throw outs. The first breakthrough, or bit of luck, came from under the bed in the dust; a folded bus ticket with a series of pencil numbers, various combinations produced a valid telephone number in London. A second item found tucked in at the bottom of the bed between the top sheet and blanket looked like a rouble (Soviet Union) banknote.

One telephone call to London had extra police officers on duty outside all Soviet block embassies. For no other reason than methodical police work, the local Constabulary found themselves back at the farm track where the ambulance had been found containing the two Syd's. Sure enough they found the burnt out remains of a motorbike with sidecar. Dead end on the man. Back to the dead in the Department 13 mortuary.

All foreign members of all embassies in London have photographs stored at the Home Office. File upon file arrived at the mortuary to see what identification could be made. Without a face it was difficult. Clothes were of no use as they belonged to Grace. Any clue with undergarments? No labels in the bra. Someone had been careless. The underpants label had not been cut properly with enough left to make out the last letter of a word. Name of brand? Name of manufacturer? Name of country? To start, what language?

Special Branch (police) reported no unusual activity at any Embassy or London homes of diplomats. On review of the interviews of the group from Wales, no comment of any sort that the man when spoken to had an accent. That without doubt very significant. Few foreigners speak English without an accent. Few English themselves speak without some regional accent. Most unusual. Unusuality continued with no claim for the dead faceless female, so into cold store, just like ice cream. They do say on World cruises a number of passengers die. They have to be kept on ice.

No doubt closing the stable door after the horse has bolted, a decision was made to give 'Corsham' a code name for all future use of 'Burlington'. If the Soviets had any sleepers (spy's) in any Government department, they might have heard of the new code name making the whole process useless.

CHAPTER SIXTEEN

That the Soviet Union had spies in Great Britain/United Kingdom is a fact. How many perhaps not even the Soviets know. Perhaps many were never caught. Some who were make interesting reading. Some of those known to George, the Foreign Office, MI5, and MI6 were;

1946 Dr Alan Nunn May, Physicist, uranium used in atomic weapons.

1950 Dr Klaus Fuchs, atomic bombs

1951 Guy Burgess, Donald MacLean. Officials at the Foreign Office, they fled to Moscow.

1961 George Blake betrayed Western agents operating behind the Iron Curtain.

1961 Gordon Lonsdale, Peter and Helen Kruger, information about Royal Navy underwater weapons establishment.

1962 (October) Unknown male, dead unknown female.

Deep Earth Humanity knew who they were. 'Ewewatch' could see all. A very long list could also be supplied of those who were never caught, the betrayers who would live till their dying day consumed with secrets, afraid to tell even their loved ones. Such pathetic stupidity had never played a role in Deep Earth.

The whole research effort was focused on George's discovery of the 'Double W' wave effect in the farthest furthest outer reaches of the known universe. There gathered ever-increasing numbers of Deep Earth scientists. Many thousands working to establish what the event meant for minute Earth sitting in a not very impressive galaxy.

Much could be nothing more than guesswork with one important exception, that being the speed of travel. Speed at such long unimaginable distance continues to be measured as the speed of light. Common census amongst the scientists was that whatever it was travelled at slightly less than the speed of light. The Computrons did not agree. That itself had the exception that as yet they could not calculate where it began, where it ended, how long, how wide, how deep. Again by commonality the size having similar dimensions to the Universe, but how could they determine what dimensions existed outside of the universe?

Whatever the outcome, the Founding Protectors, existing from the first instant of the Big Bang feared for their own very existence. What did they already know? What has already been communicated to them? Could they change from this universe into another?

Poor Earth, just waiting, sitting pretty to be kicked into somewhere. No engines in poor Earth to affect an escape into somewhere 'where no man has gone before.' Deep Earth Humanity knew they could go nowhere. Earth Crust Humanity remnants already entombed with no knowledge of what would come. The one sure certainty that Earth Crust Humanity would have ceased to exist in their bunkers long before the Wind/Wave arrives.

CHAPTER SEVENTEEN

The identity of the man, of the dead woman, raised very great concern. Then information concerning the man, that his English had no accent, he spoke perfect English, prompted even greater searches. Why did the woman go to the extraordinary extreme of blowing her face away in order that she not be recognized? No matter how serious the spying crime she had committed, no death penalty would have been sanctioned. Why did she make herself invisible? What were they hiding?

In the world of espionage those recruited (not the professional employees) fall into categories; greed or money, ideological beliefs, blackmail and coercion, self-importance, living double lives to break the normality of being normal. As the lady had killed herself some of those causes could be ruled out.

Would the man have also killed himself? Why did they not want to be captured? Not only had Moscow received the doctored George report, it now knew that Corsham had a code name of 'Burlington'. No time yet to investigate where the leak had come from, in itself not important, just by changing the name does not change the physical locality. No doubt many visits have been made to 'Burlington' by those sympathetic to the Communist cause. How to stop members of the Communist party of Great Britain going on holiday in the Cotswolds? Anthony Blunt (Surveyor of the King's Pictures and later Queen's Pictures after the death of King George VI in 1952) was at some time a member of the party. Burlington became an open secret. Anthony Blunt is well recorded as being a possible spy, then in November 1979 Mrs Thatcher (Prime Minister) exposed him as the fourth man of the Cambridge Four (Philby, Burgess, Maclean, Blunt) in a House of Commons statement.

Cambridge Police received a report that a male research student had been missing from the University for five days. The Police, generally accepting that students regularly went away without thinking to tell the University authorities, took no action. Birmingham University informed the local police that a female medical student had been missing for, they thought, five days. They had tried to contact her brother, a student at Cambridge University with no success. Neither piece of information found itself married to the other; students are students, the generally accepted response. It took another three weeks for action when the Foreign and Commonwealth Office received a request from a British family living in Ghana that they were unable to contact their children at university in Cambridge and Birmingham.

The runaway man, the dead girl, were eventually identified. How had they become involved in this spying business? Why on Earth did the girl blow her face off? In Ghana the S.L.O (Security Liaison Officer (British Spy by another name)) had the task of informing the family, informing an excuse to commence investigation into the brother and sister. Both MI5 and MI6 needed to understand cause and effect. Where is the man?

That answer was resolved as soon as the S.L.O met the mother and father. They had heard from their son, now in East Germany, who had decided to move to an East German University, from Cambridge, where he would receive sponsorship to further his research into rocket propulsion fuels, they had given him an honorary degree with a very substantial budget. Nice accommodation, driver with a car, a live in cook/cleaner. He didn't mention his sister. He had permission to invite them to visit him. His new university would pay for their airfare, providing accommodation in East Berlin for the stay, the parents now very proud of his accomplishments, his progress made more quickly as if some hidden hand provided help.

To the S.L.O it was plainly obvious that this young man had somehow involved himself with East German Security, The Starsi, his rewards very substantial from his Welsh spying activity. The escape from England very well organized by ? The S.L.O knew that would be for London to resolve. Upset relatives receiving very bad news were not unusual for the S.L.O to deal with.

This family, however, was quite different. No emotion, no tears, no difficult questions other than when would the girl's body be returned. This gave him the opportunity to arrange a further meeting with this none emotional family, saying he would return when he had details of when the body could be repatriated. They commented that they would arrange the return through a London firm of undertakers.

As the houseboy escorted the S.L.O out, a young blond haired child, perhaps three and half years old, raced along the hallway, hotly pursued by another houseboy. Shouting, 'Isaac come back, Isaac.' At which moment the child froze on the spot in front of a large photograph of a young man, a young woman and a baby. The child was obviously related to the couple. The S.L.O also stopped to look. No proof but in his own mind, the couple from Wales. 'What relation was the child to them? More enquiries for his return. Do not try and reel in the fish too quickly. Too many early questions will get nowhere. Let the parents grieve in their strange way.'

An S.L.O has no authority in a country of assignment, it was always necessary to keep on the correct side of the law. On his return back to the Embassy he noticed a Mercedes with diplomatic plates passing him in the opposite direction. He knew which embassy had that designated special reference number on the license plate, East Germany. He turned the car to follow no need to get close; if he were a witch his nose would have been twitching. Sure enough the Mercedes had arrived at the property he had so recently left. Training had taught him to always try leaving a pen, a pencil, and glasses behind after a meeting to provide a legitimate excuse to return.

So it happened the houseboy let him in and there waiting in the same hallway were two faces from the East German embassy. All three knew who each of the others were. No one spoke. The houseboy returned with the lost spectacles, probably using lenses from Zeiss, the East German glass factory – the irony. As he started to leave the senior East German spy looked at him and said,

"Burlington."

The S.L.O replied, stating,

"Pay off time for the dead."

Each part smiled, a score draw this time.

In the report back to London, the S.L.O gave facts with a conclusion pointing out that 'Burlington' the code name for 'Corsham' had already been discovered by the German Stasi who would inevitably inform Moscow Central their office on a corner of Red Square.

The reason the two had been recruited remained a matter of speculation with no hard facts.

CHAPTER EIGHTEEN

Miss Moneylegs from within the 'Ewewatch' studio with Tony Computron and the Computron family with instant success resolved the communication problems of the underground establishments of Earth Crust Humanity. Communications were only possible within a country, nothing external, there were too many problems to resolve within a country without trying to communicate with other international underground places.

Deep Earth Humanity repeated the same message to all that every nuclear weapon no longer functioned. Deep Earth Humanity were just waiting to see which nuclear power would be the first to see if their nuclear weapon were in fact useless. Most countries had constructed an underground establishment of some type to protect Governments, the self-designated elite. The self-designated elite with only themselves to govern, stab someone in the back, one less mouth to feed, less waste of oxygen. Which group of the self-important could take over their own underground establishment crowning themselves King, Queen or President to Be? Where two or three are gathered together someone will want the crown.

Tony Computron continued to think that all this existed as a complete waste of Computron time. 'They are doomed!' For the first time since Barbara arrived a serious disagreement existed between them, Barbara of the opinion that everything possible should be done to help Earth Crusters.

Ian, within Corsham, effectively the outsider, called a meeting of Departmental Heads in order to establish a system of governance. When the Departmental Heads reached agreement, the rest of the community were informed. With the reality of a long slow death now understood this new system would run for a period of twelve months. There existed the Departmental Heads, all male, the most senior female then added, then a member with the longest service that happened to be a female telephonist. Out of a hat the names were produced in groups of three, each three spending a month in charge. Ian would sit as the person of continuity but without a vote in the event of none agreement of the duty three. At the request of the meeting an 'Escape Committee' came into existence that would be open to everyone.

Grace, with the Countess, sat discussing over their morning coffee if the file about the Count was complete, perhaps even as they spoke the file was having information removed. In the mid sentence of the Countess, the ringing of the telephone interrupted; much to the annoyance of her thought process. Grace arose to answer the madly ringing inconvenient machine. Grace gave the telephone number.

"Hello Grace. It's Stephen (Ward). Are you free to come to my exhibition tomorrow evening?" (A strange clicking on the line.)

Grace replied, "Mother is unwell so not tomorrow. Goodbye."

Placing the receiver down she thought he was somewhat rude, small talk about his ridiculous pictures and ladies of the night not wanted at the present, mother is still very upset. That is the priority. Grace went to sit down to pick up mother's interrupted thoughts when that crisp knock knock of authority on the front door. In definite annoyance the Countess hissed,

"Who can this be at this time of the day? No one is expected."

Grace opened the door, another threesome, George with that official face, requested 'Could they come in?' A voice of real authority when one of the other two asked if they might speak with the Countess. Grace hung up the heavy overcoats, the trilby hats and requested that the three wait in the hall. She told her mother that they looked very important, very official, not to worry as George had also arrived. Grace nosily peeped through the curtains to see a very black Government car with the driver waiting outside. No doubt the neighbours would be spying. Two officialdom with George entered, a very definite pecking order, George effected the introductions.

On cue yet again, in skipped Esamia with her usual question, "Is George in trouble yet?" Then she went on her way.

George introduced Sir Roger Hollis of MI5 (Hollis in fact Director General at the time) with Mr Furnival Jones who replaced him as Director General in December 1965. George did not say but they were the two most powerful men in MI5, the Security Service. Hollis spoke directly to the Countess and made profuse apology about the death of the Count.

"Myself and Mr Jones are the only people who have looked at the Count's file. When we were opening the file late last night, these two letters were found inside. One to you Countess, one to Grace."

He handed to each the letter, then without stopping his sentence said,

"We will leave now. George will stay in case you need any help after reading."

The three arose, the ladies clutching the letters. George showed them to the door. Hollis again,

"George, I want to know the contents in double quick time."

Then they had gone, George went straight into the kitchen to make tea. With the tea tray in hand the two remained exactly as they were, clutching the letters from the Count. George placed the tray on a table. No one spoke. Like a well-trained butler, he returned to the kitchen to listen. Corsham had received the phone call that George had to return to London not much before midnight, saying a car would collect him by five a.m. Looking at the two letters he had no doubt in his mind that Hollis and Jones already knew the contents. Why did they need someone to stay in the house to record events?

George had deliberately left the door slightly open so he could hear any conversation. He even wondered if the letters were from the Count or made up by the Security Service themselves. Who could be on trial here? Him? The Countess? Grace? All three or any combination of the three? Too much to expect that the British Government had become so embarrassed by their failure to deal with the Count's family that an attempt to correct the wrong was in the process of being corrected. What could be the real reason for the two top men of MI5 both turning up together for what, on the face of it, might be not quite normal, certainly not a national matter.

What do you do in someone's kitchen while you wait for something to happen? Twiddle your fingers? Not George. In his small notebook, he made a drawing of the kitchen layout. Still no noise. He took his shoes off so not to make a sound as he walked to the gap in the door to see what he could see. They continued sitting, holding letters as if in prayerful meditation. In the process of tying his shoelaces, Grace came in saying they had decided not to open the letters. The Countess had decided to place them by the icons in her upstairs cupboard chapel. George was thanked for staying but he was no longer needed. Her manner had no warmth.

Matter of fact, George exited the house. This result had not been in the plan. George had only been brought up from Corsham to see how they reacted to the letters.

George felt uncomfortable. Plans all messed up, no warmth from Grace. As he exited the garden he turned left, deep in personal thought, he failed to notice a Soviet Embassy car with diplomatic plates parked some 60 yards from the house. Later he received information that the occupants had good visual sight of the front door of the Countess' house, also reported to him that he had been clocked entering the house as one of three, two left, and then some fifty minutes later he left. Failure to see the car provided an unneeded reprimand recorded on his Service file.

He continued walking around a bend, now some 200 yards walked, to see Syd G leaning against a car with half a cigarette still needing to be smoked. Syd G told George to get into the car saying,

"Did you see the Soviet Embassy car?"

George did not answer.

"The D.G. could see it when he left, they have been trying to telephone you. Their (the Countess') phone keeps ringing engaged, so they sent me to wait for you, but I've only just arrived. I haven't finished my first fag (cigarette)."

Another black mark for George. He should have checked the telephone. He later stated he did. Two black marks in one day on assessment. What is the matter with George? Has the accident caused brain damage? Syd G deliberately drove past the Soviet Embassy car, as he knew he would be asked if it remained parked when George had walked past.

Some two minutes after that, one male exited the Soviet Embassy car, climbed the steps up to the front door of the Countess' house then knocked. Grace answered the door again. She knew him from the Bridge parties. She didn't like him, he smelt always of alcohol, the Countess having told Grace he had the reputation of a womanizer, particularly with those girl friends of Stephen Ward.

Grace took him into the Countess, left the room, and went to the bedroom, lying down, trying to decide if she should open her letter in defiance of her mother's wishes.

Ivanov, the Russian, made apology to the Countess saying on his last visit playing Bridge he hoped he had left his glasses here. He had tried everywhere else. Without any deviation from her thoughts, she pointed to the table his glasses were there. He picked up his glasses with great skill picking up the two letters, in one continuous movement.

"Shall I let myself out?"

An affirmative nod. She did not notice the speed of exit or

that the receiver had been taken off the telephone. To the Soviet Naval attaché speed must be of the essence, perhaps an hour if lucky. Back to the embassy, steam open the envelope, make copy of the contents, reseal the envelope, return to the Countess in a different car, make apology for his error. Bridge is a great game of bluff or counter bluff. The plan went like clockwork, the driver parked some way away from the house on the other side of the road. This gave Ivanov the opportunity to run, so that when the Countess opened the door his face looked very red, his breathing heavy. Spluttering out an apology the letters were handed back to the Countess. That shocked her. She thought Grace had taken the letters upstairs when Ivanov arrived. Then in deep thought, 'I must not tell Grace the letters went missing for about an hour.' She knew his excuse would be false. Had he read already what she did not yet want to read? Whilst Ivanov returned the letters, the Embassy staff made another copy. A brief report written out praising Ivanov, all into the diplomatic bag to Moscow.

When she awoke, Grace came back downstairs replacing the telephone together. The Countess was still sitting looking at the letters on the table. To avoid letter conversation, the Countess looked at Grace asking, (really stating)

"Were you rude to George when he left? You had better try to contact him to say sorry."

Grace knew the Countess had given her sensible advice. Knowing how difficult it would be she decided to telephone directly to the Home Secretary, where Charles answered the phone. Explaining that she needed to contact George urgently, Charles told her that he would contact that place (she assumed he meant Corsham) to speak to George and to get him to telephone her. It would take time in any event. He would call her back within the hour. She replaced the receiver to hear that 'click clicking' sound.

Charles contacted the 'DG' office at MI5. George had been brought back to the offices by Syd G the hope at MI5 that either the letters had been opened or better still that George could be on hand for the envelope opening, therefore he needed to be back in the house. Charles contrived the excuse that he could not speak to George, therefore Grace could not. However a message had been delivered telling him to call Grace.

Grace waited for the telephone for five or ten minutes. Then continued with the family daily routine, thinking had she so upset George that in fact he would be reluctant to call her back?

Syd G collected another vehicle from the car pool, collected George with two other staff members. 'DG' expressed concerns that the Soviets might still be outside, or nearby the house, so he wanted the two staff members to ensure that George could enter without observation. Syd G had specific instructions. George was to sit behind him in the back; the two were to be dropped off one to sit in the front passenger seat, the other drop off behind. Syd G proceeded to about two hundred yards from the house, one drop off from the front seat, on past the house. Another two hundred yard, second drop off from the rear. The all clear came if the two crossed outside the house of the Countess. No crossover, this visit aborted. Fortunately the cross over happened, Syd G pulled up outside the house, alighted from the driver's side, opened the door for George, and waited till George had entered the house. Syd G noted Grace opened the door smiling. Happiness at the visitor.

Corsham underground community found escape planning a great release from their entombment. Close to Corsham existed a much smaller underground facility now in communication; from both places a tunnel would be dug to create a communication passageway.

Some fifty years earlier at Corsham, the team that assembled in Wales started to enter a routine of thinking the unthinkable, concern openly expressed that the team leader, George, spent so much time away on matters they knew nothing about. To think the unthinkable. What if Corsham took a direct nuclear hit? The center of command no longer operational. What if the reservoirs were poisoned? So easy to drop a chemical substance into the water supply, population dying before the poisoning discovered. What if a volcanic explosion blocked out sunlight for a long period of time? Project one year then project five years. What happens with no direct sunlight? What if a life form from outer space visits Earth? What if sunspots prevent all communications, not just for hours or a day, but also for a prolonged period? What if a dictator seizes control of the United Kingdom? What if the Soviet Union fell apart? All these kept the team busy drawing up detailed plans, over and above everything else, planning for nuclear attacks.

The Corsham Underground team of fifty years later had continuous volunteers for the tunnel-building project. The greatest problem encountered was how to ensure both teams were digging to a point where they would join up, not so easy without surface land surveys. Ewewatch with the Computrons now controlled any permitted communications between centers of Earth Crust life. Within Corsham, a discussion seemed to start from nowhere as to increasing the population, allowing females on the staff to become pregnant, certainly the medical facilities could cope. Certainly the team of medics could cope. There existed no married couples. In fact previously relationships were not allowed. Debating intensified around, 'Do you plan for tomorrow when tomorrow is not there?' If that hiss hissing sound continues everyone will be driven mental long before a new tomorrow.

Following Grace into the hallway, George could see Syd G pull away with only himself in the car. George assumed that the other two staff members would be on duty somewhere within eyesight of the house. He thought to himself he had spent more time here recently than in his own hallway.

Ever thoughtful, always planning, the office had provided a

small size brown suitcase, an overnight bag, clean shirt, pajamas, shaving equipment, tooth brush, toothpaste. Grace took it off him, also hanging his coat, his hat. Without any formality, without any warning, she stood on tip toe, reached up, held his hand in both hands, planting a memorable kiss on his lips. George took her waist, hugged, held her tight, almost squeezed, her lips separated for a moment to say sorry.

Into the room they walked, hand in hand, receiving an affirmative comment from the Countess,

"I assume you are friends again."

George hated mixing work with pleasure. Why did the Office keep asking him to use his friendship with Grace, what did they want to discover? Thinking to himself, 'I am a Foreign and Commonwealth Office man, now asked to head, 'A think the Impossible Team'. I am not a spy. I have no training. I am in the process of sliding into what I do not want to be involved with. George knew the Security Service wanted him to have a sleepover so did the Countess.

Looking George in the eye she said,

"It is a Bridge evening, can you play?"

George replied in the affirmative although a bit rusty. In triumph the Countess smiled at Grace telling her to prepare a guest room (not the only guest room) and when ready, come and collect George to show him to his room. Without any motive or planning, Grace prepared the next room to hers, in her own mind because it had a separate bathroom and toilet. George expressed concerns to the Countess. He had no formal dinner suit. She, amused, explained formal attire wasn't necessary for the men as they were mainly foreign nationals. "However, you will see that many of my Lady friends do make a substantial effort as I will. It is one of my lady friends who is ill and that is who you're standing in for."

The lady didn't know she was ill until the Countess telephoned her explaining she wanted the new friend of Grace to show his ability at Bridge. Lady friends of the Countess knew from experience to fall in line with her wishes (demands), the

Countess concluding by saying, "If you feel better, come over later."

Grace had just walked past her mother, that click clicking sound as the receiver went back on the phone. Again the Countess dialed, this time to Stephen Ward telling him not to bring any of his young ladies with him tonight as the new male friend of Grace would be playing. He is someone important in the Foreign Office; therefore young models were not appropriate. Without any doubt in her mind, the Countess knew Stephen would telephone his Russian friend Ivanov with the spicy gossip, a new contact for Ivanov from the Foreign Office, for Ivanov another good contact to tell Moscow about, if only he could stay sober, promotion could be much quicker.

Grace took George up into his guest room, gave him a quick tour. Yes, big enough to need a tour. Laughing, she said she would leave him to unpack. Items not provided in his little brown suitcase were laid on the bed, slippers, jumper, dressing gown, towels in the bathroom with soaps and smelly things. Even extra handkerchiefs. Enormous would adequately describe the bedroom size. A very large treble sized bed, wardrobe, dressing table with mirror, and various chairs to sit in. One invited him to sit in front of a window. A garden would be an injustice. A small coppice at the end. Within the coppice another small property, a single story bungalow, very obviously part of the big house. Beyond the coppice and into the park. Working in the garden, an elder man with perhaps a son or very young brother. As if a sixth sense told the two they were being watched, they looked up at the window. The younger waves as if to the figure in the upstairs window. 'Who are you two?' thought George. She had crept up behind him. Answering his thought, Grace explained they were Grigory with his son Peter. The mother did all the cooking, all the housework (with the help of Peter) for the Countess. The married couple, Grigory with his wife Natasha, had been with the Countess ever since the Count and Countess moved to England. The Countess' Russian family had employed the father of Grigory forever.

"Come on, I'd better introduce you now that they've looked up at the window. Before we get there, be warned, Peter is very possessive. We grew up as children together, not as master and servant, but as family."

She led him to the corner of the room, opened what he thought must be a wardrobe, there another staircase going up, going down. Grace pointed out she had the same cupboard onto the stairs; these were the servants stairs when the Regency house had been built by an eccentric trader who made money in the Far East. Down they went, George did but should not have thought, 'What a fantastic place this would be to live in, to bring up children,' thought dismissed. In fact they went down one floor then into the basement then into the garden. Standing there looking up, this is a magnificent four story regency house with a paddock more than a garden. Obviously the bungalow must have been stable blocks for the horses. They went through formal flowerbeds, fountain, then into the vegetable garden where Grigory with Peter were working. As if from behind the copse, Natasha joined the get together. Peter, older than Grace, in his early thirties, strong, well developed muscles, a shock of black hair, perhaps 6ft 5ins, he towered over all except George. He practiced martial arts, a good friend, and a bad enemy. Introductions over Natasha invited Grace and George into her house, had produced tea pre-empting them saying no, accompanied by a 'Peter size' slice of Victoria Sponge. To Natasha, Grace seemed of little interest. She wanted to know about George. Under the barrage of questions, Grace had to intervene to say that all George could say was that his work in the Foreign and Commonwealth Office had to be kept confidential. Walking back to the main house George sort of laughed that he had been interrogated. George also noticed Peter keeping a watchful eye on the two. They went back into the house by yet another ground floor entrance. Natasha followed behind them off to prepare a light evening meal, then some snacky things for after Bridge. Apparently the Countess had already gone to dress for Bridge, Grace explained they would both reappear in their dressing gowns to eat.

"Let me take you to the Library," an instruction not an invitation. Along another hallway, at the end a double oak door. Grace opened the lock, he followed her in.

"No one comes in here without the Countess or myself being present. You will see why as you look around. See you in my nearly nightie in an hour."

Off she went, key in lock. George paced out the length, 80 feet; he paced out the width seventy feet and along every wall bookcases. At some time the window had been blocked in. No, he had made a mistake, the wall behind him was not books, portraits then a length of locked display cabinets, underneath the whole length a safe for each display cabinet. Without conscious thought he realized that along the bookcase walls each one had its own language, one for Italian, one for Russian, one for English. In the middle of the room, another display cabinet, again locked, full of sets of playing cards, magnificent hand coloured, each one had a little card stating date of use, date of purchase. He could see no card with a date after 1899, then slightly to one side a card table with four chairs with various packs obviously to be used. George knew well he should have used this free time to go for a walk to report to the inevitable watcher. He now tired of this silly game of spy or by spied upon. Out came a pack, he played four different hands himself, only so he could get back into the routine of predicting the next card. At Cambridge they gave up on playing cards as only George would win, Bridge his specialty. He mused, should he play as well as he could, or lose a little? For the Countess, Bridge was a very serious way of life. She would think it grossly insulting if he did not use his skill to his uttermost. Still predicting cards, Grace returned to say,

"Mother has been waiting for you to start eating."

What small talk can you make with two such elegant women in their dressing gowns? Contrast upon contrast the meal. Everywhere the hand of Natasha, home baked bread, fresh salad topped with boiled eggs, home made jams, of course, more Victoria Sponge. This served on fine china with silver service. This meal, no feast, literally the best of home cooking with hot tea with lemon or tap water to drink.

"George," the Countess began, "my friends tell me you have been appointed to run a new department to think the unthinkable."

Grace stopped eating; George dropped a full spoon of strawberry jam onto the fine linen tablecloth.

Grace, "Mother, how can your friends know that?" George mumbled something about sorry. Grace again,

"So the grape vine is already searching if George has any skeletons in his past."

"Of course, what do you expect me to do Grace?"

Silence, the Countess started again,

"I will take your silence as confirmation. Have your people thought about Communism ceasing in Russia and the Soviet Union. What would that do for the Cold War?"

With his mind racing, George had never thought of that, never a mention from those in the Soviet section at the Foreign Office, he again stumbled over the one word, "no."

"Come on mother, let him eat. He must be hungry. Talk to him after Bridge."

Still no silence as the Countess went on to give a short summary of each and everyone of those attending. George knew of all the English names of the women. He knew none of the diplomats. He had never heard the name Stephen Ward. Of the English woman, almost without exception, widows of deceased politicians, one whose husband had been a private banker (her and his names the same as the famous bank). One man who he felt sure owned one of the major auction houses, one other man who George knew to have been an Ambassador certainly in Moscow, possibly Berlin. However, George would have to enquire from Grace.

During the same part of the day as George sat spilling strawberry jam on the fine linen table cloth, Roger Hollis in the MI5 Office for no apparent reason asked if a file existed separately to that of the Count, a Countess file.

Tunneling work at Corsham proceeded slowly. If it had not been for all the enthusiasm work would have ceased. In the excitement of the idea it had been forgotten that the whole complex had been constructed in a quarry, both teams repeatedly came upon large boulders that seemed to have been placed directly in their path. Slow, but for Ian a focus of attention, already he found out that in some of the smaller, less well-equipped bunkers, fighting factions had formed in order to take over the bunker. Definitely one group had killed others so as to preserve their own lives as long as possible. No other site had entered into the same discussion as at Corsham regarding commencing to produce babies to preserve or create another generation to be left for the future. Any scientist with any possible relevant skills was trying to determine when a breathable atmosphere would return to Earth. (The scientists in Deep Earth could give them a precise answer as to year, month and day. Earth crusters would not believe the answer if it would be given to them.) Everywhere Ian knew that suicide had started to be used by those who considered no future existed in their coffins in the ground. Better dead than pretending to be alive. With acute foresight, Ian created a steam room, in one of the furthest rooms. No doubt backing into the quarry itself. Objects were placed for those needing to be aggressive to let off steam. Almost immediately, the pastime of greatest pleasure consisted of footballs with the faces of World leaders painted upon them, kicked at a device some of the Scientists made which measured the speed as a football hit a metal square about two feet by two feet. Various footballs needed repainting nearly every day such was the venom felt for those who contributed to the end of civilization, the self-centered, and self-interested so called political elite.

Within the hour, Roger Hollis received a file on the Countess, inside one hand, written note referring to a file that had been created when the offices were at 73-75 Queen's Gate, Kensington. The office existed there from the end of 1919 to 1929. 'An archivist is going to be very unhappy to have to find that one,' he thought. 'That's why we employ archivists.' Hollis gave no priority so the request found itself at the bottom of the pile of all other outstanding file requests. Retaining the file, he made a note of his visit, and then placed the file in the bottom draw on the left hand side of the substantial pedestal desk. He sent a note to Registry that he had kept the file as he was working on it.

With the meal complete, the Countess asked George if he would wait in the bedroom until Grace collected him. She wanted to present him to everyone at the same time; mainly she didn't want him cornered by Ward and Ivanov the Soviet (no doubt a spy). George was more than happy as he could manage a nap, a snooze, forty winks, could he though, have some Bridge playing cards. Please.

The Countess, again directly to George,

"My friends tell me that you play very well. I expect you to play to win, no being nice. This is a very serious Bridge Club, with several County players, past and present." This instruction was exactly as George had predicted in his own mind. He rather felt like a naughty boy sent to his room, painful memories of those sisters with their friends who used to torment him. He did nod off in tiredness, dreamt of Grace, then awoken by the provided alarm clock, washed, shaved, clean, he waited to be collected. Already he could hear the noise of chattering guests.

The lack of coordination outside the house by the Security Service and Special Branch, later received severe criticism. They were out there like bees around a honey pot. At least one member of a Foreign Security Service had already been spotted. Two from the Security Service, one in a mini apparently with engine problems with an emergency repair vehicle in front (unable to say if it looked like RAC or AA) inside a photographer taking pictures of guests arriving mostly in their chauffeur driven cars, diplomatic people by taxi. Security Service staff were on duty on behalf of the Foreign Office; they only had interest in one person, Ivanov. If anyone should be interested in Ivanov it must be the Security Services unless the Foreign Office had an agenda with Ivanov that they wanted to keep secret from MI5, supposedly on the same side of protecting 'Britain' in the process playing games with each other.

Grace knocked on the guest room for George to come out. She looked stunning. A deep red two-piece, long skirt, top lowly cut and gently puffed short sleeves, a real princess. Remembering his manners, really a comment from the heart,

"You look fabulous."

A polite smile, a polite thank you. Holding the skirt so as not to trip over as she went downstairs, he followed. Into the room, the Countess instantly took him by the hand, speaking clearly with absolute authority.

"Everyone, this is George, a friend of Doctor Grace, our friends at Cambridge University state his Bridge is of the highest quality. Make sure you make him work."

As always, the Countess looked elegant. All her lady friends looked elegant, George noticed not one of them wore any jewellery other than a wedding ring with this wealth not one diamond sparkling on anyone, that is with the exception of the old Ambassador who had a single diamond in his tiepin. George much more interested in the statement, 'Our friends from Cambridge'. Did the tentacles of the Countess reach everywhere?

George, without exception, proved to be the star, very much to the pleasure of the Countess, then onto the drinks and food bits and pieces from Natasha. Plenty consumed with Natasha always producing more. Nothing fancy, nothing expensive. All from the garden.

Everyone waited their turn to speak with George, no one more so that Ivanov. Then George found himself cornered by

Ward and Ivanov. Grace came to his assistance. Grace flared up to Ward as unpleasant as George had ever heard her,

"Don't try and involve him with yourself and Ivanov. This is our home, not your recruiting ground." She held George tightly by the hand and pulled him away to go to the Countess, who somewhat reprimanded Grace with the comment,

"Leave them alone, they're harmless."

"No," replied Grace, "Not harmless and Stephen is using the girls, even you say Ivanov is a Soviet spy."

That spat over, normality returned with guests starting slowly, one by one, to depart, thanking the Countess for a wonderful evening. Ivanov reported he had left a bottle for Natasha to say thank you for the food. One of the last to leave was the boss of the International Auction house. He descended the steps, turned to his right, to the side of the house. In the dark he received a parcel with the comment, 'as usual.' The last to leave, Stephen Ward, who as he put on his overcoat asked Grace to come to his exhibition, bringing George as well. Grace made no reply, only a polite goodnight. Grace then explained to George that she and mother would return to their bedrooms then return for a little supper before bedtime that Natasha would leave for them. Natasha collected the bottle gift from Ivanov, leaving the big house to return to the bungalow. Peter was waiting to escort her back. With the last guest leaving, those on outside watch (spying) packed up their tools of the trade and melted away into the blackness from where they had arrived. They say spying is a black art. None of the lookers on reported the parcel leaving the premises. The after Bridge supper plain and simple just as the previous meal had been, except that the Countess started to consume the bottle of wine provided by the visitors. Grace, with George, both consumed half a glass each, the Countess taking the rest of the bottle to bed. Grace helped her mother, now a little light headed, nowhere near drunk, into her bedroom asking George to wait. No mention of the letters by either lady.

'Ewewatch', fronted by Miss Moneylegs established a well run routing of filtering out all communications, allowing only those approved by the Elders. Perhaps a form of censorship on those messages which were obscene, trying to organize the take over of bunkers, giving false information about the future, just downright insurrection. Commonality to everyone in every bunker all around the Earth that mind-numbing hiss, hiss, hissing noise. Earth Crust Humanity had not the faintest idea that the noise emanated from the Founding Protectors. Miss Moneylegs asked Mason plus Barbara if they could meet in the 'Ewewatch' studio. She knew Tony Computron would come as well, Bruce the dog already sitting on his chair made of gold besides Miss Moneylegs. She started a discussion by saying that in her opinion the main problem in the bunkers centered on food supplies with the majority having little more than two years supply. There were though some very noticeable exceptions, like Corsham, the Command Bunkers (i.e. those were the political elite expected to live) had much greater food supplies. Corsham had been built with storage rooms for food to last for some seven years for seven thousand inhabitants. That being extended if the fresh produce growing area proved more successful than the limited trials had shown. In the city built under Moscow, for the elite direct access through the Kremlin, the food growing facility had continued in constant production for years. Original specification required the facility, Bunker H2, to be self sufficient for 30000 people for thirty years. Washington in America had similar bunkers, that under the Greenbrier Hotel again stocked for thirty years and that under the East wing of the Whitehouse, the Presidential Command Centre. Every country had one, take Beijing (China) the Dixia Cheng complex, it is claimed it could house six million, the population of Beijing when the complex had been built to protect against Soviet invasion in the 1970's, how long the six million could survive, open to speculation.

She continued, 'that is a short list, many others were self sufficient but 99% had limited food supplies.' She therefore felt that the three might consult with the Elder Elder Elders if they could expand the food sources of Deep Earth Humanity into Earth Crust bunker world. Tony Computron explained he and the Computron world would not agree, mainly, he felt, why should the elite in the bunkers be further protected. In his opinion, if the bunkers existed for every person then the Computrons might think again. In his opinion, the political elite built these places in secret using money from the ordinary people and was guilty of never telling the ordinary people. Deceit, fraud, self-interest. Bruce agreed, chuckling to himself. Yes, dogs do chuckle. 'If only that elite could see me sitting on a seat made of gold, worthless down here. Who decided up there that gold had value as a store of wealth? Probably the government that had the most.'

Mason agreed with the computron. Why perpetuate these people? Would they do the same for anyone other than themselves? Of course their interest is self, self, followed by more of self. Barbara threw out the comment that in retrospect these groups did stick together. How often did a defeated politician come back in another political position? Get defeated in a European Country election then back as a member of the European Parliament. Get sacked as a manager of a football team, come back as a manager in another country. Get the sack from the job as the chief executive, come back as a chief executive of a competitor, especially if it is out of legal jurisdiction, and pass on trade secrets.

Miss Moneylegs felt her idea had not been well received by her colleagues, well intentioned to preserve those above by taking food from those down here. She had to agree, 'why preserve the self-centered?'

All scientists in Deep Earth were now effectively dealing in trying to understand the George 'Double W' effect. In simple language the 'wave' or 'wind' in the furthest points of the universe appearing to make stars jump. They were concentrating on a galaxy which Earth Crust scientists called MAC50647-JD which Earth crust scientists had calculated as being 13.3 billion light-years from Earth, and another galaxy SXDF-NB1006-2 as being 12.91 billion light years from Earth, so the light of these two galaxies had been travelling to Earth from almost the beginning of measured time starting from the 'Big Bang Theory'. As regards MAC50647-JD Earth Crust scientists believed the galaxy to be much smaller than the Milky Way however, it was forming stars at a much faster rate. Concentrating on these galaxy started to show startling discrepancies between the equipment of Deep Earth Humanity, rather like trying to use a steam roller (Earth Crusters) instead of a space rocket to visit the moon. Truth had to be accepted that these Earth Crust measurements of deep universe were subject to substantial variations when compared to information from instruments of Deep Earth scientists. The distances involved were beyond the brains of Earth Crusters even the simple basic fundamental of the speed of light had almost no comprehension, speed of light calculated at 186000 miles per second, 700 million miles per hour approximately, compare that to the distance between the Earth and Moon, about 238900 miles. So light from the moon takes 1 and a quarter seconds to reach Earth. The distance from Earth to the Sun is 93 million miles so light from the sun takes some eight minutes to reach Earth. Beyond that speed or distance difficult to comprehend.

Science in all branches in Deep Earth readily accepted the wind wave theory from studying the two galaxy movements with other distant galaxy movements, consensus existed of a major event. Trying to explain their description centered on an effect similar to that of squeezing, more squeezing of a balloon, the center getting smaller and smaller, the two ends expanding, filling up with that which had been in the middle, producing a shape like that of an old fashioned egg timer, two bulbous ends, a minutely thin middle.

Now the expectation that almost like in human reproduction the first cells dividing into two. That ended the agreement, some projected that the two divided parts of the Universe would split away from each other, others projected that exactly in the manner of growth from one cell into a living form, the one would divide into two, the two divide into four and continue. Fundamental new astro-physics, no wonder the Founding Protectors were in ever-hissing hiss mode. They in theory had no idea where their future would be. Not only were Mason, Barbara and Miss Moneylegs troubled by the theory, the community of Deep Earth Humanity were likewise troubled. Having discovered this new information there existed no new projection as to if or when the Earth would be affected or the Galaxy in which the Earth existed, the Milky Way. For once the collective of Computrons could provide no immediate answers, other than expressing concern that events would happen quicker than expected. They were much influenced by that hiss hissing of the Founding Protectors, one alarmist Computron decided that it could be the death call, the Founding Protectors knowing their time had gone, they have existed since the Big Bang, since Planck time, what hope of that almost new planet called Earth? Then some of the Computrons expressed the view that the Founding Protectors must have a mechanism to protect themselves. Logic had to suggest that if they existed at or around the Big Bang they must have some mechanism of protection, with no knowledge or contact from them, other than hissing, difficult to understand what the profound knowledge could be. How could they manage to pass through solids, a wonder beyond Earth people's knowledge?

Grace returned from escorting the Countess into her bedroom then before she could sit down a sound of a movement at the front door letterbox. She immediately entered the hallway, switched on a light, intrigued to see what had arrived so late at night. Opening the box attached against the door she found a brown envelope with the word 'Official' in black letters on the top left. Typed, half way down, somewhat to the left of center the name, 'George', no surname, no address. Exiting the hallway Grace turned off the light, George still sitting as before, handing him the brown envelope with more than a hint of sarcasm commented,

"Your post sir. Come on, open it up. Who is sending urgent letters to somewhere you don't live?"

The letter addressed to Mr G came from the under secretary at the Foreign and Commonwealth Office telling George that for the time being he should not return to Corsham. Instead he should use his old office in the Foreign and Commonwealth Office. The Prime Minister, through the Cabinet Secretary had requested that the person who had written the Cuban assessment should be available to the Cabinet on a daily basis. Each day a driver would be provided to collect him from home, wait at the hospital whilst he had a daily check up, then return him home in the evening. Corsham had been advised of his delayed return. Immediately handing the letter to Grace, he, the Foreign Office and anyone else in the loop waited for Grace to say, George.......

She handed the letter back, saying,

"Are you so important they are unable to manage without you?" Then back into general chitchat each attempting to discover a little more about the other. George eager to explore the web of contacts that surrounded Grace, more particularly around the Countess. Grace eager to find out about George with his family. Time progressed, Grace yawned first, then like an illness, George yawned, obviously bedtime for both. Having turned off the downstairs lights, George followed Grace up the stairs. For once both minds were enacting the same scenario. What do I do when we get to the first bedroom door? The first bedroom door would be that of George, then Grace, then the Countess who Grace had previously escorted to bed.

At the top of the stairs, turn left, there the little chapel lights were on, trying to tiptoe past, Grace had put her finger over her mouth so George knew not to speak. Perhaps the squeaky floorboard had creaked in the past, George had not noticed, this time it did squeak loudly enough for the Countess to turnaround.

"Mother you are crying." As Grace spoke her words were still in her mouth as she knelt next to the Countess. Not the scenario that the two had contemplated when a moment or two before they were ascending the stairs. Brain racing, George thinking, 'what is the correct thing to do?' He had the status of new family friend, certainly not close enough to even consider following the lead of Grace. He felt he should, and then decided he should not. So for one of those long moments, he stood glued to the spot, car headlights into rabbit eyes. Time moved very slowly, that damn glue fixing him to the floor.

By good fortune, with more than a tear on her face, the Countess begged his forgiveness, then more good fortune with Grace offering an escape plan.

"George go into the kitchen to make some tea, you should know where everything is by now. We will join you in a minute or two."

Utter relief in his head as George downed the stairs, managing to switch on too many lights then into the sanctuary of the kitchen. He had almost filled the kettle with water when he found Natasha behind him. She took over, back again to being a spare watsit. "SIT" Natasha told him with herself busily making things ready. The Countess arrived arm in arm with Grace, the three ladies all talking to one another. George definitely felt like a spare watsit. Sit still, keep quiet, drink more tea, his mind wondering, then interrupted by the Countess insisting that he should stay with them for the next few days, lucky George, his wish granted.

It was difficult to judge which of the two youngsters looked most pleased, the Countess telling him to bring enough clothes here to last for a week. 'More easily said than done with a high proportion of his clothes already collected and sent to Corsham.'

Whatever had caused the tears, George felt he should exit, say goodnight, leaving the three ladies alone to chatter. In his own mind, the missed opportunity now expanded into at least another five or six nights to make appropriate advances to Grace.

He made a quick list of matter to be discussed with the Office first thing (now later that morning) making sure the driver collected him from here, not his home. Climbing into bed, the smell and feel of clean linen sheets reminded him of his mother and the tormenting sisters, tonight sweet dreams.

Alarm clock set for seven; sleep overtook him, then into dreamland. A vague memory of the alarm ringing, could not remember, switching it off, then a shaking of the arm. Then she stated,

"Strong breakfast tea for the sleepy head. It's 7.30am. Natasha will cook you some breakfast at eight." Instructions given, Grace left. He remembered that she was still on a few days holiday to compensate for the stress of the events that had befallen her in Wales.

Obviously the shirt fairy had visited, his dirty shirt from yesterday hanging clean on a coat hanger. Which of the three found that in the night, instead of musing about clean shirts, he would have been better advised in thinking whom and when had someone been in his bedroom? Not thinking straight from the accident or another type of emotional upheaval.

Natasha produced more homegrown food, scrambled eggs on toast (mental note to look for the chickens), more toast, butter, jam, and a pot full of English tea, the new trend of tea bags not yet encroached into meals here. During breakfast there was no conversation from Natasha. Neither Grace nor the Countess appeared. However he could already see Grigory with his son Peter working in the garden. A knock at the door, one driver, one car, not a Syd this time. Natasha opened the door to let him out, collecting the milk bottles as the driver opened the car door.

By the time the car had travelled perhaps two hundred yards, the empty kitchen he'd left moments before was full of masters and servants. Had the five been waiting his exit before having a board meeting? Or was it coincidence or politeness? With the board meeting breakfast completed, Natasha handed Peter a key with the instruction to take the morning off.

George was now at the hospital to receive his daily early check up, and found himself not in the waiting area but straight into a private area. Perhaps the check-up took fifteen minutes, no more, then back into the car arriving at the office no more than fifty-five minutes since he left the house. His replacement at the Foreign and Commonwealth office deferred to George when he entered the old office, then gave George his old desk back. George back in his old office as directed by the Prime Minister.

The staff was much less friendly than when he left. What had been going on in his absence, he wondered. All the latest information about Cuba had been prepared ready for his assessment. Information fell into two distinct interrelated activities of the Soviet Union missile build up in Cuba. Firstly, details of the arrival in early October of Soviet aircraft capable of carrying nuclear weapons. The basic information he had seen in the paper work delivered to the ambulance, this new information of much greater depth recording multiple sightings. Secondly, reports dated 14th October 1962 of photographs taken by an American US spy plane of launch sites for medium range missiles. A map provided by the Americans showed such missiles could reach most American cities. Then a last minute note attached identifying a large number of Soviet ships in the Atlantic believed to be heading for Cuba, with information that they were carrying equipment related to missile launch sites. George made two additions to his previous advice;

1) Royal Navy Ships, air reconnaissance aircraft to report on any Soviet or Cuban vessels seen at sea, including those of satellite countries.

2) Contacts of any existing known source connected to the Kremlin to be constantly advised that her Majesty's government could mediate if asked to, suggesting London as a neu-

tral venue.

The new amendment circulated by the Under Secretary to a very restricted 'need to know' group of ministers. Then George contacted the Under Secretary by internal phone to ask if he would arrange to chair a meeting with legal advisors sometime that afternoon to see what options existed to stop Soviet vessels on the high seas to search for nuclear missiles or their parts, what could be legally undertaken within International Law. George received a message to say 4.00pm would be the time of the meeting in room 534 Main Building.

At the meeting, those dry factual legal eagles gave the exact legal possibilities of action possible. Factual but useless, until a legal advisor laughed saying,

"Get one to stray into our territorial water, then the law is really on our side."

George, now more than tired asked the driver to take him to his flat first so he could pack a suitcase. Arriving at the flat George could not find his key. He must have left it in the bedroom last night. He had always kept a spare with an elderly spinster next door who did his laundry for him. She opened the door, taking the key with her, thinking to herself, 'when will he stop wearing those stiff shirt collars?'

George had invited the driver up to his flat in Belsize Park while he packed. No milk, so black tea. But there were sugar cubes. A bachelor flat is a bachelor flat, functional not comfortable. Bathroom needed a good scrub, no crocks in the sink awaiting washing. George shouted,

"Help yourself to a biscuit, green tin, second shelf."

The driver found the tin empty. Looking around (not being nosy) everywhere dwarfed by a huge table/desk. Papers clearly marked by subject, at one end matters for research, large sheets of used or yet to be used blotting paper. A waste paper basket overflowing with ripped up papers. Only one photograph on the table that of the family when George would be twoish sitting on his mother's knee. He thought, but didn't report, 'this could be a heaven for a foreign spy. They might not find anything, they would have lots of fun though.' Two chess sets both with games in progress were at the other end of the desk table, the driver wondered who he could be playing against.

When George emerged the driver immediately took the very large doctors type bag from him, then proceeded to the car. George assumed the driver played Chess as on the one chess board the King had been moved.

Deep in thought in the back of the car he tried to come up with a plan to get a Soviet ship into British territorial waters. Climbing the steps into his temporary home with the driver behind him with the bag, the door opened by Natasha informing him the Countess and Grace were out. She instructed the driver where to leave the bag; Peter would carry it upstairs whilst he had some tea. Enquiry by the driver as to what time he should collect him in the morning received the reply from Natasha, "Not before ten, he is still recovering." 'That's that' went through George's mind as she led him into the dining room, whipped off a tea towel from the food underneath, instructing him to eat she brewed the tea. (Almost like mother had done before he went off to University.)

Returning with the tea she asked him if he wanted to play chess both her husband and son played seriously. George thought to remember to look for the flat key in his room. Having had his light tea, as Natasha called it, she informed him the Countess would be back with Grace not before seven thirty, therefore dinner would be late tonight at eight fifteen at the earliest.

When he entered the bedroom the very substantial doctors bag had been placed at the end of the bed. First though he looked into the top drawer of the tall boy checking on the key. There safe and sound. Unpacking he placed the clean handkerchiefs on top of the keys, second drawer undergarments with socks. Shirts hung up in the wardrobe, with another suite, then sports jackets, trousers, ties. In the base of the wardrobe, another pair of shoes. Back to the third drawer down for nightwear, nothing for the bottom drawer. He opened it in any event to find packs of playing cards, two chess sets, with a collection of pens, paper, and blotting paper. Down into his bare bones, he found himself having a bath. When they returned, both ladies called out, 'hello' as they walked past the bedroom door. Two minutes later, a knock on the bathroom door.

"George do you need any help, remember I've seen it all before," giggled Grace. With the water gurgling down the bath plughole, he threw the robe around him and exited. They were both in the bedroom, the bed now covered in parcels. It looked like Christmas. Sitting in the chair by the window the Countess spoke,

"Now George be gracious, (funny using that word) we have spent a super afternoon together buying you some clothes."

The names on the bags spoke out exactly where they had been buying clothes. How easily a man can be embarrassed by gifts.

The Countess,

"Come on, otherwise, we will have to open them for you."

In total, never before felt embarrassment, he duly opened packet after packet, box after box, he would be clothed as a new man for years to come.

Eventually entering into the spirit of this financial kindness, from time to time, he went into the bathroom, tried items on came out to be inspected by the Countess. In a new working suite, three piece with waistcoat, he even managed a twirl, the Countess clapped. He thought,

'It is as if someone measured all my clothes before the shopping started. He knew a large sum of money had been spent on him.'

With much happiness the Countess departed, leaving the two alone. Grace said,

"Mother is so happy, she says you're the son she never had! Now let me help you put your new clothes away."

At which point the Countess put her head around the door to tell them to dress for dinner.

"Grace be a darling, go and advise Natasha we will dress for dinner. We will eat in the main dining room." Another moment for the two to be together lost. How many more rooms existed for the 'main dining room' tonight. Obviously more bedrooms on the floor above his bedroom, then a basement, next they will tell me of an underground tunnel linking the house with the old stable block. Perhaps I should ask Grace for a guided tour. George almost forgetting his official purpose here of looking at the two letters still in the chapel. George didn't want to deceive the trust and friendliness of this strange family of employer and employed.

A gong sounded for dinner. He hid behind the bedroom door until he heard someone walk past, then he appeared. They were walking along together. From the back they looked like twins in identical long dresses, long sleeves, high collars. He interrupted their conversation when they reached the top of the stairs.

"Shall I go first?"

"No," replied the Countess, "You haven't been to the main dining room so you will need to follow." George thought, 'just like a poodle.'

(In the Deep Earth, Bruce the Dog indicated to all that he objected to this thought of George as it indicated poodles, and therefore dogs, were only good enough to follow, not lead.)

The two ladies in front, George behind, they walked to the library. As they approached the library door, on the opposite side of the wall, someone, moved to slide across a wooden panel, on the other side Grigory in butler's uniform welcomed the Countess. Taking her to her seat then correcting it for best comfort, he indicated to the two youngsters, Grace to sit to her left, George on the right. All three were looking at George, he looking around. This room was beyond opulent.

His home table desk had been commented on many times for its length, this table could seat fifty, perhaps sixty, the three of them at the top end nearest the sliding wall. Grigory in his best white gloves offered each water for their only glass. Somehow at the same time placing his foot on a large felt circle on the floor in-between the Countess and Grace, somehow under the floor there existed a mechanism connected to the kitchen to say food could be served.

Neither of the ladies had on any jewellery again, a total contrast to the table with silver service, exquisite glass, fine porcelain, around the walls chairs to sit in after the meal. The walls decorated with paintings. George knew some of the famous Russian artists, they were all represented here. Then at the other end of the room a grand piano with more chairs with music stands to make up a quartet. Natasha now in black uniform handed over to Grigory three bowls of soup. He placed them in front of the three then offered bread. Everything had home made stamped upon it. Always having been the center of attention, George several times had to bite his tongue as the Countess pontificated over a wide range of subjects. He had to concentrate, in other words, stop looking at Grace, as the Countess had the increasing habit of saying,

"What is your opinion Georgee?"

Every time she said Georgee that young lady had to control her giggles. Soup dishes taken away by Natasha she returned with three plates for the main course, a small piece of chicken, potatoes and vegetables, all in total contrast to the fabulous surroundings. Out came the afters, banana with custard, water always available. That ended the meal with the Countess leading the way where tea, green or black, with milk, without milk, with lemon without lemon, arrived from Grigory. Then the two were gone; to George it felt like an Alice in Wonderland world. Needless to say the topic of conversation, the only topic of conversation, what had gone on in the diplomatic world?

Fortunately the papers were full of 'The Cuban Missile Crisis' with every editorial discussing what would happen next, the two 'K's' confronting each other, Kennedy and Khrushchev. George with all this so called fact, mainly speculation, felt he could talk a bit so concentrated on the problem of 'if only the West could catch the Soviet shipping red handed with missiles and missile parts as cargo.' He also felt he could pass on the joke of the legal expert who laughingly had said,

"Get a ship to stray into our territorial waters."

Now the Countess had heard the gossip she started to talk about her past with the Count, he wondered how many times had Grace heard this? None of the three had noticed Grigory came in, while George had been talking, to replace the pots with new fresh teapots. Chatting continued until the telephone rang, it was Stephen Ward to speak to Grace, Natasha told the room.

'Fiddlesticks,' thought Grace.

"George, he is going to ask me to go to his exhibition. Will you come with me? He and that Russian friend of his worry me."

"Of course," George replied.

When she returned it was to announce that she and George would be going to the exhibition at 7pm the next evening whilst commenting that the phone was still making a funny clicking noise. George thought for a moment of his new team at Corsham, in his own mind thinking this heralded a very bad start for the new project. They there, he here, they having no knowledge about his absence.

At Corsham, some fifty years on in time, speculation grew that the two tunnels under slow painful construction should be within perhaps 10 or 11 inches of each other, with correct calculation, only another five inches digging on either side. Ian through the 'Ewewatch' stream, nobody had any real idea of where it transmitted from, and more importantly, who controlled the same, had painstakingly built up a map of all operating bunkers in England and Wales. Off the map statistics were being compiled of personnel on site (male and female) projected time that food stocks would last. The team around him expressed surprise at just how many underground bunkers existed. There were in fact many thousands of survivors left. Without really having a plan in mind, brains constantly battered with that hiss-hissing scream, to start talking with 'Ewewatch' to see if communications could be extended into Europe, then the rest of the world.

Much to his surprise, 'Ewewatch' (with Miss Moneylegs) replied to say they were working to see if it could be possible. Tony Computron thought, 'what idiots, it would only take him and the computrons a millisecond to make the connection.' The Computron community felt Earth Crust Humanity should be left alone to cease to exist over the next few years. They were even more convinced when the simple task of joining the two tunnels failed. Someone had got the measurements wrong, they had gone in the incorrect directions and now had to construct two parallel tunnels some eight feet apart. If outside help could be found this must be the moment. Emergency sirens ringing in both centers as those green electrical lights were chasing all over the two tunnel entrances. Those inside quickly as possible exiting the tunnel. Electric flashed everywhere inside shooting all over the entrances. They lasted ninety seconds and then it was all over. Over too the safety officer who drew straws to be the first inside, the unlucky one started to crawl in. His expected return running late, later, the second security officer readying himself when out of the entrance came a distorted, altered figure.

The Safety Officer took control. A hand stretched out, a voice,

"Hello I am from Corsham Two B, your man has gone on to say hello to our lot."

Loud clapping.

Breakthrough.

'Pathetic,' thought the Computrons. 'What good will come of this?'

With the clapping continuing it had become the Livingstone Stanley moment again.

Still in the main dining room the young people were desperately hoping the third would say goodnight as she went off to bed, but the Countess continued. Eventually George yawned and made his apologies, saying 'Goodnight', as he headed to bed.

Grace looked at the Countess,

"You're staying up deliberately?"

"Yes," she replied, "I am still waiting for information on his suitability for us."

Both ladies retired to sleep the night away, one dreaming and one planning, which one dreaming? Which one planning?

The same routine as the previous day prevailed the next morning. George ate breakfast alone; Natasha cooked it, no sign or sight of the other ladies. The same driver, the same route to hospital, then into the office.

No updated news about Cuba, no new Secure Security reports from Havana, Washington or Moscow. All over the country there was a heightened sense of anxiety. Some people were starting to stockpile basic foodstuffs, described in newspapers as the selfish elite. Behind the scenes a great amount of hurried activity at National and Local authorities.

It would be hard to imagine that a threat of nuclear annihilation existed with the populous going around with normal levels of activity. It was almost impossible to describe the atmosphere, as there had never as yet been such a war. No one knew what to expect.

Almost nobody believed that mass annihilation could take place, so the nuclear powers could destroy one another there would still be many habitable places left particularly south of the Equator. The concept of a nuclear winter existed in theory. The streets of every major city continued with hustle and bustle as normal. No doubt the elite with their vested interests making their own plans for their own survival, like at Corsham.

For George the day in the office felt like the lull before the storm. A world on the brink of extinction.

Not far across Central London from the Foreign and Commonwealth Office the head of that famous auction house still had on his desk that parcel handed to him following the last Bridge evening. Having cut the string undone the brown paper he kept looking at the contents. He had been receiving similar parcels once a year since 1951, this contact one of the reasons he had made it up to the top job. Each item since 1951 produced high commissions, whenever the catalogue made it into the public domain the providence always stated, 'property of a titled family.' No other information. To date nothing had surpassed what he kept looking at, now the time had come to share this once in a lifetime find with two of his experts. Experts that were respected worldwide. Twice since 1951 the items were so important they were not auctioned, they were sold by private treaty to institutions, then available to the general public at large to view.

In came the two experts, the first head of books and manuscripts, then somewhat not so senior, maps and prints. Turning around the brown parcel to be in front of them the head looked for the expression on their faces. Silence. One commented, 'the Holy Grail.' The other, 'There is no record of it ever existing. It's always been assumed there must have been one.'

So the auction house boss asked the obvious,

"What sort of value?"

More silence.

Agreement that the head of books and manuscripts should speak to the main institutional curators inviting them to individual private viewings, all conversations not to enter the public domain. So what price for the original set of 1610 John Speed maps of the English and Welsh counties in original hand colours, each signed John Speed and saying 'My original map.' All 67 maps, including the various proof alterations, in total 287 maps. Valuing the 1610 atlas maps relatively straightforward, but the real value in those 'Various proof alterations,' some were in collections but many had never been seen before. The complete history, each signed by John Speed. Where had the collection been for all these years?

After much discussion a figure of not less than £50000 the point at which to start negotiations. Having come up with such an amount one of the accountants received the task of giving this some meaningful value. What could £50000 purchase? Having an interest in cars, he decided to use current purchase price of new cars and then new houses. The list;

Rolls Royce Silver Cloud III	£6277
Mercedes 300 SL	£5417
Jaguar E Type	£2036
Ferrari 250 GT	£6272
Morris Mini Minor Super	£557
Austin Mini Cooper	£640
Austin Healey Sprite	£622
MG MGB	£949
House detached London suburbs	£9750
Cotswold Cottage with land	£4500
Semi detached house, Manchester suburbs	£3250
Cash for investment	£9730
Total	£50000

Note, a newly qualified accountant would cost a salary of £1250 per annum to look after the accounts full time. That is a little bit more than average as the position is a little different to most.

Negotiations on the sale continued with the proceeds to be transferred to the usual Swiss Bank account in Geneva where all previous transfers had been sent into the account names 'Scotia Isles.'

For George it had been a day of little activity on the Cuban missile crisis until at about 3.30pm a very excited member of yesterday's legal team raced into the office. (Legal team. Race. Foreign Office. Are words that do not normally appear in the same sentence).

"George, you'll not believe it. A Soviet ship called the Sarucla on the way to Cuba has asked for help to get into the docks at Plymouth. From what we understand the Captain with the Political Officer have gone mad smashing up the navigation system. This is what I jokingly suggested yesterday would be the only way to get a legal opportunity to board the ship to see what the cargo is."

George, "Have we notified the Americans? What arrangements need to be made when the ship docks to get as many specialists on board as possible? Have we notified the Soviet embassy?"

Excited lawyer,

"The request for help came directly from the Soviet Embassy who needed permission to send Embassy staff into one of our military restricted areas. At the moment, the Soviets have a car, the Americans have two cars, and we have a bus all heading to Plymouth. The Navy has already appointed a Captain Groves to undertake all coordination. This event is very unexpected."

George decided he had not been asked, so would not volunteer to go to Plymouth. Anyway, he wanted to go out with Grace tonight. If it had not been for his near death experience he would have questioned that a joke request had now entered the realms of reality. More than one person in the Security Services thought, too good to be true.

In London the Soviet Embassy had accepted the offer of a frigate to escort the stricken Sarucla into port with a best estimate of arrival into Plymouth at 3 am the next morning. With the excitement dying down George decided to make a file note of the information, passed no comment, other than to say 'disturb me (wake me up) if necessary during the night.' (Always good for a few bonus points even though he had no expectation of being disturbed.) So the driver took him back to the temporary home.

Grace met him at the door with a hello kiss saying dinner would be early so they could go to the 'Ward' exhibition. In the lounge, the Countess asked him,

"What sort of day have you had?"

Then without thinking, almost a confessional, he started,

"Remember me saying that one of the legal team had joked that what we wanted was a Soviet vessel on route to Cuba to break down. Well one had. It will be in Plymouth in the early hours of the morning."

He didn't even think that he shouldn't have revealed such information, however the Countess did and therefore decided to change the office subject.

"We thought (I decided) we should eat first them you two will have plenty of time to change. Peter will drive you in the car."

'The car' news to George that the family had a car, to polite to ask what sort.

"Which one do you want to go in Grace?" (which one, how many are there, George asked himself).

"Leave it to Peter to decide," Grace said, "But not the Rolls Royce otherwise Ward will have an expectation that we will purchase some of the pictures."

Sitting around the dining table, Natasha produced yet another 'egg based' meal. Who is the vegetarian? George never that partial to eggs, more of a roast beef, Yorkshire pudding, vegetables man. For conversation he enquired how should he dress for such an exhibition?

"Wear the new suit with shirt and tie," the Countess instructed. Then the Countess advised him, "be careful whom you speak to, particularly those Russian friends that Stephen has. Do not let those young models of his start asking you for favours or money. You may well see some important people you wouldn't expect to see, remember everyone has a private life, even royalty."

With that, the Countess excused them from the table saying she would inspect them before they left. Two of her lady friends might still be around when they returned, just carry onto bed.

Peter arrived with the car, a good solid comfortable Rover 95 or was it the 110? George was never that good with cars. On arrival Peter said he would collect them again at 10.30pm.

Artists' exhibitions can be found in some very strange locations, as this one was. To George it looked like a church building no longer used for the original purpose, now dedicated to holding monthly exhibitions of up and coming but not yet famous artists. Yes, George did recognize some of the guests, however he was more surprised at some of the portraits (portraits were the speciality of Stephen). Did these famous people sit for him or had he used photographs freely available, then draw his portrait?

Everyone knew Grace. Everyone asked about the Countess. Grace introduced George as a friend of the Countess, saying he was fantastic at Bridge and staying with the Countess whilst moving into a new position at the Foreign and Commonwealth Office. The Countess hoped that when he had settled in his new position he would be a regular attender at Bridge evenings.

Wherever possible George decided not to speak. He stood silently behind Grace so that whenever they had their backs to the wall Grace would place one hand behind her back so that George could hold the same.

By 8.30pm the place started to empty at which time Stephen suggested they go back to his place for a drink. About ten or twelve made affirmative noises so the group walked a short distance into Bryanston Mews West, just behind Marble Arch, where the property stood. One of Stephen's young ladies offered a glass of wine to the incoming party. There already seemed to be a party of sorts in full swing, with three of the girls with several older, well-healed men. Grace again uttered, 'be careful,' as the Soviet Naval Attaché, Ivanov, made a beeline to communicate with George. Somehow, in one movement, Grace stood between them. It had not been an obvious attempt to keep them apart, certainly no sense of rudeness, she intervened to protect.

George mused that somehow these social skills are in-built to the aristocracy, perhaps they watch from the womb when their expectant mother's keep their bump out of harms way. To the casual observer the three would appear to be conducting ritual dancing, Grace between two men. Outside the Mews property, George had noticed a Morris Minor convertible and a Trojan three-wheel bubble car. Somehow he assumed they belonged to the girls, from what he could understand they also lived here, permanent or temporary not made clear.

Time had moved on giving Grace, with what appeared to be a sixth sense, the start of uneasiness. Something in the air made her very uncomfortable. Stephen clapped his hands for silence, moved towards a picture on the wall, removing it saying 'now for the real art'. With the picture gone a largish two-way mirror into the bedroom showing two of the girls with whips chasing one of the two men previously seen. As the guests jostled to gain the best viewing position, Grace had George out of the room and into the street before you could say, 'cockrobin.' She exploded into anger and pulled George to the nearest red telephone box and exploded into greater anger when the Countess answered the phone. No one can use profane language with the same effect as the aristocracy.

George understood that Peter had gone on to see some of his Russian friends before coming back to collect them. Grace told the Countess they would walk home so Natasha should tell Peter of the changed plans. From the red telephone they stood by in Marble Arch a walk back home would take little more than twenty minutes. Grace held his hand tightly setting off, so they were alone, surrounded by hundreds and hundreds of passers by, but they were alone together.

She talked; he listened, about everything and nothing. A car pulled alongside them, Stephen Ward stuck his head out of the passenger window, Ivanov the driver of a Soviet diplomatic car. Stephen shouting, really imploring, 'can we talk?' Grace walked to the window, spat in his face using unlady like language saying, 'stop curb crawling you dirty little pervert.' Still pleading, Ward screamed, 'Don't tell your mother, Grace.'

"Too late you nasty man, I've already told her by telephone."

They were still holding hands; George could feel her pulse racing. She was very very angry. He pulled her away; Ivanov put his foot down, two scrapping cats, separated. (At the trial of Stephen Ward in July 1963, Janet Barker, 20, a known prostitute told the jury that Ward brought her to his flat in Bryanston Mews to have sex with a man she did not know. Janet Barker also whipped the client receiving £1.00 for each stroke. She also said she had seen the hole in the wall (mirror.))

George placed his arm around her waist, her heart thumping away; he knew she did not like the man. When they approached home the two lady visitors were in the process of leaving.

"They've had a sort of board meeting," Grace whispered in his ear. Immediately they entered the hall, the Countess sounded incensed that her little girl had been so upset. Grace recounted what had happened with George saying 'yes' or nodding in all the right places. After her upset little girl had finished, mother, (not now a Countess) recalled do you remember me saying Profumo, Ward, Clivedon, and then getting a very immediate response from the Home Secretary?

"Well, my friends have been listening to the Westminster grapevine. A major scandal has been kept out of the public domain involving those three names. The details are not clear, ministerial jobs are at stake. Stephen Ward is involved, from what the ladies found out he is the central figure, so for the present I still want him to play Bridge to hear any information directly from the horses mouth."

Pulling a face, Grace indicated she would not be downstairs when the Bridge meetings took place, so to compensate the Countess indicated she felt tired; leaving them on their own a last. With the door closed, with no one talking, it is difficult to know what they got up to. Neither pretended to be part of the Swinging Sixties, however, George had removed his jacket when they reappeared, Grace definitely adjusting any clothing so that it fitted where it would have fitted before. No clue either when they arrived at the first bedroom, that for George, a peck on the cheek from Grace and nothing else. Both noticed a ray of light dancing out from the slightly open bedroom door of the Countess, obviously on parental patrol. In the event, two adults had crossed the line from being friends into a serious relationship. Only a few days earlier when setting up the Corsham Unit, George stated he had no serious relationships that would prevent him spending his life split between the London Office and the Corsham Office.

Whilst George slept much activity surrounded the Soviet ship damaged at sea, trying to enter port at Plymouth. At some time around 11.00pm the limping vessel escorted by a frigate, sent out S.O.S. flares followed by automatic gunfire, the incident lasting some six minutes. Still, the vessel continued on course for port. No request for help. The captain of the frigate to do nothing other than report. On land the reports were shared with those interested groups patiently waiting to board the ship. Had the frigate been behind instead of side by side those items thrown overboard during the six minutes of mayhem might, only might, have been seen. Two items, both bodies, were found several days later in different locations at sea.

Some fifteen minutes after the gun fire the frigate captain received instructions to get a group of four armed marines onto the Soviet merchant vessel, they to hide until intervention proved expedient. A deafening foghorn from the frigate as grabbling irons were secured on the railings, the four were on-board, undercover, ready. It was important that no action of any sort was taken and heads were kept down. Waiting in the offices on the dock side the Americans were arguing with the Soviets as to who would get the stricken vessel first, for the British security personnel the answer only to easy. They were already on board and therefore had the capability to stop any group from getting on or off.

So much happy singing came from within the stricken ship that the Marine Commander decided they could take up more advantageous positions. To the Marines, a party in full swing now had all the crew loosing all interest in anything to do with the vessel. They had to assume someone had to be steering, some still must be in the engine room, a very jolly ship for one reported in such distress. What really had the crew done?

Within reasonable time she came up dockside with the frigate still in attendance. Singing laughter continued, as the engine went to stop some crewmember somehow forgot to put on the generator lighting. Pitch black dark, the singing, the laughter gone, pitch black silence. Gradually a few lights came on from the dockside, and the four marines started to sweep the vessel. No crew were found anywhere. Blood in plenty in the Captain's cabin, blood in plenty in the political officers private quarters, no Captain, no Political Officer, no crew. A mass escape. Phone lines, any means of communication used by the three waiting countries. No 10, Prime Ministers do not like being woken up, took an instant decision to stop any news agency getting even the hint of a mass escape of Soviets. Who would possibly believe in the media or the general public that no connection existed between this event, the nuclear missile crisis, the possibility of a nuclear war. Headlines could come thick and fast, like, 'Soviet Specialist troops land on British soil, Nuclear war comes closer.' If a news blackout existed would the Soviet media or the American media report still make mention? Only time would tell. Another instruction from No. 10 on advice from the Foreign Office, 'no attempt is to be made to capture. See what happens.'

In various states of despair or euphoria, the London Diplomatic Visitors set back on their return from Plymouth. On the return journey a car from an Embassy stops to allow those in the boot to get into the car proper. With no one to ask for permission, a detailed search began of the deserted vessel. Without comparing notes, each of the marines passed the same comment, 'the singing on the ship were all western songs, sung in English.' It would be no good hunting for men with strong Russian accents.

George came down for breakfast, again no ladies, Natasha again on hand preparing exactly the same breakfast as the day before. All normal except she looked as if pale from lack of sleep. George made polite query as to her health, to be old Peter had received a phone call in the middle of the night to say one of his friends had been taken ill. Peter had left in the Rover to visit his friend but had still not returned home.

Syd G, on duty again, set off with George in the car to hospital and then to the office. Sometimes even the Foreign and Commonwealth Office is a hive of activity. When George arrived today was one of those days. Within a very large conference room a hub of activity was coordinating the search for the escaped Soviets, each Government department had a series of desks with hurriedly made signs; Home Office, Police, Security Service MI5, Intelligence Service MI6, Foreign Office, Army, Navy, Air force. Then in the middle a very large operational map of the United Kingdom, not the sort of map available to the general public. At the back of the room a display board plenty big enough for everyone in the room to be able to read. Information to date limited saying;

Time and Date

Escape from Plymouth

Looking for 18 to 25 Soviets.

Then numbers from 1 to 25 in columns for any information on individuals. No information in any one of those twenty-five columns. (The number 18 to 25 coming from the number of cabins or bunk beds counted on the ship.) Telephones were busily ringing, a buzzer in place to signify an entry onto the display board, as yet unused.

Some escapees were already deep inside an embassy. Where were the others? A small army of scientific military experts spent much time searching the vessel with the finest 'tooth combs'. There were large quantities of general cargo destined for Cuba. No one could find anything remotely military, remotely missile. To save face for somebody, somewhere up high, a decision came down from 'up there' that the vessel should go into dry dock for a complete external examination. Placing a vessel in dry dock with all supporting structure takes time. Foreign Office niceties called the Soviet Ambassador in London into the Foreign Office to receive the information about dry-docking directly from the Foreign Secretary. As part of ambassadorial training, a diplomat has to learn when to keep quiet, when to shout loudly. For the Soviet Ambassador the events were enough to give him an opportunity to shout loudly. Since Khrushchev (who became Soviet Leader in 1955 after the death of Stalin) at the United Nations had taken his shoe off and used it to bang on the table shouting that the Soviet Union had its own nuclear weapons, taking the shoe off banging the table had become the norm when Ambassadors became upset. So the

Foreign Secretary expected the event when the Ambassador followed Khrushchev's way. Prepared, the Foreign Secretary invited a representative from the Embassy to watch the dry dock event.

"Perhaps your Naval Attaché, Mr Ivanov should go to Plymouth?"

The Ambassador reported back to the London station KGB chief of the offer. Now his more immediate concern, 'did the British know that Ivanov although called Naval Attaché had always been in London as a spy? Or did they not know? Or were they pretending they did not know? Bluff, double bluff, triple bluff?' To the KGB Chief the answer was straight forward, Ivanov invited so Ivanov must go!

The Ambassador dealt with the niceties thanking the Foreign Office for the kind offer. 'Ivanov will go. How should he travel? Alone or with someone from the Foreign Office? And what about accommodation?'

Replying the Foreign Office stated he could travel by himself, drive or take the train. Hotel accommodation would be paid for out of the 'International Goodwill Fund' (whatever that might be, another creation for the moment?) For Ivanov a difficult dilemma. Moscow Central would be expecting reports of naval activities of ships arrivals, departures; the British will be watching every move to catch him in the act of spying. Ivanov needed to be seen, then not to be seen, he contacted Ward to ask if one of the girls had a car. They could drive him to Plymouth, staying with him until his return. Ivanov knew most of the 'Ward Girls' literally 'inside' and 'out' from various 'romantic' late night encounters. Ward arranged for 'Bea' to be available. She would drive the Morris 1000 convertible and bring the bikinis! Careful, she might sting.

Ivanov now had plenty for the security people to report about, mind you, he knew his file would be full of such liaisons, pleasure mixed with business. These arrangements all above board, anyone could listen if they were interested in his plans.

About an hour later, a female member of staff caught a

London bus travelling down to Oxford Street, entering a well known shop of ladies clothes she made a purchase of a small item then went to the public telephones. On a five pound note, she telephoned the number Ivanov had written down. When the person at the other end answered she said,

"Have you a 1693 Edition of the Nuremberg Chronicle?" then she placed the phone down. She spent the five-pound note before exiting the shop. Then back to the embassy and reported to Ivanov and got on with her normal secretarial duties. What Ivanov knew, and MI5 probably assumed was that those arrested as the Portland Spy Ring where not the only Soviet agents established by Gordon Lonsdale, the Soviet spy. Gordon Lonsdale had been created as a deep cover Soviet illegal with a false identity and nationality. His real name, Konon Trofinovich Mology, was the son of two Soviet scientists. Selected as a child of ten in 1932 to train as a spy he grew up (having been officially sent) with his aunt in California where he received his education, excelling in languages and returning to Moscow in 1938 at the age of sixteen. During the Second World War he joined the NKVD (forerunner of the KGB). In 1954 he went to Canada to establish a false identity, obtaining a passport in the name of Gordon Arnold Lonsdale. In March 1955 he came to London, enrolling as a student on a Chinese Course with the School of Oriental and African Studies. At the same time, he also set up a number of companies with interests in electrical type products. He came under surveillance by MI5 when he was seen meeting two people, already under surveillance, Harry Houghton, a clerical officer at the Underwater Detection Establishment at Portland. The second person was Ethel 'Bunty' Gee, his girlfriend, also worked at the Underwater Detection Establishment as a record keeper. Lonsdale went to London in October 1960. He had a meeting with Houghton in November and was then followed by MI5 to a bungalow in Crawley Drive, Ruislip, belonging to the antiquarian bookseller and his wife, the Krogers. They were Lonsdale's Support Team, his radio operators, later it was discovered that they were actually Morris and Lona Cohen the veteran American KGB illegal agents. At the trial at the Old Bailey in March 1961 all received prison sentences, Lonsdale twenty-five years, The Kroger's, twenty years each, Houghton and Gee fifteen years each. A long-time concern of the Security Service was that with the Soviets having spent so many years and so much money on developing Lonsdale, Morris and Lona Cohen as illegals, there must be a possibility that Moscow had other such illegals in Great Britain.

The phone call made by the Russian lady from the famous London store had the intention of contacting one other illegal. For that illegal the contact would be made by the question, 'Have you a 1693 Edition of the Nuremberg Chronicle?' Any antiquarian book dealer would know that the Nuremberg Chronicle in fact had a publication date of 1493.

Tony Computron, in Deep Earth, could identify exactly where in Plymouth the phone call had been received, who exactly had received it; a pillar of the community who had run a small business in the area for many years. Married, one adult child long since left home, a wife who had been a librarian on the mobile library ever since 'Books in the Community' started.

Having received the alert telephone call he knew that contact could be expected at any time. So he had to keep absolute normality, the usual routine, until a Morris 1000 convertible driven by a young lady with a male passenger pulled into the garage concerned about overheating. Overheating in clouds of smoke. The young lady explained everything had been running well except for a stop at some toilets twenty miles away. After that, the problem started. Exiting the car, Ivanov walked around a little then approached the garage owner asking,

"Is there a book-binder in town?"

Repairing the car continued as if nothing had been spoken.

"Who is paying the bill?" enquired the garage owner, then saying, "come to the office so I can issue a receipt."

Ivanov followed into the office, paid the bill, collected the receipt. The garage owner then said,

"You had better take this small can of water just in case." With that the Morris 1000 continued on the journey to the hotel. Entering the designated bedroom, 'Ivanov' immediately stated it had no view of the sea. Transferred to another room, he walked into the bathroom saying that it smelt. Then another room, and another room. Eventually he liked a corner room that led to the fire escape. He explained once he nearly died in a hotel fire in (never finishing the sentence). He felt he could do no more about finding a room that had not been bugged. His only task to get back to the boss in London the small can of water; everything else would be part of the spying game. They unpacked, shared drawers, wardrobe space roughly 80% to her and 20% to him. How is it possible for a lady to take so many clothes on a four-day away day? Mind you, what about the shoes! A female centipede, the dresses, the skirts, the 1960's mini. So 'Bea' now in situ decided she would get ready for the evening meal. She said about thirty minutes. Ninety minutes later she declared herself ready. Ivanov was happily asleep so she left to go out hunting for a client or two, or three or four as it was only early evening. As she left he decided to give the 'watchers' something to do. For two hours he walked around town with a newspaper tucked under his arm. Stopping to look into shop windows, walking backwards a few paces as if something missed on first view. Jumping on a bus, good for someone had left a newspaper so he swopped newspapers. Getting off the bus, crossing the road, and then crossing back to the bus stop. Waiting for the next bus, getting on and getting straight off before the bus moved. Sitting on a bench in the town center bus station, then running to get another bus as it pulled out. Missed the bus, jumping into a taxi asking to be taken to the hotel. Straight into the bar for a well earned drink and chaser (a tot of whiskey). That activity will give the watchers plenty to write about. Wonder if they searched for the original newspaper. In fact, he had not been followed the watchers were much more interested in fitting listening devices into the new bedroom.

Back in the bedroom, he decided Bea had found a customer for the night so he played another of his spy games sitting on the bed saying his prayers in Russian then speaking out loud every fifth word. That is very much how the four days went, she sleeping during the day, working at night, he spending the days at the dry dock watching nothing being found as the ship continued to be searched top to bottom. Really his only concern to get the can of water safely back to London. On the return journey home, they stopped off at the garage again. This time a bag of naval uniforms was handed over. Bea had done her task well with a nice assortment of uniforms from her various sleeping partners, and she had made good money as well. As the Morris pulled away the clothes were already in a hidden room (really a flat) as the remaining four crewmen turned themselves into Naval Officers. One after one over the next few days they caught the London train creating new identities in the metropolis, and then continuing their various journeys to be close to reservoirs around the country. Each had a small packet of chemical poisons to throw into the water at a given signal. Ivanov again received 'brownie' points from his boss who took the tin of water into the small laboratory in the Embassy basement. Having emptied the small amount of water, two small packages were opened in front of the boss for a quick examination prior to making a copy then forwarding the original in the good old diplomatic bag to Moscow. Of the two packages, one showed those underground passageways underneath the military base at Plymouth, the second indicated a number of places off shore where a submarine should be able to hide outside of all shipping lanes. In fact, Ivanov felt like a dog with two tails at the success of the mission. Time to get out drinking.

In Deep Earth, Bruce the dog took immediate objection to 'a dog with two tails'. He had heard the expression before. Why not say, 'a human with two tails?' Why should his canine friends be demeaned? Tony Computron for once showed great interest in the ship activities, this had obviously been a project long in planning and suddenly taking advantage of the Cuban missile crisis. Why though had two members of the crew been killed? Why their bodies thrown overboard? He was much more interested in the growing number of illegals during this possible nuclear war. Why had antiquarian book dealers been used to set up various Soviet spy networks? Tony Computron knew it had been a classic case of what had not been very valuable to Soviet Libraries becoming very valuable in the commercial Western antiquarian book world. History would show how many really valuable first editions started to arrive into the book world in the late 1950's, early 1960's. Useless pieces of paper turned into greedy profits keeping a willing group of helpers, always waiting for the next book gift. Not money for old rope, instead, money for old paper. Ever bemused by the pathetic activity at Corsham and the other nuclear bunkers, he proposed to the Elders that a time record counting down to zero (the time a bunker could no longer support life) be placed in the top right hand corner of any visual displays still operating. The Younger Elders immediately thought this a sensible idea but would a number of displays be better showing bunker life with different levels of staff, obviously the longest survival for each bunker would be if only one person remained, the rest taking their own lives, or just going for a walk outside into certain death. Barbara, Mason, Miss Moneylegs were horrified at the suggestion particularly when taking into account that Corsham and others were talking about producing babies as a new generation. Tony stated if they want to survive they need information. With information a logical decision can be made, but the logical answer is as plain as the nose on your face. Fewer people, longer life span for those who remain. The reality is that what they really expect is some magic fairy to produce food every day so that the real life or death decision does not need to be made, cowards to the very end. Barbara went off in anger, the Computron did not move. Bruce the dog ran after Barbara to be her friend.

At Corsham, Ian had exactly the same thought as the Computron; to survive numbers have to be reduced. A cull is needed. Can we put people to sleep for a long time (years)? What about comas? We have more ability to manufacture drugs than manufacture food, or the obvious, can we get more food from elsewhere to bring here. Even that could only be a temporary measure but worth talking about with the community. Certainly they had some transport; they had many 'space suit' type clothing with air bottles. Why didn't we think of that before? A simple start could be made to the supermarket in Corsham.

Scientists within the Deep Earth community now spent every moment studying the wind/wave. There existed no let up in the sound noise level of the Founding Protectors, if only they could be communicated with! Is the noise their method of communication? That simply idea set off a whole series of new experiments to see if the noise could be a communication language from the beginning of time.

Mason suggested that the cell he had been kept a prisoner for a time could be useful to the scientists as no noise could enter the cell other than the Founding Protectors passing through. The construction of the cell kept every thought, every sound away from the space inside. (Mason had been placed into the cell for thinking unacceptable thoughts, just before the Whale anomaly arrived.) Mason continued remembering George before his death had speculated that one adult computron had a greater capacity than all the computers on Earth crust if they had all been connected together. Mason therefore suggested as many computrons as possible should be in the cell, then all the computrons should assemble in one place to concentrate on the communication void. Tony Computron immediately requested not to go into the cell, as he did not like confined spaces. Miss Moneylegs giggled and thought, "I knew he had a weak spot." She thought Tony gave her a dirty look. Barbara had returned telling Miss Moneylegs to leave him alone. The Computron most definitely smiled. The Computron hierarchy went off to think through the logistics of how so many hundreds of thousands could be in one place at the same time. One of the research scientists had found information from the library that a long time in the past a group of Communist Scientists had speculated that a speed faster than the speed of light had to exist, or previously existed, giving their reason based on how quickly the Universe had grown after the Big Bang. No research could be found, just the statement of thinking. It is not easy to understand that when it is stated that a solar system (for example) 10 million light years away, the measurement represents a distance and a look back at the universe in time. Really better descriptive dimensions should be used to explain the double meaning. If therefore a speed of the George double W is greater than the speed of light, then new calculations needed to be made as to when the Milky Way would be affected. Is that why the Founding Protectors were so angrily noisy?

Miss Moneylegs had genuinely found herself bemused so she sidled up to the Computron and fortunately started with the correct though of, 'I don't understand.' Tony Computron, now happy to explain as she admitted failure.

"The problem is that using Light Years means that it is the Light distance that is measured to state where an object is. What you really should say is that the object was there ten billion light years ago. You are comparing seeing that light today with what that light looked like 10 billion years ago. If you could then zoom from Earth today this moment in time with real time light, the object would have moved, changed, disappeared. You must remember when you look into the Universe you are looking at a past, not a present. Then to confuse minds further, the past is at lots of different past times. Imagine your old school ruler. Place it length ways with the longest number nearest your eyes. You know that the distances all along are different but you are looking at the whole different distances all together at the same instant in time."

Miss Moneylegs,

"Wish you had been my science teacher."

A happy computron smiled (perhaps). Barbara got in the act by asking,

"Does not light degenerate as it travels? How can it be the same say, one billion years ago and to day? Does not light criss cross the Universe? How can you be sure that light from one place does not merge with light from another place? Take the Sun and the Earth. Light is not consistently on the Earth; only parts of the Earth receive light as it rotates. But surely if light travels why cannot the light from the sun be all over the Earth regardless of the rotation?"

Tony, with some friends, went to think about some of those questions, but they should not be distracted from the conundrum and all Computrons were supposed to trying to resolve. However, Tony as a parting thought indicated that the measurement of the speed of light is as in a vacuum. Is it safe to assume that the Universe exists in a vacuum? All fourteen billion light years really existing as a vacuum???

CHAPTER NINETEEN

For George, the same routine as the previous days, no Countess, no Grace, just himself for breakfast with Natasha. Out of politeness he asked (but not really interested) if the friend of Peter showed any improvement from his illness. 'No', she replied. George had been disturbed several times in the night by noise from the old stable black. Collected by Syd, to hospital, back into the office. The front door had only just closed behind him when the Countess and Grace arrived for breakfast. Both wanted to hear from Natasha what had been going on during the night. What had Peter been doing?

The breaking news on the radio continued firstly to be about the escaping Russian crewmen. Where could they have reached? Various sightings had been reported literally from Land's End to John O'Groats. No captures. Usual warnings, 'do not approach, they are armed and dangerous, report directly to the Police.' The second story, the Cuban Missile Crisis. Soviet ships carrying missiles with missile parts were midway across the Atlantic heading for Cuba. Then back to the main story now suggesting that they were not seamen but spies. Reporters from various parts of the country interviewed members of the public who were sure they had seen a spy. Out came the stereotype descriptions, beard, shifty eyes, gun bulging in a trouser pocket, rucksack with a picture of Lenin, dirty wellingtons, smelling of vodka, looking at women, asking in a strong Russian accent the way to the nearest army barracks. One report said a spy gave a

Birmingham shopkeeper a rouble bank note instead of a pound note, and then he ran away not even taking the food he had purchased. Various sightings said he had a patch over his left eye, others that he had a patch over his right eye. A report from the driver of a school bus that two Russians got on his bus asking for Fylingdales, he knew they were spies because their English was too good for locals. (They turned out to be two experts from the Ministry of Defence in London.) The Police investigated each and every sighting giving the information to the local Special Branch Officer who then handed it on to his Security Service (MI5) contact.

Continuing with the news the farthest north sighting was just outside St Andrews, the home of golf, in Scotland. Do Russian spies play golf? 'Bunkered at the 19th' the headline in a heavy weight national newspaper. A politician from one of the minor parties in Westminster decided that to attack the Soviet Union would ensure his name appeared in the newspapers, on television and on the radio. He suggested all sporting events should be cancelled whenever a team or a person from the Soviet Union took part. Start by banning football teams from the 1966 World Cup, to be played in England, who were communist states. He got his headlines. None were immediately captured, the whole event well planned, well executed by, as yet unknown. Could this have been another group set up by Gordon Lonsdale? Perhaps a sleeper from a long time ago. Perhaps some form of secret society from the very center of power that believes communism could have been prevented if the Russian Royal family had received help.

Tony and the other computrons were consumed with work on the George Double W effect, but a few of them around Tony did smirk (?) with the knowledge of what really happened to the disappearing crew of the Sarucla. Then a Computron threw the radical though, 'could they actually have been British spies making a run for home before the start of the expected nuclear war carrying important secretive combinations for launch sequences of the Soviet missiles, to be handed to military intelligence to create a blocking/failure sequence numbers in reply to the originating firing sequence? How to give abort signals to the oppositions missile attack that would create a no loose nuclear strike advantage?'

With the George Double W effect now consuming all scientific and computron minds a very uncomfortable fact (well estimate) that no one could calculate the speed of travel. A growing consensus consisted of a believe that the speed of light was as if a tortoise when compared to the 'wind/wave' hare!! The critical question, 'when would the Earth with the moon, be affected had not even entered the world of gestimate.' Nevertheless the senior of the Elder Elders decreed that Deep Earth Humanity had to inspect every nook and cranny looking for any structural defects in the world of Deep Earth Humanity. An initial search that in Earth Crust years had a planned programme running for fifty years, followed by repair, reconstruction programme with a time estimate of five hundred years. That hiss, hiss, hissing sound now a part of every day life, there constantly and never ending. A programme of development that Mason followed with intellectual amazement centered around a project that could only be described as being like individual eggs. Early on the computrons advised that when (note that when) the Earth entered the Wind/Wave anomaly it would be like a 'cork' thrown in the 'Niagara Falls', rolling, turning, up, down, sideways, all happening at the same time, hence the idea of individual eggs to protect the individual inside. Mason thought real science fiction to which Tony Computron, receiving the thought replied, 'no practical science to us,' continuing, 'a failure rate will also be expected, as with the bird not every egg will survive. Unlike you Earth Crust Humanity, we are making long-term plans for an uncertain future. Your Earth Crust politicians could not even comprehend planning for fifty years.' Mason knew he could only agree. Shortsighted political class had been infecting Earth Crust, only contemplating today and never tomorrow. That infection was spreading into all people everywhere. My self-interested today! Let tomorrow take care

of itself. Such a selfish, ignorant lack of communal interdepend-
ence. The egg idea only existed as a conceptual thought, Mason
new he would not he here to need one, incredible planning for
five hundred years in the future. Could King Henry VIII have
made plans for space travel, or the then Pope have made plans
for super Italian sports cars, and here the crunch not just thinking the idea but creating the plan for the idea to come to exist.
Like planning to create one only world wide language, one only
world wide government, one only world wide currency, one
only world wide religion. Barbara knew the computrons were
waiting for Tony to have one of his fundamental thoughts, she
knew from his strange expression, so he began.

"You Earth Crust people never sorted out your transport so
it did not produce carbon dioxide gases. Less that 150 years of
poisoning deliberately the air you breath. Without air, suffoca-
tion. What vested interests prevented the development of real
alternatives? The vested interests of governments so as to have
mass employment in car factories? The vested interests of the
capitalists not wanting their investments in plant and machin-
ery to have a zero value? The vested interests of Unions having
many members all in one place? The vested interests of the oil
producing nations?"

Tony continued,

"What about 'magnets'? What about capturing the speed of
light? What about using the natural speed of the movement of
the Earth around the sun?"

The Computrons all sort of nodding. All thinking the same.
'Feeble brains of Earth Crust Humanity.' Then they were back to
thinking about the George Double W effect. Even Bruce looked
deep in thought. 'Dogs can pull a sledge on snow, or with wheels
when there's no snow.' Mason, Barbara, Miss Moneylegs all
looked at him, the thinking dog for man. All four returned to the
library screens to catch up with George only to be interrupted
by Esamia with another of her starting statements,

"Our class thinks that your scientists should have harnessed
heat produced by the human body to create individual means

of transport. We also think you could have done the same with the human poo, produced in abundance every moment of every day."

As usual off she went without waiting for a reply. Back to the Library screens to catch up with George, the Cuban Missile Crisis, for the Earth Crusters.

To George hospital had entered a routine of pointlessness, his near death experience a very recent past event. Pointless arguing with the office Lords and Masters, go with the flow. Back in his old office again the quiet reception from his once oh so friendly staff, he still had no explanation for their indifference. The replacement for George again deferred to him, offering George his old desk and chair back. As George sat down the 'top secret' daily file again handed to him updating the latest information on the 'Cuban Missile Crisis,' a new note had been added to the first left hand page, written in red saying, 'we do not believe the Americans are giving us all the information (real word intelligence) in their possession.' The heads of both MI5 and MI6 signed the short note. Not really a surprise to George, it had never been a secret to anyone that he believed the 'special relationship' had always been one sided in favour of the Americans. Never more so since the recent British spy scandals. He looked up. Everyone in the room was looking at him.

"What has happened to my once friendly team?"

No response.

Again, "What has happened to my once friendly team?"

Again, no response. A lady, he knew her as Carol, cleared her throat,

"Everyone in the Foreign and Commonwealth Office is saying that you were dead, covered all over in green, then the green went, then you were alive. It is difficult to communicate with someone who died then is still alive."

George thought and asked his replacement to stand by the door, keeping it closed and allowing no one in. Now I am going to walk past each of your chairs, give me a thump or a punch, make sure it is I. By the time the person in the fourth or fifth chair had given a punch the room entered a state of giggles. When he arrived by Carol she stood up, smacking a resounding kiss on his lips. An uncommon like cheer went up (within the Foreign and Commonwealth Office, never). Then a knocking on the door, within the room a scurry of activity as naughty staff returned to their allotted desks. Another knock as the door opened from the inside, a stern head masterly voice,

"What is going on? Its work time not play time," and departed. The room again burst into giggles. George returned to his Top Secret File, his old staff back to normal relations. Every Christmas party for years afterwards all remembered the Carol kiss.

Esamia skipped back into the Library, her usual question, "Is George in trouble yet?" Miss Moneylegs, "Only a little bit." Esamia again, "Mason, the class wants to ask you something." Miss Moneylegs again, indifferent. Barbara recalled her good experience. Bruce the dog decided to go along with Mason.

A young boy started,

"In 2008 your world had a banking crisis when people all over your world suffered capital and income loss as a result of bad, if not dishonest, banking. Our question, why didn't ordinary people take action?" Mason simply replied,

"What action could be taken?"

The class with one thought,

"Start a penny rolling, or a dime or the lower value coin of any currency."

Mason, "I don't understand."

So the young boy explained,

"With your technology of texts and emails you could ask your friends to make a bank transfer to you of 1 penny. Then they could do the same with their friends and so on and on, ordinary citizens would have then clogged the system up with very little real cost to themselves. Here, we could have told you exactly how many transactions each bank could perform before a malfunction would set in, so simple, so easy. Mason, our question, why did no one think to take control of the banks in such a way?"

Mason was lost in thought; he kept thinking what the young boy had said, 'so simple, so easy.' He excused himself from the class just repeating, 'so simple, so easy.' Barbara and Miss Money-legs were both amazed at the simplicity of the children's idea. A banking crisis literally caused by transactions of no value from which a bank would find it very difficult to make a charge. Seized up systems unable to generate commissions (profit), what would the bank do then poor things.

To George very little had changed on information in the secret file but it would be beneficial to have all the information the American partners had, even better to know what the Soviet enemy knew as well (that really would be impossible.) Who first had the idea of an American/British meeting remains unclear. A meeting took place in the Foreign Office with lead players from the 'spies' of both sides. The afternoon meeting produced no new information for the Brits other than the American spy agencies were under very great pressure from the President to explain how the Soviets literally got under the radar for so long as these missile sites were constructed. It was as if the failure of 'The Bay of Pigs' intervention had placed a fog over the American eyes. George received instructions to visit the 'Head of 5' when the afternoon meeting had finished. George knew exactly what he would want intelligence about, those damn letters. George played a straight 'bat' explaining they remained unopened by the Countess and Grace. In the later investigation the use of those words, 'unopened by Grace and the Countess' were to save him recrimination. His driver took him from '5' back to his temporary home. George was now beginning to get bored with the imposed routine.

On the route back George told the driver he did not want to go back home yet but asked to be dropped off in Saville Row, as he wanted to buy a new three-piece suit. The driver did as he was told, George saying he would take a taxi home, the driver dismissed. Fortunately for the driver he went straight back to MI5 headquarters informing his superiors of the changed plan.

Logging the change, the superior thought nothing else needed reporting, he certainly had no detailed instructions which required him to sound alarm bells.

George found himself with the freedom to do what he wanted. George looked into various windows, walked into a tailor he had used in the past, asked, after some discussion, if they could get him some samples of light summer type cloth, blue with white chalk stripes. Tailors do not ask questions of clients but for George this more than an unusual request. (George could not explain he would be working underground in air-conditioned, temperature-controlled environment). He walked to the end of Saville Row, turned into Vigo Street, left toward Regent Street, crossed Regent Street then walked into Glasshouse Street, the outer extremities of Soho. Into the land of seedy gangster infested pubs then the smoke ridden strip clubs of every shape, every size, and every price band from not expensive to you need real money to be here. He had as yet no fixed destination just to wonder around until a pub or club took his fancy. With the strip clubs there was no shortage of scantily clothed ladies (many not so young) enticing him over the threshold with the comforting words, 'First drink on the house.' At best a watered down variety of the cheapest whiskey. George thought the '3 S's, smoke, sleaze, strip.' Gangland Soho meets the naive. It was best if the punters were foreign and spoke very little English, just enough to put the frighteners on. Only one object, to extract the maximum amount of money. Unfortunately one of the best sources of money those now de-mobbed from conscripted military service. Conscription, two years of enforced military service, came to an end in 1959, so it was only the stragglers the late deferred entries that were left. The new target had to be the increasing number of foreign tourists. Soho, its reputation, China Town, all must be on any sightseeing tour. Throw into the mix those many theatres along Shaftesbury Avenue so from 10.00pm a ready made supply of the inquisitive. The days of cash before credit cards. A 'fagen' world of pickpockets at the height of their profession with a progression of operating streets and clubs. As a newcomer starting on the periphery and with time, progressing to the more lucrative center. Pickpocketing for cash in hand. They say the gangland bosses had policemen in their pockets, from pickpockets to police in pockets, Soho gangland.

Barbara, with Miss Moneylegs was expecting the arrival of Esamia. Before she asked the usual question, Miss Moneylegs thought to her, 'looks as if George is about to get into trouble.' No response, obviously another matter of importance on Esamia's mind. Sure enough she started,

"You Earth Crust people sent cards to each other for birthdays, that time you called Christmas. In the class we were wondering why you never had 'a sorry day' when you owned up to a wrong done to another, or 'a thank you day' when you said thank you for a kindness you had received."

Barbara replied, stating the obvious,

"Card making organizations would have progressed those ideas if anyone had thought about them. To a card organization you could not have too many reasons to send cards." Then without stopping for breath, "the cards were never cheap and then there were postage costs on top."

Esamia had gone.

George had half a pint here, another half a pint there, no strip clubs, only pubs. Time now going towards dinner in his temporary home, he couldn't decide whether to phone in saying 'eat without him' or not to phone as that further extended his freedom. Common sense prevailed, there a faithful red telephone kiosk inviting him to place his coins to phone. He felt fortunate that Natasha answered the phone. All he had to say to Natasha was the simple fact,

"I am delayed. Dinner will be over by the time I get back."

He felt comfortable that he did not have to make an excuse or lie to the Countess or Grace, both would ask questions.

Another half a pint in another pub and in his mind the matter in hand now clear. From all streets in Soho George knew how to get to Soho Gardens. He had done it many times before. He looked around the Square on his arrival, receiving more than one invitation for a good time. They were certainly not hanging around the usual tree or the usual bench. Most unusual for them not to be about this was always their time. Easy to miss one, but the two were always, always, together. Another young lady made the offer of a good time when he replied, 'no thank you,' she shouted after him, 'can't you get it up luv!' A few who heard looked around. George continued looking for the two. He knew at this time it must be too early for them to be tipsy (tipsy, not drunk). Another hour and he would not expect to find them, at this early evening they should be about, they always had been in the past, the two together, safety in number. So he started a second look around the square. The 'can't you get it up luv!' came over when she clasped eyes upon him.

"Come on, I've see you before. You often come into The Square."

George acknowledged the comment in the affirmative but she was not who he wanted to find. So he went around the outskirts of the square, the once imposing homes of the affluent. In the 1600's, just inside the wall built to protect Londoners from attackers perhaps those from Scotland. Looking down alleyways not the most sensible way of proceeding as he looked more like a plain-clothes police than a punter. (Strange how in English you get such different meaning words beginning with the same letter, in fact Soho in three 'P's', prostitution, punter, police.) Down one alleyway, the word 'pervert' reached his ears. Then from another, 'he's alright, he's a politician out for the night.' He thought there must be a gent's outfitters nearby; so many of these men are in the same raincoats. It was not raining, flashing, flashing red light down another alleyway, again the haunted plaintiff cry of 'want a good time mister?' Obviously there were money shortages in Soho tonight.

He wondered if it would be worth asking if any of the girls had seen the two he wanted to find. Better not, keep looking. He knew a little bar in one corner of the square where he had met them in the past, worth a try. Arrival at the solid door, the smell of cigarette smoke mingling with stale beer wafted out onto the pavement. Pushing the door open his eyes, his lungs pitched into the toxic air, he starting to cough with the second step. Everyone looked up to examine the unwelcome stranger; locals, not part of the usual Soho scene, only used this bar. A quick look around, they were not there. He exited urgently into the fresher outside air. His level of anxiety starting to rise. Not yet concern or alarm, only a mild sense of anxiety. His spur of the moment decision to find the two started to look like a failure. Then the worry of partly deceiving the Countess, of deceiving Grace, now wishing he had gone home for dinner instead of the adventure into freedom. No doubt they would be discussing what matter of national importance had kept him at work. He could not telephone to extend his excuse. First better to try one other possibility. He walked to the far corner of the Square, crossed the road, standing in front of what in its day would have been a fine Regency four-story town house. He started to climb the stairs up to the front door. No point in looking into the basement flats, they were not the sort of females he wanted. At the front door an impressive lion headed doorknocker requested his hand to give a sharp knock. Nothing. A second sharp knock. A female opened the door.

"You! Are you coming in or going to stand around for all to see."

Down a corridor she opened the second door on the left. She went in first, he followed. Another female voice.

"What do you want?"

Somewhere in the building a very good saxophone player at work. The second female repeated the question, adding one word, his name.

"What do you want George?"

George in his own mind still not sure why he had come to see Joy and Heather, his sisters. After the end of the Second World War their father had continued as a City Stockbroker having success eventually becoming a partner. He died unexpectedly when George had entered his teens; their mother shortly after

George left University. His father's wealth passed to the mother then on her death, equally between the three children. Sufficient for each to invest in a property for themselves. Neither Joy nor Heather had married, each pursuing a career, for Joy in photography, for Heather, portrait painting. Together they purchased the Soho Square property to be close to work, always saying that one-day London property would be very valuable. From the start they had created two basement flats. This income providing enough to meet the house running costs. Since Mother's death, George kept in touch visiting them perhaps twice a year. They had never been to his flat. So George started,

"You are both listed as my next of kin with the Foreign and Commonwealth Office, my new appointment is that I will be absent from London two or three weeks every month."

Having said his news he arose to leave when Joy said exactly what he expected.

"We're a bit short, can you lend us £50?"

George had come prepared handing over the £50 which he knew from the recent past would not be repaid. Heather shooed him back to the front door, closing it behind him. No thank you, no goodbye. He knew they were embarrassed so the baby bunting of long ago childhood kept quiet. They struggled in their chosen careers, neither had success either with photography or portrait paining. Part of his money would go on drink. They were not habitual drunkards. The rest hopefully saved for another day. At the bottom of the steps, he turned left heading towards Oxford Street where there would be taxis. At the end of his sisters house, an alleyway. As he passed by a severe blow to the head, at the same instant, a sharp needle into his arm. George was dead to the world.

CHAPTER TWENTY

The Countess had set 9.00pm as the time to start asking questions with no George back she contacted the number Grace had been given to report to if George had been taken ill. The Duty Officer did not waste time, immediately sending two members of staff to visit the next of kin. The sisters confirmed George had visited them much earlier in the day and he was fine when he left.

"No! He did not say where he would be going only that his new appointment would take him out of London for two or three weeks every month."

Barbara and Miss Moneylegs turned around waiting for Esamia to arrive. She always arrived at a critical moment in the life of George. Still no Esamia. Barbara expressed the thoughts that the hiss, hiss, hissing noise of the Founding Protectors had merged into all other noises now no louder or quieter than it had been. Certainly whilst they had been so preoccupied with George the noise presented no annoyance anymore. Tony Computron expressed concern that with the noise level now constant no progress could have been made with regards to the wind/wave phenomena. Still, where is Esamia? Does this mean that this is the time George gets into trouble? Is it so obvious that she did not need to come and ask them? Tony Computron knew. If a Computron had lips they were remaining sealed.

A Duty Officer does not like staff to disappear, particularly someone as important as George. He now had a priority standing list, the Duty Officer followed procedure to the letter. Within the hour the loop of need to know had been informed, Special Branch had been notified with a photograph. Out of respect for the Countess, he informed her of the basic facts. "No information yet."

All the phones started never-ending calls, this would not be a normal case, and this would be a long night. He had been in no doubt that National Security could be at risk. More importantly, the Prime Minister relied on the man for advice during the ever-deepening Cuban Missile Crisis. The Duty Officer brought in all available staff, many already turning down the bedclothes when the 'Back to Office urgently' phone call interrupted home life. Where had George gone? Could he have relapsed? (Check all hospitals) Could he be trying to get back to Corsham? (Check all railway stations) Had he gone for entertainment in a Soho nightclub after visiting the sisters?

At least two groups were preparing for a long night, the security world staff, the Countess with Grace joined by Natasha, Peter with his father, perhaps at least one more group as yet unknown. Still the Cuban Missile Crisis progressed to greater danger.

George moved a little, obviously remained alive, bright lights instantly all around him. Back into induced sleep, the lights went out again. He thought he heard a male voice, "too early for him to be of any use, more time needed for the drug to get through the system." Dreaming George thought he could see pictures of himself around the room, sketched as if drawn by 'Ward', or perhaps his sister. Naked pictures. Another voice, a female "Give him a shake time is moving on." Another female voice, sounded Russian. Then asleep again, feeling of being uncomfortable, feeling in danger. Those pictures, 'did I look naked?' Impossible. Why am I here? Someone roughly pulled him up so his back found support from the bed headboard, his head fell forward. Then someone held it back. He felt unclothed, flesh rubbing against his upper legs, flash, flash, flash. Light on, off, on, off, on, off. Someone pulled his feet so he lay flat on the bed. More unclothed flesh sitting on groin, then an up and down movement going on for about thirty seconds, all the time flashing, flashing lights. His mind racing. No green flashing lights. Moved again, feeling flesh underneath, what am I on top off? Moved up and down, flashing, flashing lights. Convinced a male voice, "now two of you, top and bottom, make it look 69." More flashing, flashing. Another prick in the arm, dead to the world again. Then they tidied up with professional pride, made sure plenty of George pencil drawings around the room, tied a handwritten note to the big toe on his left foot, exited locking the door as they went. Job well done waiting for the outcome, leave the trussed turkey to himself, she having made plans with the others kept the door keys returning alone to George, having liked what she had been playing with wanted more. De-clothing, she quickly had herself positioned for maximum extension making more photographs of the trophy. At the critical moment he moved. She felt rejected. In the process of cleaning herself, a knock at the door, unclothed she made it to the eye glass peep hole within the door, she looked, glad to have slid the bolts into place on her arrival, two of Soholands well known night club bouncers doing the day job of putting the frighteners on someone. Who were they expecting to find?

Now a thing like a truncheon brought down heavily with an intimidating crash, the door held. A good full swing kick, the door held. Well within their ability to smash it in. On of them looked in through the other end of the eyeglass peep hole. Impossible for him to see inside. Mumbling curses of disgust they left. She turned quickly to dress prior to a very quick exit. George had moved, slouching into the headboard with his eyes now open. He could make out a female body, his eyes would not focus, and words were in his mouth failing to reach his lips or the female form. She looked very tall, perhaps 5ft 10 inches, very slim, dark black shoulder length hair, if she had been under age he would not have been surprised. She had left, George went back into dreamland thinking about the nymph like figure, then Grace, then the nymph like creature, the Countess waving a finger in his face telling him he had been a naughty Georgee.

George awoke with a thumping headache, a stinging sensation in his arm. He had no clothes on, naked on a very large bed, the only other piece of furniture a chair with his clothes neatly folded on the seat, his jacket hanging on the back of the chair. All around the room there were pencil sketches of George in compromising positions with two young females. A vague memory of the tall one with dark black, black hair, brain working overtime. Every turn in the maze spelt 'trouble'. I am in deep trouble, the obvious compelling question, 'who wants me compromised? What do they want?'

The note on his toe, 'You will be contacted about the photographs.'

He dressed, took some coins from the heel of his left shoe, starting walking to the door, tripped over a wire, landing full facial on the bed, coins rolling everywhere.

Raising himself he followed the wire to find a telephone under the bed. Picking up the receiver, a dialing tone, the phone still usable, and a deliberate plant to find out whom he would telephone. He dialed a London number, a female voice answering, 'London Pavement Company.' He gave a name and then left the receiver dangling over the bed. Whoever dialed that number would get the same reply. The Security Service had many such emergency telephone numbers, only senior telephonists dealt with the array of such special numbers, an emergency call from a staff member.

George knew it would not take long for a team to come to see his embarrassment, it would not be the first compromise set up the team had dealt with, certainly in these 'Swinging Sixties' it would not be the last.

Through a small window George could see the moon, so near and yet so far away. Yet in the distances of the Universe the distance between the Earth and Moon is nothing. How long would it be before man got to the moon? How long before an Earth colony could be established? Strange how we only see the one side of the moon. Could something live on the other side, the dark side? What would Earth be like without its moon? Strange word that, moon. Who thought that name up? He sat there thinking as the team arrived. The team had taken less than eight minutes to arrive. George in quarantine was driven away to the same hospital he had been visiting every day. This would not be a quick ten-minute check-up. Someone had the common sense to telephone the Countess. Charles gave her no information other than George had been found, that he had been taken to hospital for a routine!! Check up. Rather like 'Department 13' a specialist medical team with a permanent matron. The team to examine every last hair on the body of a not yet fully awake George. Enough blood taken for testing to keep blood specialists happy for days. Enough urine taken to make a small pond. (How do you explain to a loved one that your job is testing urine all day, every day, all year, dedication to humanity.)?

In George's circumstances not starting with the whack on the head, no in this instance sign of any sexual activity. Every word spoken by the medical team was recorded, every minute detail recorded. All he kept thinking about centered on the female saying 'Can't you get it up luv," he convinced himself that he had met her before; she made herself so obvious in talking to him twice. Where oh where had he met her in the past? After all the examinations, the long debriefing, a clear picture appeared of an attempt to set him up for something. For George the worst had yet to happen. Firstly he received instructions to go along with the blackmail, he really didn't want to be a spy. Enough is enough. Secondly, he would have to tell the Countess, more importantly Grace, an untrue set of facts. George was very very unhappy. How had he managed to get involved in the unpleasant world of spying?

He returned to his temporary home, obvious they had all been waiting all night for information. The Countess set the agenda by insisting no questions, 'he will tell us when he can.' Instant relief for his anguished mind. As if to prevent any further discussion, she went on to say that she would open the letter from the Count. After breakfast Grace confirmed she would do the same.

Neither Barbara nor Miss Moneylegs could understand why Esamia had not appeared during the latest George crisis. Barbara decided to make sure Esamia had gone to school. Not knowing exactly where she lived, school would be the most appropriate place. Emptiness described the school, no teachers, no pupils, nobody. The walkways were empty. Where had they gone? The Earth crusters had been so preoccupied looking at George they must have missed something.

To Barbara it was much more alarming to realize that Tony Computron had also gone. Did she miss his departing thought? In some distress she reported back to Miss Moneylegs, Mason, could not be found in their home, the two of them were alone. That hiss, hiss, hissing remained as intense as before. Back to Ewewatch the all-telling eye of Deep Earth Humanity.

Before they arrived they could hear distant music. Barbara received a tug on the sleeve, in her Sunday best, Esamia had arrived. 'Come quickly, you must dress in your best. It is 'the Wedding Day.' Pushing, running the two back to their home on route trying to understand what had happened to their Wedding Day Invitation.

The music now louder, now nearer, Esamia now had a hint of anger in her thoughts. 'Come on hurry up, or I will be in trouble with my parents.' Barbara threw on her best 'made in Deep Earth' outfit, Miss Moneylegs still making up her mind. Esamia was now really angry.

'Just put something on, now you have made me late. Do you not understand, it is rude, very rude, to be late.'

On leaving the home the start of the procession had already arrived. How to describe dress for the occasion? Rather like sixties flower-power people meet English Morris dancers. Colour in abundance, noise all around from little bells attached to every costume, even managing to dull out the hiss, hiss, hissing noise. Some were dressed as Kings, Queens, Jacks, Jokers, as if from a pack of playing cards. All. Everyone, taking part, initially subdued even Miss Moneylegs cheered up. Some two of three miles of Deep Earth Humanity on the move. (Later they found out similar events were taking place all around Deep Earth.)

Somewhere, eventually the terrible three were found. Mason, Bruce and Tony Computron. Where had Mason managed to get such an outrageous costume? Tony Computron with bells all over (must be a joke in that statement). Bruce the dog with a straw hat wedged over his ears with a saddle on his back made entirely of bells. The two underdressed ladies joined the Terrible Three, they were laughing at the inadequate dress of the ladies. In gentlemanly style they were given some bells of their own. Bruce offered his hat (declined), Tony with some of the other naughty Computrons offered the two ladies a ride on their shoulders (declined). From behind his back Mason handed them two Easter bonnet type hats (accepted).

In walking, more like dancing, Tony Computron explained that the marriage time only happened once a year making the day a holiday everywhere in Deep Earth. No need to worry about rainy wedding days as it never rains down here, thought Barbara. With the music at the front the Earth Crusters soon realized that as they passed houses, those to get married joined in behind the music. Then holding hands with their soon to be husband or wife. There were now thousands upon thousand in the procession. All for a time forgot the hiss, hiss, hissing sound of the Founding Protectors. No worry about keeping up with the 'Jones' in this wedding when Tony explained 386 couples would all be married at the same moment in time. They arrived at one of those immense open areas that Bruce often roamed, probably a stage (in Earth Crust language covered by a tent like structure). Then row upon row of those swing things that Barbara had seen in the classroom. Miss Moneylegs thought they looked like spiders. She still dreamt about her first encounter in Deep Earth, when she landed in spider world, only to see them laughing at her. (Yes, if you listen carefully all spiders used to have a belly laugh at Earth Crust humanity when it still lived.)

The marriage took place, with an Elder Elder on the podium stage, sending the thought 'You are married let the celebration commence,' that was it. Now celebrating would have been a lesson for Earth Crust humanity if it had still existed, very happy people without the need for alcohol to take away inhibitions. No smoking, no drugs, only the constant jingling of millions upon millions of bells. With the celebrations in full swing (well perhaps ringing) Tony Computron explained that after the marriage those flying carpets would take the marrieds away to a holiday area, then when they returned each couple would have a property (home) of their own. Sometimes their parents moved to a smaller home, sometimes an existing property would be turned into two properties, particularly if a parent had died. If you like a granny flat. Or sometimes a completely new home would be constructed. It all depended on individual family circumstances, so when you arrived back after the wedding holiday each couple immediately had their own home. Mason asked the practical question, 'why all marriages only once a year?' The Computron looked puzzled, as did all those receiving his thoughts. 'It is part of our life cycle. Part of the living community, part of Deep Earth Humanity tradition. Our way, our judgments, our life cycle, no wars.'

Bruce the dog enjoyed the freedom of the weddings, freedom that made him think of his man 'pet hate', (Yes! A dog does have 'pet' hates), travelling in motor vehicles. Why did those Earth Crust Humans keep putting us in cars, those terrible 4 x 4's, then leave windows open when the vehicle travelled so us dogs put our heads out then getting eye infections. They never understood the sick feeling of confinement in the back of a vehicle. When the doors are opened we then get into trouble for running out into freedom, fresh air, and freedom. Earth Crusters were so happy driving cars they thought their pleasure extended to their pets. Perhaps if dogs wanted to go in cars they would take a driving test.

CHAPTER TWENTY-ONE

With dinner finished the three went onto the more comfortable chairs. The Countess opened her letter with loving care, in her own mind, her own decision, she would read it aloud. Quietly Natasha joined the group.

"My ever dearest,

With despair I write, if you are reading my words, a terrible event will have taken place."

At that moment a house brick smashed through the front window landing not far from the feet of George, a note attached. A loud voice from outside, 'Go home commi and stop your missiles.' Then a second brick. Before the second house brick hit the ground George jumped up, made for the front door, jumped the steps, off in chase. In the not too far distance a figure could be seen running, already chased by one male figure, behind him another male figure. Four men at speed heading for ??? George ran as a man possessed.

The Countess picked up the note which said, 'Go home Commi bastard.' She showed no emotion, told Grace to telephone the police, then sat down again with the note in her hand. The police were very close getting to the house in slightly less than two minutes. Had they been on duty, a coincidence, or a tip-off? Some three minutes into the chase George over took the second pursuer. George knew him by sight, giving him an instruction to telephone the office then get back outside the house to resume his surveillance duties. Definite progress for the first pursuer, who was making obvious gains. A bend in the footpath, a passer by tripped up George, then with George still on the ground he pushed a piece of paper into his hand. George had exited the chase.

He stood up, brushed himself down, read the piece of paper and then carefully placed the paper into his trouser pocket. So the brick thrower had achieved the appointed task of drawing George out of the house for the accomplice to hand over the paper, then the unexpected bonus of identifying two men from the British security world. With George re-entering the house, he passed the police in the doorway having been told by the Countess no complaint was to be reported. Peter and Grigory were already placing wood over the broken window, a temporary fix until the morning.

George explained he had been knocked down in the chase that prompted Grace to give him a quick medical examination. Little grazes, no doubt bruising tomorrow. The Countess spoke quietly with a degree of anger in her voice.

"I will not read anymore of the letter someone has already read the contents. The letter is no longer personal or private."

For perhaps that lifetime of memories of no more than twenty seconds absolute, complete, silence. George asked the question on all the others lips, with continued anger in her voice.

"Life in Russia had been dangerous during their courtship. The wrong word would have caused them both trouble. For protection, when they wrote the left side of the last page would have a small indent, that small piece of paper would be inserted in the letter, the small piece of paper no bigger than one eighth the size of the nail of the smallest finger. The letter always inserted into the envelope folded, the fold placed in the bottom of the envelope, the piece of indented paper within the folded letter. In opening the letter that small piece of paper would fall out, nothing on it just a little piece of a paper."

There had not been any such paper when she opened the Count's letter, at the best someone had already read it, or it was a falsehood. George could only respect the simplicity of the security system (just like Moscow rules).

The Countess again,

"Grace, open your letter with care. Shake the open letter on the table. See if the security is intact."

No piece of paper exited from the envelope Grace had been gently shaking. She gave the letter to her mother overcome by the deceit she burst into uncontrollable crying. George received a stare from the Countess telling him to take control. With him comforting her the Countess helped by Natasha, left the emotionally drained room. How do you comfort someone with a lifetime of emotion erupting in an instant of time, deep breathless tears of anguish?

George would always forever remember that next morning. He awoke with Grave lying on his numb left arm. She lying sideways against his body, her legs wrapped around his legs. Around the bedroom items of female and male cast off clothing, their intimacy prolonged. She had not experienced such close contact with a man before. He edged slightly to the right, she did not move, he wriggled his arm a little, she did not move. He slid his arm out from underneath her exhausted body. Now the difficult part, untwining the legs. She stirred and he froze. Grace back asleep. (Hope I didn't snore, he thought). Wish I could ring in sick, only one telephone down in the hall. Wriggle the first leg, limpit like she stuck on. She rolled to the left, one leg free, she rolled back again. George still in a second leg lock, starting to feel uncomfortable. He smiled to himself about the tickle spot, some two inches down from the small of her back, a gentle tickle, she pulled the legs up attempting to protect from any further advance. George swung two legs over the side of the bed into freedom.

He arrived downstairs for breakfast, Grace still asleep. For the first time he had company. The Countess already in her day clothes, siting, drinking green tea. George knew she had been waiting for his arrival. Her words came as an aristocratic understatement.

"Thank you for taking care of Grace. Let us hope she is not pregnant."

George really did blush.

"Now George, your people either know what words were in the letter or are desperate for you to tell them."

George gave a nervous cough, blushed again.

"I want you to tell them exactly what took place with the exception of the way the Count and I knew that letters were genuine. Can I expect your full support even if you find yourself in that world of white lies, stretching the truth."

George now on stronger ground.

"I do not like this spy and be spied on business. I will ensure that both yourself and Grace are fully protected."

As he spoke he wondered if he might regret the promise at a future date. Raising himself up from the table the Countess gave him a kiss on the cheek, leaving him to have his breakfast. As she left the room Natasha walked in with his boiled egg. Had she been listening? Again to himself. 'I hope I don't end up with egg on my face by undertaking the request of his Countess.'

He had not really finished breakfast when Natasha opened the front door to let in the driver. Fortunately one of the Syd's had been given the George duty. On route to hospital he had further news on the bricks thrown through the window saying that the thrower had lost the pursuer when using the underground. Continuing,

"After hospital you have a meeting with some of the big names in the Foreign Office. They expect you there by 10.30am."

Hospitals inevitably run slowly behind appointment times when the patient needs to keep another appointment. Doctors have a built in working day clock that runs more slowly than clocks used by the population at large. It is accepted normality that medical appointments run late. Woe betides the patient who is late. There exists two different standards; even with the weight of the Foreign Office behind him his appointment ran late. The previous days when he had no fixed time to be back in the office, they ran on time.

Syd could see time running late so he telephoned the office to report events and received instructions to get George into the office immediately and to return to the hospital with George in the afternoon. George found himself bundled back into the car. Hospital management went into meltdown in the blame culture. Why? Who is responsible for the failure to keep to time for the especially important Foreign Office patient. Management spent so much time (therefore money) on who had messed-up that the money wasted could have been used to employ another nurse for a year. The blame culture was more important than the nursing staff, unless, of course, a nurse could be blamed to the mess-up. The most senior of manager's telephoned his Foreign Office contact to make profuse apology asking if he could be informed when George would return for the check up so that staff would give priority. (In other words, other patients will run late.)

Arriving at the Foreign Office main entrance George found a male private secretary waiting to rush him into the meeting. Yes, rush and Foreign Office, obviously more important than George had anticipated. A polite knock of an impossible larger than life double wooden door receiving a sharp response. 'Enter.' The private secretary opened the door, walked in front of George then introduced him.

At the far end of one of those immensely long mahogany tables sat four men. The table was so long that a team of craftsmen would have built the table within the room itself and it was never to be taken out once constructed. George found himself ushered to one side of the table, opposite three from the Foreign Office. On the same side as George separated by two chairs sat an obvious outsider. The Permanent Secretary, George had met him before, introduced the Foreign Office head of security and the senior member of the Soviet 'desk'. Then again the Permanent Secretary,

"Let me introduce you to Mr Stephen Ward."

Ward stood up, reached to shake hands with George. Neither of them said a word. Again the Permanent Secretary,

"This is a highly secretive meeting. Our minutes will explain only the most basic facts of the meeting, who took part, that the subject matter was the Cuban Missile Crisis (George thought, 'I'm slipping further and further into this merky spy world'). Other than the four of us no other person is in the loop. We are going alone on this one. Neither our friends at MI5 or MI6 are aware of us asking Mr Ward to use his contacts with Mr Ivanov of the Soviet Embassy to see if a dialogue can be started with Moscow to resolve the Cuban crisis."

"George, you will be kept informed by Mr Gray (Head of Security) of developments. Mr Gray will take total operational control of dealing with Mr Ward and Mr Ivanov. I repeat, we do not want MI5 or MI6 involved."

Mr Gray then spoke,

"Mr Ward, would you please inform your friend Mr Ivanov that we would be favourable to discuss a resolution to the crisis. Would you please arrange your first meeting as soon as possible but definitely before 5pm today? Please advise me where the meeting with Ivanov will take place."

With that the meeting closed, Mr Ward escorted to the door by 'Gray' who handed him over to a uniformed security officer to escort 'Ward' out of the building. George, not having been dismissed, remained in the room then received the further briefing that no-one in government knew of the intention to start a dialogue. (In later history it always appeared the other way round, Governments wanting the Security Services to produce reports favourable to the action the Government intended to take).

Tony Computron, having come to see Barbara, watched for a

few moments then directed her to look into the office of Mr Gray, Head of Foreign Office Security. Enlarging the picture, Tony again directed all to look at the top item in the out-tray. A simple note from the American friends reading,

"Lee Harvey Oswald arrived back in the U.S.A in June (1962) having spent three years in the Soviet Union. He now has a twenty-two year old wife and a baby daughter. We (American friends) want to find out any information on what he had been up to in Moscow."

A note from Gray on the bottom of the page,

"Forward to Embassy in Moscow, low priority."

Tony Computron again.

"Now look at the screen in America, specifically New Orleans."

Miss Moneylegs gasped; she could not believe the scene in front of her eyes. She was looking at Lee Harvey Oswald, now chairman of the Pro-Cuban Committee, handing out leaflets saying 'Hands off Cuba.' Miss Moneylegs thought, as did Barbara, how could this man, obviously known to the American Security Services, manage to kill President Kennedy? Could he really have gone out of sight so quickly? Had a lapse happened around this pro-Castro sympathizer who had spent three years in Moscow, in the Soviet Union or did something more sinister happen? A conspiracy? As Tony Computron thought there were not than many Americans going to live in the Soviet Union. Why had he been lost? Misplaced? Under the security radar. Miss Moneylegs kept thinking, 'I had no knowledge he had spent so much time in Moscow, the arch-enemy in the Cold War.'

She to the Computron,

"Can you give any more information on what events really happened?"

"No," he replied.

That was that. Journalists do not like the 'no' word, even about history. Miss Moneylegs, now sidetracked onto Lee Harvey Oswald had determination in her eyes to track him down starting with him boarding a plane to Moscow, to get onto a plane he would need a Soviet visa. How did he manage to get that? What about money to live on? How did he live? In a hotel or a flat? Did the Soviets recruit him as a potential spy? Did the Americans send him to spy on the Soviets? 'That Computron would give me answers,' she thought.

On arrival at his temporary home, a tired looking George found the Countess opening the front door to let him in. That's unusual, he thought. In one of those voices when you know you are about to get a telling off, (think of that teacher at school that haunted you when in trouble) (George instantly thought of the two in a bed of the night before.) No, 'how did you get on at work today or what did the hospital say', those polite half interested questions, this he could feel would be a knife in the back for the kill. No Grace, had she already felt the displeasure of the Countess? No Natasha, no pot of tea. He could feel his heart beating increasing. Now hoping his face not turning red with anxiety, hold my breath words are forming with her lips.

"George, you and Grace slept together under my roof last night. Do you think that is what a gentleman would do in someone else's house with their daughter? You have only known Grace for a few weeks. Is that what the Foreign and Commonwealth Office teach you to do in this modern world?"

(He knew his face would be getting redder, heartbeat now pounding.)

"What do you think the Count would say if he remained alive? Knowing him it would probably be pistols at dawn. What example are you setting to Natasha and her family, certainly not what my Bridge playing friends would expect. They would soon have you branded a cad, despicably taking advantage of Grace when she had lost control of her emotions. Grace is so embarrassed that she washed and ironed the bed linen to hide her misdemenor from Natasha."

George could sense the climax would be at any moment. In his mind he had started to pack his suitcase. Would they let him order a taxi? How could he explain being dismissed (thrown out) to the Office, at least Corsham staff were not in the loop.

"Now young man," (that's ominous), then repeated. "Now young man, I think you had better consider your situation in this house (his mouth now dry like cardboard). Do you really think you have acted as a good guest?" (Please get it over with thought George.)

Exactly on cue, in skipped Esamia, with one, two, three friends. No it had to total all her classmates.

"Come on in. Look there's George with the Countess."

She'd not said the usual, "is George in trouble yet?" as it was plainly obvious to all that he had trouble written all over his redder than red face.

"Keep watching," Esamia gave instructions. Had she watched all this before? Without warning that hiss, hiss, hissing sound increased a few decibels. Could the Founding Protectors be watching an uncomfortable George as well? "No," it had to be a more serious matter.

George desperately wanted to make an apology, to say sorry I defiled you daughter.

That hiss, hiss, hissing sound again increased in intensity. With acute disappointment, everyone received the same message, to urgently return to their emergency meeting points, for Deep Earth Humanity, that meant 'get to your home,' except for the emergency services who reported to their place of work. Continuing the thought process, 'Scientists have detected an unexplained anomaly that is bombarding Earth Crust with something best described as like large head shaped bullets. When they hit the Earth surface they violently explode sending out a chemical substance saturating the landing area. Scientists do not yet understand what this is or why no earlier detection happened from the astronomical instrumentation."

Miss Moneylegs raced to the Ewewatch studio; Earth Crusters in their bunkers hearing the exploding noises existed in a high state of anxiety. To them they sounded like an attack. Without any consultation, Miss Moneylegs gave an emergency announcement, speaking to all Earth Crust underground establishments in the same instant of time.

"You are probably hearing continuous explosions above ground. Earth is encountering some form of meteor storm. Without an atmosphere to burn up the small meteors they are exploding when they hit the surface. There are millions upon millions currently falling all over the planet."

Tony Computron congratulated her on the quick thinking explanation as logically every part of her statement had a basis of fact. She concluded the broadcast by stating an update would be given in fifteen minutes.

CHAPTER TWENTY-TWO

For (nine lives) Ian at the immense underground base at Corsham the 'Ewewatch' broadcast came as a great relief. For a few moments near panic had set in with the horrific exploding noises going on above them. With nowhere to go it had been a salutary lesson in the fragility of their imposed imprisonment. Two of the specialists dealing with attempts to extend communication links asked to see Ian to suggest that they were convinced that they recognized the voice of the 'Ewewatch' announcer. When the next update broadcast came, would everyone stop their appointed activity to hear if anyone else recognized the voice.

Precisely after fifteen minutes the enormous screen at Corsham burst into life, a smiling Miss Moneylegs sitting as in any newsroom.

"Hello Corsham," (sounds like votes being cast in the Eurovision Contest). "Two of you thought you knew my voice so here I am, the missing Miss Moneylegs. Greetings also from Mason and Barbara." Then she went off screen, only her voice continuing.

"The meteor shower is ongoing, another update in fifteen minutes. Speak to you then Mervyn and Simon at Corsham."

At Corsham you could have heard a pin drop. Mervyn looked at Simon, disbelief. Ian looked at both of them. Everyone near by looked at them. From near obscurity into the limelights. Questions flying in all directions.

"Where is she? Is this place bugged? How did she know they were at Corsham?"

Another profound feeling of not being alone. The noise of the meteorites became louder, the hiss, hiss, hissing nearly turning into a scream. Founding Protectors understand what? The beginning of the final end or the beginning following the Earth Crusters end?

Miss Moneylegs looked up from her broadcasting studio desk to see some of the Elder Elders disobeying their own instructions that all should return to their safe houses. She knew this would mean trouble. That Computron somehow shrank into the corner. He knew when trouble might explode. For Elders to not obey their own instructions showed the seriousness of their actions. Having dealt with senior management at the B.B.C (British Broadcasting Corporation) Miss Moneylegs had learnt not to start such a conversation, only to respond after being communicated with. Never interrupt the demi-gods of management, their voice is more important to them than any other voice. Politicians are only interviewed so as to shoot them down in flames. Modern bull baiting, modern spearing the otter. Then mother of all profound thoughts, "Humans can't see in the dark, they need light to see." Is the optic eye so constructed that only light activates it, could that be why the human brain and body has a created biological frame only to function in daylight time. Dark time only to be used for rest/sleep patterns. So much carbon emission was produced to create artificial light yet from the beginning of Earth Crust human time it is only in the most recent past that artificial electric light came into existence. Not a chicken and egg conundrum. Humans' first then electric light. Now the whole human existence needs artificial light. Imagine the chaos of automobile transport in the dark with streetlights, without vehicle lights, as good an indication of any that Earth

Crust humanity ended up trying to live a twenty-four hour day using a body/brain created to function in daylight.

The Elder Elder addressing Miss Moneylegs.

"Preliminary results from our scientists indicate that the objects falling all over earth are the 'waste' produced by the Whale Anomaly (whale poo). The main constituent is oxygen."

Miss Moneylegs repeating to herself the whale anomaly poo is oxygen.

"We need you to inform Earth Crust humanity and advise them that they must conduct their own tests to examine the height that oxygen levels have reached."

"Can't you give them that information?" requested Miss Moneylegs.

Deaf ears, the only response. She knew yet again she had gone beyond the realm of acceptable behavior as judged by Deep Earth Humanity. She did exactly as the Elders had instructed. Somehow she knew that if any Earth Crusters thought breathable air existed outside of their bunkers, the first to try would probably suffocate. What about those Earth buried insects or small creatures still hidden away? Would they be able to exist on the surface? Somehow she knew the answer to be yes!! Miss Moneylegs decided to make the statement as brief as possible saying,

"The meteor bombardment has produced small amounts of oxygen everywhere. The level is very low, insufficient to support human life."

That information quite enough for the present. Disbelief always the character trait of humanity. Obviously a plot by Miss Moneylegs and co to keep all in the underground tombs. Inevitably someone somewhere would have to try for themselves. Doubting Thomas's? Inevitably the old 'Cold War' protagonists, unknown to each other, found willing bunker members eager to prove their manhood. It was not like the 'Arms Race' as neither knew what the other had started.

In Nevada (U.S.A), to the east of the Urals (Russia), the large underground bunker facilities both decided to put a 'toe in the water', who, how, volunteers or conscripts, perhaps drawing names out of a hat? As always, volunteers prepared to die would be ideal. In Nevada without any hesitation a Marine Sergeant offered his services, some 6ft 4inc, blond haired, rippling muscles, many times offered promotion he preferred to be hands on, out of politics. A man's man leading by example, his record clearly showing if a job needed doing he would be first to step forward. In the underground bunker, as big as a small town, he felt claustrophobic; he would rather be dead than spend forever in this one place. Already politics were overtaking reality within the enforced community. Damien wanted to escape.

On the east side of the Urals, not a great distance from Dammatov, Sergei, some 6ft 4inc tall, blond hair, rippling muscles, in fact if you placed him next to the American Damien then they looked liked twins. Sergei did not like the military. A scientist dedicated to extending food growing in underground facilities throughout Russia. His passion was long distance skiing. His extra salary paid for underground working funded his passions for fresh air, for freedom of open spaces, biting ice, cold wind blowing into his face, ice crystals encasing his beard. Sergei volunteered for one last visit to the surface. He knew he would take his last breath in freedom from the dungeon.

Tony Computron, the other Computrons, never failed to understand the apparent in-built stupidity of Earth Crust humanity. What was American Damien, Russian Sergei, doing going against the advice Miss Moneylegs had given? Why did these people with no factual information go against the simple, straightforward advice? He thought in his own mind to when Earth Crust humanity turned from an agricultural society into an industrial society. The ever-growing need for fossil fuels to power mass production, the ever-increasing production of carbon gases, for what long-term future? In some three hundred years from Industrial Revolution to carbon induced extinction. Could no one, no government have had a means of production not based on fossil fuel? Such financial power passing in less than an Earth crust lifetime to those man made borders (countries) with abundant oil and gas. What should have been a financial gift for all was retained by a few. Did Earth Crust humanity not understand that they had not produced these abundant riches but life hundreds of millions of years ago? Somehow the industrial revolution produced a financial revolution employing millions upon millions, all playing at chasing bits of paper, bank notes, bond certificates, share certificates, mortgage documents. What did they contribute to the well being of Mother Earth? How could they have coped if the greater stars in the Milky Way had ranked Earth as a junk status financial planet? With that hiss hiss hissing continuing Tony Computron speculated what the 'rating agencies' would make of 'junk status' Earth. Perhaps they knew how close that came to reality during the financial crash of 2008/9. Earth Crust humanity brought to near collapse by 'Financial Instruments', the posh name for bits of paper. Every Computron knew that any one Computron could conduct alone all the activities needed to run a stock exchange without the need for super computers, dealers, lawyers, accountants, back office staff. Compete a baby Computron against a super computer the 'baby' would win with the greatest of ease every time. Turn off the electric, the super computer is dead, not a Computron who produced their own supply of power!

Mason, Barbara, Miss Moneylegs, all well understood Tony Computron's thoughts. From where they were now their past life felt pointless. Tony Computron had not finished. 'Any other Computron would have undertaken the role of a world political leader with ease, making judgment on fact, not sentiment, not party bias, not human frailty. Not loosing train of thought by having to eat, sleep, defecate. Again that badly constructed human body wearing out in less than one hundred earth crust years.'

Damien and Sergei, the unlikely twins, died the first moment they left their dungeons, they did however become a welcome tasty meal for those Earth living insects.

CHAPTER TWENTY-THREE

George sat like a naughty schoolboy still trying to say sorry to the Countess. She, the Countess continued,

"The Count and I were virtually kept apart other than in company, we were by the judgment of today, what you would call an arranged marriage."

Looking into his crest fallen face, her eyes more piercing than her words, his heartbeat pounding at excessive levels, she delivered the fatal blow, the ultimate mother protecting the chicks, the Captain telling all to abandon ship, her Churchillian voice,

"George I would like to arrange for you to marry Grace."

Cheering from the Esamia gang, stunned silence from George. Where was his mother to protect him? Again the Countess spoke,

"George, do you hear what I am saying? George."

Motionless, statuesque (Esamia with the gang all saying 'Yes' as George couldn't speak, not of course that the Countess could hear them, or could she??) From behind one of the ceiling to floor lined velvet curtains, Grace broke out into hysterical laughing, then appeared, kneeled in front of George saying,

"George will you marry me?" (Ecstatic cheering from Esamia and co.) Everyone now holding their breath. Grace, with the Countess in the room, Barbara and Mason who knew his after this time life, and Esamia with the other friends of Deep Earth humanity. They of an age that would make them grandchildren of George, even the scientist friends of George in Deep Earth were glued to the screen. Folk law even had the Elder Elders watching. How long would everyone be holding his or her breath for? George looked greenish.

In the registry department of the Security Service (MI5) the file request from Hollis found itself to the top of the in tray for the routine work of that day. A junior clerk spent the whole of a Tuesday getting dirtier and dirtier as she rummaged into past files. With no success she placed the file request on the desk of her line manager adding a note 'UNFOUND'. Miss Merchant picked up the request with the attached note the next morning. She had been with the Service for many years, slight of figure, well dressed, wearing spectacles dangling from a cord around her neck, her experience knew that many old files had been cross referenced to be attached to more recent evens. She set about searching each of the annual cross-reference letters going through each entry one by one. Each year was contained in a huge ledger bound in red leather with the year in gold lettering on the spine and on the front cover. Access to the ledger room had restrictions the key kept by the superior, the key signed in and out, the superiors desk blocking access to the Ledger Room with just enough room to squeeze past when allowed entry.

Miss Merchant left as usual back to her home in Highgate West Hill, in crossing the road a vehicle travelling at speed ran straight over her killing her instantly. Onward sped the hit and run driver, a black salon car with none of the two witnesses seeing the registration plate, one absolutely convinced they remember a 'C' the other convinced that they saw an 'O' or 'D'. Miss Merchant's superior had left some forty minutes earlier to return to her home at the very top of Highgate West Hill. At some two o'clock in the early hours of the morning the emergency services were called to an inferno fire consuming the house. Miss J, her name in the service inside. Her last action had been to neatly fold the request with its note, walk into the ladies toiler, close the cubicle door behind her, adjusting her clothing so that the folded request fitted perfectly into a pocket on the inside of what could be called lady hockey players knickers, not her first such action definitely not an expectation of the last time. For the Security Service to loose one member of staff in questionable circumstances raised alarm bells, to lose two within hours, a calamity of monumental proportions. Department 13 were activated to go to the home of Miss J, the civil authorities had taken care of a road traffic accident of Miss Merchant.

Within hours, in the middle of the night, all departmental heads were back in the office. Hollis chaired the meeting. The two deaths could not be a coincidence; an immediate investigation must take place in Registry. Head of Internal Security to immediately start in Registry, line managers who had never worked in Registry were moved to assist with the investigation. Registry would be closed for seven days. Registry staff arriving as normal were taken to individual rooms to be interviewed. They were then dispersed to other departments for the time being. London slept. The press officer was to make no statement; there was no need as of yet to inform Government ministers. Instructions to the press officer were to ensure no press linked the two deaths. No information was to be given that they worked for the Security Service. Hollis had not forgotten he had a pending request as yet not answered by Registry. Two of the usual undertakers were to be employed to deal with formalities, as small a notice a possible in the Times asking any relatives to contact the appointed undertakers. The notice for Miss Merchant was to be placed immediately; the notice for Miss J was to be delayed until the undertaker received instructions.

At the home of Miss J it took until early afternoon for the fire brigade to damp the fire down. Police set up a security cordon announcing to all that the structure was damaged. By mid-afternoon the investigation by the Fire Brigade team (actually Department 13) started work.

The first task was to find a body. Most neighbours went about their daily routine as normal, but several 'rubber necks' stood around, one junior from the local Highgate newspaper wondered around trying to make an interesting story before deadline hour. (An unfortunate mix of words deadline and death). Within the detached property little remained of the roof, of the upstairs bedrooms, they were a tangled mass on the ground, the upstairs would have had three bedrooms, a bathroom and a toilet. Downstairs there would have been a kitchen, living room, dining room, small study and a toilet. The property had no garage, a long back garden, and a shorter front garden. On the left side of the property there was an entry gate connecting the front and the back. The front garden had a well-maintained privet hedge with a gate leading onto the footpath and then onto the narrow road that lead onto the main Highgate West Hill Road. There was no lamppost outside the house, the nearest was some fifty yards away.

CHAPTER TWENTY-FOUR

Somewhat earlier, around 4.30pm, on the day that Miss Merchant had been killed in the hit and run accident, Ivanov had met Stephen Ward and Mr Gray (Head of Foreign Office Security) in a public house in Highgate village, a regular meeting venue for members of the security world. The landlord always had a table in a quiet corner with a reserved sign. Gray already sat with a pint of bitter, smoking, when Ward arrived with Ivanov.

Ward was in his element as the center of importance and made introductions between the two men. Gray asked the two what their 'tipple' drink would be. Ward would have liked a gin and tonic but in a pub decided on a pint of the best bitter. Ivanov opted for a large whiskey as someone else was paying. The drinks request was no surprise to 'Gray' who had watched Ivanov more than once before. No need for niceties 'Gray' handed a carefully worded typed message to Ivanov asking him if he would 'telex' the contents to the Foreign Ministry in Central Moscow. Certainly both Gray and Ivanov knew the message would be sent to Moscow Central, the home of the K.G.B. (Soviet Union Security Service) first so that Ivanov would gain his 'brownie points'. The meeting was over almost as soon as it had started. Mr Gray left them with their free drinks paid for by the British taxpayer. Ivanov felt empowered enough to purchase another round of drinks. The Finance Department at the Embassy would have to approve the vast expenditure or run the danger of the accusation of preventing peace talks.

For once Ivanov would be in the right. He knew he was on a high, perhaps one more drink prior to setting back. That now made three double whiskeys, barely scraping the surface of drunkenness to a man that started the day with vodka before breakfast. Now happy or tiddly (mildly drunk) Ward impressed on him the advantages that both could enjoy by acting as the 'go betweens'. They parted outside the pub, Ward collected by a female driver in a Morris Minor, Ivanov thankful his car had a 'CD' plate.

A very happy 'spy' set off down Highgate West Hill contemplating what rewards he could ask and expect to receive. His C.D. (Corps Diplomatique) car registration number plate guaranteed to keep him out of trouble with the police. Speeding down Highgate West Hill he though he hit something, then a sickening thud as something went under the wheels. In reality he could not remember and certainly did not care. Goodbye Miss Merchant, corpse diplomatique.

He went back in the Embassy in Kensington Palace Gardens shaking with excitement. He immediately sought the office of the K.G.B station chief. Without even time to sit down his boss had read the typed message and escorted him to the outer office of the Ambassador. Those within the office were immediately dismissed then Ivanov joined his boss in the main office. All humans need to feel important, even Soviets.

A note from the Security Service (MI5) Archives

'Ward says at the height of the Cuban Missile Crisis ... Ivanov brought another Russian official (Vitalit) Loginov (Charge d'Affairs) to see Ward. We had practically a cabinet meeting one night.'

Within his own mind 'Ward' kept repeating the thought 'gong'.

A 'gong', is slang for an award from royalty and government of the day for services to the country, well that's the theory. 'Ward' felt the successful conclusion of his Foreign and Commonwealth Office assignment, perhaps a Knighthood (Sir) or a Lordship. The odd thought already crossing that thought process Lord Ward of Marble Arch or just Lord Marble Arch, recognition for saving the world from possible Nuclear War. He certainly knew of one royal that could promote his expectation, his name in the New Years Honour List. A very good party to celebrate afterwards. He even started a mental list of whom to invite, then reality again set in. To be positive he decided to make head and shoulder sketches of those with whom he had meetings at this important time in his life. Ivanov already done.

Miss Moneylegs, back in the Ewewatch studio explained the stupidity if the 'two twins' Damien (Nevada), Sergei (Damlatov). With their instant death going against the advice she had given. Even as she spoke a screen could be seen showing Jupiter expanding then contracting as if it was like the human heart. Could Jupiter be the heart beat of the solar system, not the four billion year old sun? An effect of the windwave. Heart beat a recollection of her first undercover work as a reporter, heartbeat pounding in the early days fearful of being found out. For three months undercover in a factory (yes production line) making those microwave ready to eat quick meals. She did at that time enter the realms of vegetarianism having witnessed what went into a 'ready meal'. Her first day started at 7.00am in a very large warehouse unit on the edge of town with the name Home2Organic. There was no indication of what went on inside the grey painted building with no windows. Reception was not easy to find in one corner of the huge box. Thereafter the entrance was through a special 'staff only gate' at the back of the box. Entering reception gave no idea of what went on inside, six not comfortable chairs, a coffee table, no magazines, a unisex toiler, a large uniformed man sitting at a desk with a locked door to his right entering into the box, oh yes and music. She soon learned that if it had been one of the supermarket buyers that area was transformed into comfy armchairs, an attractive young lady behind the desk available to serve suitable hot drinks.

From the entrance Miss Moneylegs went into a windowless side office, signed her contract of employment, signed a confidential non-disclosure agreement, signing up to work twelve hours a day at adult minimum wage with no overtime, Saturday or Sunday a compulsory working day. With agreements signed she received a locker key where her working clothes would be, an in house laundry providing clean white overalls every day. (A common joke from the workforce went that the laundry really provided 'soup' from the specks of food left on the daily overalls.) The routine was tiresome, mind numbing, no need to think. Production lines are no good without the magical ingredients, so one third of the enormous box a storeroom for ingredients from all over the world. Then within the 'golden store' where prime quality ingredients were kept for when a buyer visited, always by appointment. Ingredients of the very, very finest quality. For normal production the cheapest cheap from anywhere in the world. Any products that failed the stringent requirements of those bulk buyers' ideal for the production line. No one knew what really went into those ready microwave meals. Miss Moneylegs undercover report once published resulted in acclaim from the public, threats to her life from the fast food industry, practices that made headlines;

1) Tasting spoon residual placed back into production.

2) Spitting game, who could spit furthest along the production line.

3) Management inspection always finding good reasons to place back into production raw materials (food) previously considered bad or out of date e.g. rotten moldy meat.

4) The international game of football chicken carcass. Simply two sides made up of the same nationality, the goal, and the production line getting a complete carcass into a cooking vat.

5) Female staff played a nail clippings competition. Each day

finger and toenail clippings were produced, a total made, daily score record kept, then toe and fingernails entered into production.

6) If management 'pissed off' staff, new ingredients would be added by the pissing staff. Reprisal, that sense of relief when a convenient ingredient substitute needed. If you are producing ten tons of curry on a shift, not difficult to hide rotting meat, everything adds to the taste.

Then management played a game with the customer.

1) Weights slightly less than the content weight, easy for 225grams to be 223grams instead. Anyway, who weighs the contents of a microwave meal? To the customer blind to if the weight includes packaging, always a little more water.

2) Contents always altered to include a percentage more of the cheapest, say 2% extra carrot with 2% less meat.

3) As far as possible make all ingredients sound as if produced as 'British'. Who can really tell if a lump of meat comes from the rolling grassland of the Cotswolds or the dirty slaughterhouse of an East European factory farm?

4) How many consumers can tell the taste difference, horse-meat or beef, chicken and turkey etc. etc. Forget about free range and battery.

Miss Moneylegs well remembered the three or four days of public outrage until the supermarket publicity/public relations' executives joined forces to produce a story. All good 'PR' professionals have a good story on the back burner ready to unveil, a never ending chatter from celebrity world. So off the back burner a story about a well known female 'celeb' who didn't know who the father could be of her latest child as to quote 'she had been sleeping around a great deal at the time!!!' Good scandal with unlimited license to name the potential father, accusation, denial, counter accusation, any clue in the child's name of 'Chelsy'. After the lull of a few days 'ready to eat' meals selling robustly again, the 'Chelsy' story ran for another two weeks. Miss Moneylegs did manage one last story from her undercover assignment, she had discovered that one trick to keep a customer happy entailed finding a new supplier in some far flung corner of the Earth then inviting the supermarket customer to go visit that 'far flung corner' to inspect. Now supermarkets are very strict about 'benefits' not allowing suppliers to pay for such jaunts (buying trips). For the supermarket buyer not unusual to find their economy ticket had by magic been turned into first class on arrival at the airport. Same at the destination hotel, basic economy rooms turned into top of the range 'suites.' "Mine host' British supplier would have instructed 'mine host' far flung supplier that the various celebration meal/parties should include a liberal sprinkling of young unattached. Within the industry well understood that 'buyers' would be attracted back again and again if they found a friend in that 'far flung corner', the ultimate if buyer and supplier both found a friend.

Miss Moneylegs' thinking returned to Jupiter, the wind-wave theory, the beating heart, heart and love, back to George. George still looking greenish, the words from Grace, 'George will you marry me,' Esamia with her friends now holding hands in a moving circle including Mason and Barbara, in the middle of the circle, 'Bruce' going around in circles attempting to catch his wagging tail. Instantly they all ceased activity as George kissed Grace on the forehead. Without a word he stood up, held Grace by the hands, sitting her down in the chair he had just vacated, then kneeling. "Grace will you marry me?" to him that had to be the correct way, him asking Grace. Grace replied, "Yes." Already the Countess had plans for an engagement party. Only one daughter, it would be a social event. Esamia with the gang in unison punched the air all expressing the same thought, 'Yes.'

Somehow the engagement appeared in 'The London Times' announcements column the very next morning. In normal circumstances George would have questioned the London Times carrying the story so quickly, in the euphoria of the days he did not ask such an obvious question. Equally the question of how had an engagement party been organized for the coming Saturday at 'The Ritz' in London. Could it be he no longer had any control over his own destiny? Who could be in control? Who could be sure that a marriage would take place? To make the plans, had he come compliant to the predetermined wishes of some other? With all the joyous happenings Miss Moneylegs had not noticed a fire raging in an underground establishment in Poland. Now observing the event she quickly determined that most of the six hundred occupants were in fact American not Polish. Her instant assessment that this base existed to listen to conversations in Russia, Germany, and the Baltic States. Friendly Americans, perhaps the Polish were fed little titbits of information particularly about their best Russian friends? With the fire raging all that the station commander had an interest in consisted of burning every available document therefore adding to the fire. Staff had for some time talked about him having flipped his lid, they were in a trap. Nowhere to go outside, the fire raging inside. Why did someone not kill the commander or set about damping down the fire? Somehow they had no reality, wondering about as if in a dream.

Mason, who had been paying more attention to the events than the others had noticed the Station Commander pressed a purple button and that all around him was covered with a mist. Whatever the mist contained, whatever item of chemical warfare had been released, the Commander and his human like zombies, fried to death. For what purpose only the Station Commander knew. Did he not understand that in this changed world, secrets were of no interest? What a waste of Earth Crust Humanity. He must have been a mad man. Tony Computron, reading the thoughts in his usual matter of fact way, let it be known that the Station Commander had a few moments before been tested positive for the 'Aids' virus.

A small scrap of paper, card, the investigating officer discovered in the devastating fire in the home of Miss J had trace marks of coming from the Registry at the Security Service. Investigating Charles received the information.

CHAPTER TWENTY-FIVE

George entered a world of quietness, becalmed, perhaps only an illusion. Natasha and the Countess entered into frantic, never ceasing organizational activity. Somewhere, someone decided that the marriage event would happen thirteen days after the engagement party, on a Saturday at the Russian Orthodox Cathedral in West London. Guests for the engagement party were simultaneously invited to the wedding with polite information that it was only a small wedding present not an engagement present in addition. Dispatched back into the office everyday George had little idea of the organizational skills swinging into place. His only real task was to give the Countess a list of those guests he would like to invite. His list struggled. Family etiquette necessitated his two sisters be invited but then who else? A quiet meeting with the head of the Security Service provided the list of work colleague who should receive an invite to the engagement party and wedding, some names meant nothing to George; a friendly female staff member of senior staff from Corsham, both Syd's the drivers, Charles the secretary, the rest of the names had no meaning for George.

For good measure the Countess informed Grace that she (the Countess) would invite two hundred to the Ritz party and four hundred to the church wedding, followed by a reception at the Mayfair Hotel. Grace invited only nine.

George, if he had not been consumed in doing nothing, might have been expected to remember that the Ritz and Mayfair were almost next door to one of the Security Service Offices, a fact not lost on Stephen Ward when he received his telephone invitation from the Countess who told him not to bring any of 'those girls'. Bring Ivanov. So who could be playing into whose hands? George gave his list to the Countess who gave no comment except that George must telephone and invite them himself.

Within the guest list itself; there was much discussion as to why the wedding would take place so quickly. General gossip centered on Grace being pregnant with George doing the right thing by her. Had they known each other long enough for George to be the father?? No discussion though in front of the Countess. For these intimate friends she told they had no need to wait. They had everything a newly married couple would need; house, car (she never said cars), both were in work and in any event, Grace had a private trust fund with substantial income to live on. None of the wedding party could say it was all a result of George needing to get back to the Corsham Underground base. Though many couples did get married very quickly with the possibility of the Cuban Missile Crisis on the brink of producing a nuclear war. For hundreds of years the threat of war, the threat of going into battle never to return, the threat of the lovers being separated has produced instant marrying plans. Wedding plans were not only being made on Earth Crust. Esamia had talked the teacher into allowing the class to have their own wedding, copying George and Grace as much as possible. Their teacher not quite sure of the educational benefit, but it would be fun. Esamia had been doing her homework about European royalty telling everyone that whoever played the part of Grace should be called 'Lady' Grace. Esamia by sheer luck found herself playing the part of 'Lady Grace'.

The Countess took it upon herself that the engaged couple

entered into no more premarital activity, she had almost forgotten about the Count's letter or non-letter. George asked the Countess with Grace he vexed question of where to buy an engagement ring. Grace looked at the Countess who knew the answer, an explanation that the family tradition provided a selection of engagement and wedding rings going back for hundreds of years. Grace knew the tradition; the Countess would take the two of them to the family bankers where the family jewels were safely kept in a safe deposit box within the vaults. Tomorrow morning would be best.

Peter drove them in the Rover to the bank obviously with clear instructions to wait in the car for as long as necessary. A doorman opened the car door at the back passenger side holding out a white gloved hand to the Countess. He then escorted the Countess up the eight steps into an imposing entrance. Here another guard in top hat and tails escorted the Countess, Grace and George in tow, to a large boardroom table on top of which were substantial leather bound ledgers. (No computers yet). A bank officer in morning dress arose from the table greeted the Countess leading them to a long marble staircase leading down out of the banking hall. (George whispered in the ear of Grace, "Has your mother, mother not Countess, spoken to anyone yet?") A graceful tap from her shoe to his ankle was the only reply that obviously meant 'keep quiet'.

Why did a banking hall create the same hush as when in a cathedral?

Prison like bars at the bottom of the stairs were immediately opened by another guard as the Countess arrived. Then on into a very plush side office (office an unjust description to the opulence). Sitting, the Countess handed a deposit box key to the official in the morning suite, who she now called Sir Peter. Before he left to obtain the deposit box she said,

"Sir Peter, you may have met my daughter Grace many times. This is her future husband (no name). Perhaps you will have time to chat with him at the engagement party?"

Sir Peter returned with a guard carrying a largish deposit box with another guard in hot pursuit. Sir Peter opened one lock, retiring out of the room saying he would be available when the Countess required him. One guard stood outside the door with his back into the door, the second returned to wherever. From a chain around her neck, the Countess produced another key, placed it into another lock, turned the key and opened the box. On top lay black fabric, velvet George thought, then an item in purple cloth that the Countess did not look at. Next a tray with rings, the Countess closed the deposit box. Addressing Grace and George,

"These are the family rings. You are at liberty to choose anyone that you would like."

They were precious, all precious and valuable. Then to Grace,

"If the one you prefer is too big or too small, Sir Peter will have it altered overnight."

Grace counted fifteen rings. In looking at each one on her finger the Countess explained the family history of the ring. She reminded Grace that in Russia the wedding finger would be on the opposite hand to the English tradition, and also that in the 1700's and 1800's diamonds were less popular than many other stones. As Grace continued her on-going ring finger trying, the bank provided a small mirror. The Countess took out a leather bound, gold coloured diary size book that she handed to George.

"You are holding much of the family history in your hands, with each item in the deposit box listed with a detailed description, the name of the last owner, a history of where the item was purchased and the history thereafter to the present day. Some of these jewels have not been seen in public for several hundred years. None have entered the public domain since the Russian Revolution, since the unification of the Italian state."

Grace had progressed to a choice of three rings. As though he was a mind reading he predicted the next question from Grace.

"George, which ring do you like? They all fit perfectly."

Esamia with her gang now playing at guessing which George would choose. Strangely the girls of Deep Earth humanity all chose the same one, the boys were all different.

Sort of helpful, George pointed to the one on the right saying, "I don't like that one." Now they were down to two. George knew that the Countess would give the final advice, in effect making the choice for Grace.

Pointing to the cluster ring on the left the Countess produced from a box a necklace and a tiara.

"This is a set of three. If you chose this ring, the tiara and necklace make a set. You could wear them on your wedding day. They belonged to my grandmother, given to her be a member of the Russian royal family. None had been seen for some ninety years."

Grace looked at George, smiled, and squeezed his hand.

"What do you think future husband?"

Cambridge University debater was lost for words looking at the precious family jewels. He had no knowledge of what to say. He kissed the Countess on the cheek attempting to say thank you. Grace giggled trying on the three items together. Even wordless George admired the beautiful elegance as if all three had been made all those years ago for Grace to wear. A gentle press on a table bell by the Countess had Sir Peter back in the room as if he'd been waiting outside.

The Countess explained the decision. Would Sir Peter arrange for a staff member to deliver the ring to the Ritz to the Countess who would give it to George to give to Grace? She would inform Sir Peter nearer to the wedding when to deliver the necklace and the tiara to her at home.

Having been escorted in the same routing except that Sir Peter handed the Countess a sealed packet of bank notes, the first time George had ever witnessed a member of the household with money, with the Countess placing the money into her leather handbag. Descending the entrance stairs George noticed that Peter stood on the pavement talking to someone, that someone seeing the group of three approaching left Peter very quickly, making haste to merge into the City commuters. In his own mind George felt confident he had seen the person who knocked him over during the chase after the brick throwing incident. Without enquiry Peter volunteered the information that the passer-by had been asking for directions to Soho.

CHAPTER TWENTY-SIX

T he home of Miss J continued to be searched with no information relevant to MI5. However under instructions instigated by Charles, who was heading up the investigation into the Registry, all items found in the burnt out residence were to be moved to a safe warehouse and laid out on the warehouse floor. This was by necessity a time consuming job with photographic evidence of even the smallest bits and pieces. No one had any idea what he thought could be found. The only other people in the loop were the Head and Deputy Head of '5'.

Sometime after lunch on Thursday all three were contacted urgently to immediately go to the site. For convenience all three travelled together in a staff car with a driver. The police moved the cordon as the staff car approached. As the three alighted from the vehicle the senior investigator trudged to meet the bosses. Some ninety per cent of the building and its contents had already gone to the warehouse what remained was mainly brick walls. Ushered into an area that had been under the stairs, the senior investigator pointed around a central area, indicating the team had an opinion that this 'might be' an entrance door leading into the foundations. He wanted the top brass on hand just in case the suspicions the team had were confirmed. Hollis gave the instruction to proceed. A cast iron manhole type cover could quickly be identified. In practice a tripod type of apparatus with chains would be used for such a heavy lift. Junior members of the team quickly had it in place but were having difficulty in placing the chain hooks onto the cast iron due to the fire damage. Hollis wanted no panic, no rush; he wanted it done properly with as little damage as possible. Winding up the chain on the cast iron grate as one end raised itself; smoke poured out of the tiny gap.

Hollis gave instructions for all but three of the winding team to move away then gave a barking order for all work to stop, all to move away from the building. With a life time of experience of dealing with the unexpected his instinct was now working overtime. If he had been a witch it would be nose-twitching time. Everyone of the team he brought together and gave the following instructions.

1)	Go into unexploded bomb routine with the civil authorities

2)	All homes within a quarter of a mile to be evacuated.

3)	Residents to pack an overnight bag, take over church halls.

4)	Church halls to be manned by the Salvation Army with Red Cross.

5)	'5' staff members to be mingled within the Church groups for any, any information about Miss J.

6)	'5' to provide the dummy bomb squad. <u>No news blackout.</u>

7)	Police to man the quarter of a mile exclusion zone.

8)	The '5' government liaison team to keep the government updated.

With those detailed instructions, members of the team felt Hollis might have some idea of what would be found, none were more secretive than the Heads of the Security Service or the Intelligence Service.

Barely two hours had passed when Hollis gave the instruction for two to enter. They looked more like spacemen than security officers. The local newspaper was on hand to take photographs for circulation to the Nationals. In any event that would look good to all those in overnight temporary accommodation, adding credence to their discomfort. Also the inevitable keepsake of 'I was there'. Other than the two spacemen, Hollis and the senior of the investigating team were on hand in the burnt out shell of the house. They had contrasting dress with Hollis in his normal everyday overcoat with hat, gloves, and the senior in another space like outfit. Instructions from Hollis for the two entering were to go step by step, slowly and to note everything. When they considered it was safe for the team to enter, they were to return to the surface and then take it in turns to take in the extra investigators. To begin with they were to stay inside for no more than thirty minutes under ground.

One 'space figure' as the senior of the two people decided he would go first, the second roped to him. In the real world they were both mountaineers well used to climbing protocols.

Now to see if the very innocent of innocents, Miss J, had hidden secrets. Descending into the hole, smoke filled everywhere, not dense, not thick, wispy like. Eight steps down, both were on the cellar floor. Number one indicated he felt it was safe to remove their masks. They were not short of breath from smoke, only from the surroundings in which they stood. They stood as if in any MI5 underground office. Detailed recordings take no account of emotion; this was to be an exception, a first sighting that they would have nightmares about until their dying day. Three dead females were slumped onto desks where they had suffocated during the fire. It was almost impossible to think they were underground to both it was plainly obvious that this must be a complex. At the far end of the office type room there was a closed door.

One spoke quietly to two, they decided to return to the surface at once to tell Hollis who without hesitation called over an assistant instructing that a wooden structure be erected without delay. A team would be here for weeks. With the two spacemen in front, Hollis behind them, behind him the Senior Investigating Office in his space outfit. Those in the front had powerful torches only available to the military, better than any electrical light, with a long life provided by not commercially available batteries.

They walked past the bodies to the far door, entered then walked through in the same order. Beyond there was a corridor with doors on both sides. First door contained an office with one female body. The second door was a toilet, the third door sleeping quarters with four bunk beds, enough to sleep eight. They went to the end of the corridor and walked back. The fourth door was a kitchen dining area with one female body; the fifth door was a communications room with one female body still wearing headphones. The sixth door was completely empty, as if it was a prisoners cell.

Hollis had seen enough. More and more information would only confirm that meek, mild; Miss J had a spying secret.

Hollis left and without delay travelled to the Cabinet office, the Head of MI6 was already seated and waiting for him. The Prime Minister arrived seconds after Hollis. Reporting at this level remains brief, remains factual, much too early for conclusions, notwithstanding the loop of need to know established, the highest level of security imposed.

Construction work at the burnt out house, without any need to worry about noise with the neighbours in overnight accommodation, produced as if a miracle, a large waterproof building with changing room, store room, working room with the cellar entrance towards the back. Any meaningful debris left on the surface was no longer of use.

With daybreak the building was completed with paintwork on the outside that was needed to blend in with the leafy suburb. Yes, painted trees with green bushes, even MI5 has artists.

Of the three who went underground, their reports to Hollis

all stated the same. That the underground office had been set up as identical to the 'Registry at 5' where Miss J worked.

That morning Hollis had arrived to watch the cellar, which had been sealed up overnight, reopened. He had with him Charles, the investigating officer from the Registry who had with him in his safe, a voluminous schedule of Registry filed numbers with a brief description of the file contents. Within perhaps the first ten minutes the theory that Hollis had come up with proved to be totally accurate. Those files in the cellar were identical in number and content to the Registry files. They were all hand written copies. Hollis had not expressed a view on that cellar type room; he stood in the middle as an operative crawled along the floor. With a spy's nose for a stink he directed to an area that would have been at the back wall with earth soil the other side. There the entrance hatch he expected to find. Opening it the operative could only watch with an expressionless face as Hollis looked into a sewer, certainly deep enough for the average sized lady to stand up in.

As all the neighbours were still in their overnight accommodation, there was only the smallest trickle of water going down the pipes. Now was an ideal moment to get men suitably dressed to carry out a search. Then a report to Hollis that in removing the bodies they were all similar in size and stature (but not in age) to Miss J. Then a report from the sleeping quarters that all clothing was the same, as if it was military clothing, having sorted the clothing into size groups the report continued there were most likely other females within the group who were absent when the building burnt down. Still standing in the room with the trapdoor down into the sewer, a milk bottle had been handed to the operative, then another, then another, sixteen in total, spotlessly clean, but bog standard milk bottles. Hollis called the underground operative back into the room. He gave an explanation that they were all in racks (like wine bottle racks) next to a tube structure large enough for a bottle to be inserted inside. Behind the wine racks were some form of machine in which the tube passed through. With the lighting they had the tube ran continuously one hundred feet or thereabouts. Hollis called all operatives back into the ground-side structure.

CHAPTER TWENTY-SEVEN

George with great relief, woke up at last on the day of the engagement party. For the previous days coming and goings had been intense, the newspapers full of a story about a record price paid for a Speed map atlas. George now had to find a way to keep out of trouble for the rest of the day without making it obvious. Fortunately, a moment arose over breakfast when he and Grace were alone. He kissed her on the lips, whispered in her ear what did she think about him (they) buying a small gift for the Duchess to give her in the evening. She returned his idea with a favourable kiss. For George that meant freedom for a few hours without even an instruction to return for lunch. The many jewelers in Bond Street would be his point of destination. First though, a walk to Regents Park, spending an hour or so in the Zoo. The Zoo was always a place of intellectual stimulation, with never enough time to spend studying the habits of other life forms. His interest now more the 'naked mole rat', strange name for something that lives in the deep caves of Earth Crust somehow with a life expectancy ten times greater than those the species is named after. As George left the house he was deep in thought, 'if humans could live ten times longer if they lived underground.' He managed to kick over two milk bottles, one with the usual note to the milkman inside. In placing them back he mused how strong the bottles must be not to have broken.

With the thought of living underground in his mind, Esamia giggled to herself, thinking 'if only he knew that ten times could easily be fifty times longer'. She also wondered about the 'naked mole rat,' what about Tony and the Computrons, clothed or naked??

Wondering around the zoo always made George think of the arrogance of humanity to enclose those who enjoyed freedom into enclosed cages of imprisonment. Perhaps when the early Victorian world first encountered these perhaps some morality existed to show the wider world what they looked like, but not now, over a hundred years later. Only human prisoners had any comprehension of locked up behind bars, freedom taken away, with eat it or leave it meals. No choice but to eat what the keepers gave you, whether zoo or prison.

He left, walking down Harley Street, the expensive home of those experts in keeping humanity alive. Over Oxford Street and towards expensive Bond Street where all that glitters is gold. Grace had informed him which jeweler the Countess regularly purchased from, with the instructions of Grace, 'Do not purchase anything expensive, we are only giving a thank you not an item of value or investment.' It happened that as George went to enter the jewelers the security doorman stood in front of him, preventing entry.

Curtly,

"Who are you? What do you want?"

Not the reception George expected or wanted. He thought, 'what's the problem?'

"Sir, clients do not have straw in their shows in here. Is this really the high class jewelers you would like to come into or are you looking for one of those high street jewelers like ...?"

The words weren't actually finished when a voice from the

street called,

"George, are you on an errand for the Countess?"

George and the doorman both looked at Sir Peter. From the outside umbrella stand the doorman produced a shoe brush with a long handle and gave the zoo straw shoes the one over.

Sir Peter said, "Come in with me and let me introduce you to the Directors, George."

George never liked the 'old boy network', 'my friend is your friend and therefore to be trusted,' the unwritten law of the City of London. With the introduction effected, he explained that Grace had dispatched him to purchase a not expensive gift for the Countess.

A jeweler to the nobility has an inbuilt instinct when to go for big money, when to go for the modest. The Director well knew the modest taste of the Countess and he also knew of some of the very, very high value items she owned.

George followed advice; a small broach costing three hundred pounds (about half the price of a small car) was selected. The Director also suggested a small inscription on the back. If George would like to wait in the guest room for an hour, the engraved broach would be ready. George declined saying he would return in an hour or so.

Walking towards Piccadilly, he noticed the newsstand boards carried warning headlines about the looming Cuban Missile Crisis. He knew too much to be alarmed about the headlines. Approaching Piccadilly, a voice shouted, "George, wait." A young lady went to throw her arms around him. She was not very tall and anyway the milk bottles got in the way. She was one of the Cambridge students. George thought fast. He remembered her face, but what on earth should he call her?

Quickly thinking he missed out the name part.

"What are you doing in Bond Street on a Saturday morning?" With embarrassing excitement she offered the explanation that she worked for a large auction house in Bond Street heading up the Russian Jewellery Department and that she was only working today to complete a catalogue of Russian Fine Art.

George could still not remember her name, she had been more of a stranger than a close friend. Trying to be friendly he suggested they go to the Ritz for afternoon tea.

"Impossible," came the reply from Jennifer (thank heavens I remembered George thought.) "But come to the office for ten minutes to catch up on the last years."

Readily agreeing, George walked side by side, chatting on route. Within the auction house she sat George down in the reception area and then went off to make a pot of tea. George mused through some auction catalogues without realizing alighting on a ring very similar to the engagement one. When Jennifer returned he showed her the picture, obviously disappointed with the engagement news, she explained that a set would be given by the Russian Royal Family to close family members getting married. During the Russian Soviet Revolution nearly all were confiscated to purchase military goods, both sides as guilty as each other. After that polite chit chat until George uttered, "Goodbye, till next time."

Jennifer was greatly excited by the information from George on the engagement ring and went to report to her department head that she had discovered a previously unknown item.

George collected the engraved broach, returned home (yes home now) to find the expected turbulent earthquake cum tsunami in full progress. Grace took him on one side to give her full approval to his purchase activity and explained that Natasha had placed all the 'Engagement Party clothes' ready for him. The three of them would have a light meal when George must present their small gift to the Countess. The high flyer of all Cambridge graduates was now required to take orders as if the new boy at a private school. His intellectual agility was sidelined. In response he went into the Library, now that he had his own house keys.

During the party, meal and dancing, George kept himself as close to Grace as physically possible with one lady after another admiring her spectacular engagement ring. George found himself introduced to one famous name after another always getting that polite tittle tattle to a point where he found out who would be at the wedding. He tried to remember faces and names.

If Grace had been pregnant any child inside her would have felt those prying eyes burning into him or her. George would whisper in her ear, 'she must be pregnant.' Grace tried not to giggle. Thereby the nature of human thought, quick marriage equals pregnant. The Countess in her most radiant persona was really the center of attention. A few people George knew of were Ward, Ivanov and another were permanently joined as if they were triplets. One gentleman took great interest, no fanatical interest, in the ring, which amused George as the admiration was mainly coming from the females of the party. He introduced himself as (George forgot the title and the Christian name) Blunt. With his name still on his lips the Countess arrived to explain that his expertise in art filled many pages of text, his expertise was often required by the Royal Family.

No engagement speech was required from George that task undertaken with gusto, needless to say, by the Countess who uttered very kind words about her soon to be son-in-law, not failing to mention his intellectual ability at Bridge. When some appointed time set by the Countess arrived, people gave good-byes, thank yous, coupled with 'see you at the wedding.'

All evening the Countess had paraded her engraved broach as if in competition to the engagement ring. Then her most intimate inner group were invited back to her home for ongoing celebrations.

George sat with Grace and felt like a spare part to the main event. Then when everything was over, they were engaged, the Countess was contented that her precious daughter had found such a suitable partner. She knew the Count would have been happy to pit his wits against the finest brain of a generation, her Georgee.

CHAPTER TWENTY-EIGHT

I n Deep Earth Mason, Barbara and Miss Moneylegs all shared thoughts on how that George had gone from the center of attention to the scientific authority to academia ignored, treating him at best as a recluse. Tony Computron with Esamia joined them. In there own ways they both had questions about the engagement party they had also been watching.

Tony, deciding he would like to be a 'gentleman' allowed Esamia to interrogate first. Esamia stated,

"Lots of people at the party talked to each other, then went away saying bad things about them 'behind their backs'." Miss Moneylegs responded,

"Another expression is back-stabbing."

Not to be sidetracked Esamia continued,

"Why did you people use the precious commodity of the brain for such a pathetic pastime? How your society would have achieved so much more with constructive intellectual thinking. Why did ladies think Grace had to be pregnant to get married so quickly? Why did they stare so obviously at her womb? Did they expect to see something jump out? So most Earth Crusters spend a very high proportion of their communication ability to talk in tittle-tattle. In my opinion they would have had a more productive life if not tittle-tattling, perhaps more constructive thought progress. Did people understand if you are 'A' then tittle tattle about 'B' then 'B' would talk about 'A' to 'C' and on and on? Somehow those who tittle-tattle most are blinded to the obvious that everyone talks about them behind their backs. Stupidity upon stupidity. Why not rid Earth Crust of the gossips? They should be locked away as if suffering with a mental illness. They only did harm to the community, or locked away to protect themselves verbally self harming!" Spoken by a child the truth was obvious. Miss Moneylegs,

"Where would chat shows have been without gossip?"

At this point Tony Computron communicated that in his opinion the human brain developed with faults and was unable to comprehend positive thinking without negative talking, on an individual, national, international level. It would have been better for Mother Earth if those neutrinos passing through Earth Crust humanity had just switched their hearts off, for all the other Earth Crust species life could have been so much more fulfilling. Get rid of mankind, have a peaceful Earth.

"As Esamia has I think finished my question is again how could Earth Crust humanity convince itself that it must be the most important life form in the Universe? Your scientists misled so often by saying this planet, that planet, could not support life as that basic element of this water is missing. What Earth Crusters should have commented is that this planet that planet could not support 'life like us.' The whole of the rest of the universe was ecstatic that 'life like us,' could not be found, no Earth Crusters, anywhere else, thank who/whatever!!"

"Why didn't those neutrinos exterminate such arrogant stupidity?"

Then a momentary change in the sound of the Founding Protectors as if agreeing with Tony Computron's thoughts.

No! Another event, they all felt the identical sensation best described that the Earth momentarily stopped spinning then in the same instant returned to travelling through the Universe.

All in Deep Earth received the same explanation. Earth with all its accumulated power had just entered a minute vacuum in space, large enough to create the anomaly though small enough for the Earth to pass over it. Again the same thought, this could exist as a forerunner of that Wind Wave anomaly, the 'Double W.' Barbara brushed her brow with ice cold sweat that had formed in the moment of fear. Miss Moneylegs and Mason also felt the same ice-cold sheet of sweat. Tony Computron still had the urge to discuss frail Earth Crust Humanity; even he realized that this would be a bad moment.

CHAPTER TWENTY-NINE

Hollis instructed that the Thames Water Company produce all underground plans of sewers in the North London area, then told that company Chief Executive that he required three of the most senior underground inspectors on secondment for some time. He reminded the Chief Executive that he had previously signed the Official Secrets Act, that the three on secondment needed to do the same. A legal representative of MI5 would be on hand when the three arrived to take them through the formality.

Hollis concluded in saying, 'speed of the essence, national security in jeopardy.' On arrival the 'legal beagle', went through the signing formalities explaining that they would not receive any additional salary, however, if they were successful in the appointment assignment each would receive a mention in the next 'New Years Honours List'. Even the most argent socialist liked to receive a Royal 'gong', particularly as each of the three were married with grandchildren.

The Thames Water Chief Executive had done the selection well, no immediate reward as in the normal course of events, his 'gong' guaranteed.

From 'legals' the three were passed over to the team leader who went into an explanation that a pipe had been discovered which had no status on the underground sewer plans. (It is often forgotten that the center of London around the Thames would have been submerged millions of years ago, also the central area is more or less surrounded by higher hilly ground e.g. Highgate West Hill etc.) The first stage of the operation was in effect to start backwards from the Cellar Sewer entrance. Muttering amongst themselves the three indicated they did not understand the panic as they had seen similar pipes in other parts of London. They had always assumed they contained telephone wires into Government offices, something secret, hence no known record.

In effect going backwards meant walking up an incline, instructions, two men in the front, one waterman bringing up the rear, two spooks in the middle. Charles continued to compare 'Registry' with that of Miss J, a new team set up to look for the other, if other, members of Miss J's team, Hollis adamant they existed somewhere within London. Further search in the bedroom complex discovered several secret cupboards hidden behind the far wall, one compartment had several British Naval uniforms, pressed, ready to be worn. So did some of Miss J's co-workers dress in men's uniforms?

In the early hours of the morning after that engagement party George awoke convinced he heard a noise in the garden at the front of the house. Throwing on jumper and trousers over his pajamas, bare feet into shoes, no other sound in the house to indicate that the Countess or Grace was awake, he proceeded into the hall, picked up his keys, exited through the front door when much to his annoyance he kicked over one of those empty milk bottles which clattered down the steps, he even placed a finger in front of his mouth saying 'hush' to himself. Turning the corner of the house a severe blow to the head, at the same instant a sharp needle into the arm. George dead to the world.

Watching in Deep Earth, Mason, Barbara, Miss Moneylegs, looked on with dumbfounded disbelief. 'Unbelievable,' muttered Barbara.

Morning panic set in when Natasha rushed into Grace's bedroom to scream, 'George has gone. His clothes are still in his bedroom. His house keys have gone.' Doctor Grace didn't panic, doctors don't panic, her first telephone call going to the Duty Officer at '5'. History repeating itself never liked, behind every action the Service looking for Soviet moles after Burgress, after McClean. Who would be the next? Rumour circulating, there may be a fourth, maybe even a fifth man (note man).

Back in the sewers of London progress was dirty, messy and slow. The experienced watermen constantly on the look out for things that should not be in sewers, in certain areas the stench was unbearable, to the watermen a normality. For the men from '5' the rats, everywhere the rats, difficult to comprehend the numbers. Every now and again a kick from a waterman sending an unfriendly rat kicked flying. Why such a human fear of rats equaled only by a fear of spiders, every one hundred feet the little group made a short stop to ensure the men from '5' were not suffering from claustrophobia. On such a momentary rest the senior waterman went into great detail on the different colour of 'pooh'. In various parts of London, not as different now as during World War II, even today there are noticeable differences between East End Docklands with West End Mayfair. The diet produces different colours, textures, and smells.

Thirty-four minutes into the walk they found what looked suspiciously similar to the Miss J milk bottle bank. Photographed, nearest locator reference noted, about turn back to the camp to look at the plans. On the return journey, a waterman explained what even the two from '5' understood it must be raining up there. The water level was rising slowly. Walking turned into sloshing, the sound of falling water all around, never a friendly atmosphere, yet these watermen have worked in this climate all their working lives. The water noise was getting louder and the watermen increased their walking (sloshing) pace and then decided to exit at the next entry/exit point. Those from '5' could see concern drawing across those experienced faces. What could be concerning them?

George came around thick headed, blurred eyes, pain across his chest, two of them sat in front of him. Tied hand and feet to a chair rather different from his last near death experience.

Watermen could have guessed what the noise could be, in the event the surging rat infested water went over the heads of even the tallest, the watermen had heard stories of such a wall of water suddenly released in the past. None of them lived for more than two minutes, their rat invested, rat eaten bodies washed up over a period of days in other parts of the outlet system, their secret discovery 'gong' with them. The families of the dead watermen did receive posthumous bravery awards, some government department providing money for the families of all five dead to compensate for their loss.

George could see this room looked and felt more like a prison cell. In front of him one man (person) seated holding a double-barreled shotgun. Somewhat to his left sitting at a table another man (person) with a telephone in front, both people wearing balaclava helmets with only slits for eyes, nose and mouth covered. Without speaking George was given a piece of paper to read. Again without speaking a telephone was thrust into his hand.

Grace picked up the phone on the other end, giving the number. George read (from the paper), "This is George. I am a prisoner. I will be released on payment of £10000 in cash, more details in an hour. A shotgun is pointed at my head, do not tell the police."

Hardly had the word 'police' left his lips than the person at the table cut the phone off. Although Grace had answered the phone, the Countess standing at her side had listened to the conversation. Picking up the phone, the Countess telephoned the Duty Officer and reported to them what had happened. She also informed the Duty Officer the family would pay up and that the Service need take no action. She would keep them informed.

Her second call was to Sir Peter at the bank.

"I need £10000 in cash, used notes. Please have a courier deliver within the hour."

Sir Peter asked no questions. Over the years he had learnt that the extremely rich blue blood client had been an important client long before his time. He also knew that £10000 represented little more than pocket money, not that anyone would guess at that. Only he and one other senior colleague knew the many investments in the names of various funds owned by the Countess. He well knew that Grace only had very limited knowledge of her mother's wealth, George had no idea.

A courier from the bank arrived within thirty-six minutes; during the wait the Countess had a discussion with Grigory and Peter. They were to prepare the Rover, Grigory was to drive and Peter was to drive a fast car. Slightly before the hour had turned the Countess, seated by the telephone took the call. At the other end George could see and hear it was the man with the shotgun. He started,

"Have you the money?"

The Countess started (don't mess with the Countess),

"The money is here in used bank notes, still in the bank seals in bundles of £500 and £100 depending on the note value. Where do you want to meet? I will be in my Rover car with my driver. George is to be brought to the car; the money will be in a Doctor's bag by my side. You can count it if you are unsure. No George, no money, I wait to meet at 12 noon. Where shall I see you?"

George could not hear the conversation, he could see the man opposite visibly taken aback by whatever had been spoken on the other end of the conversation. In front of him, the man who'd been taken aback was almost stuttering, "OK. 12 noon at the side street by the main entrance to Paddington Station. Place white ribbons on the bonnet as though it was a wedding car. Only you and the driver, make sure he wears his uniform."

Confirming the arrangement and placing the phone back on the rest she laughed. If it had not been her Georgie she would have laughed loud and long at these amateurs. She called a meeting giving instructions to Grigory about making the car look like a wedding car and that he needed to wear a hat with uniform. There was much amusement and Peter listened in.

Esamia appeared to say the next part of George's life would be very interesting then continuing, seeing this 'kidnap' why is a life of a person more valuable when they are captured than the time proceeding capture. Jumping in with both feet, Miss Moneylegs commented it must be obvious that the value is not the actual life, it is the value ascertained as to the wealth the person owned.

'OK," Esamia continued, now with a glint in her eyes. 'So if you have wealthy parents you would receive the parents money if you did not pay the 'kidnap' money. Do children arrange to have their parents kidnapped?'

Within the Miss J house there existed an air of deep-sadness. To lose five people in the act of protecting their country was always a wake-up call to so much of the mundane in the Security World. In searching for the five a sixth body came to light, all of the so called 'cable wires' from Miss J's house backwards to where the accident happened no longer existed. The instant force of the water wall carried all away before it. Going forward much of the next five hundred yards had also ben lost. Could the wall of water have been intentional? A desperate act of destruction.

At Paddington Station a wedding car arrived with five white ribbons over the bonnet. Passers bye could see a very important wedding about to take place, the chauffeur looked impressive,

223

and the mother of the bride or groom looking very elegant sitting in the back.

Tony Computron watched with interest as the every day commuter like ants bustling around the station, a waste of Earth Crust precious resources producing little for Mother Earth in return. Thinking, 'here they are, at it again, not yet twenty years from the end of World War II veering into a nuclear war to wipe out most populations in the Northern Hemisphere. How can the brains end up like wiring diagrams, hell bent on self-annihilation? What did that humanity achieve in all the hustle, bustle, pointlessness?'

Mason, who had for a long period of time, remained in deep thought looked at Tony Computron thinking, 'If you Deep Crust Humanity claim to be so clever why are you all living underground?'

From the Computron came no answer, from somewhere; all looking at each other, 'We never said we only occupy Deep Earth and you have never asked.' From all around the high pitched voice from the Founding Protectors louder, louder. Barbara felt her ears could burst open. Each of them jolted forward very slightly. Could Mother Earth have had a gentle collision, some advance warning of the Wind Wave effect. No activity from the monitoring scientists.

George looked at those holding him captive, only the one ever spoke. In turn they dress up using rubber masks to hide their faces, not funny masks, the sort that stunt men use when they pretend to be the star in some dramatic event. Other than that they were both dressed with a long raincoat, collars up, and large rimmed hat. After that George had a rubber mask yanked down his face, no space for eyes, he could see nothing, smelling stinking rubber obnoxious. Arm in arm they walked to a vehicle sitting him in the back. The other end of his wrist cuffs were attached to something metal. No on spoke. In his mind he started counting as the vehicle started to move. In his mind he knew the Countess would arrive with the money. How would those moments resolve themselves when the changeover took place?

George sat next to the Countess who helped him remove his rubber protection. Dilemma, what do you say to someone who just spent £10000 on your life? Reading his mind she said,

"Georgie, your worth much more to me and Grace. If they had asked for a million we would have paid."

For the rest of the journey George mused as to whom the 'we' were. Was it just the Countess and Grace? Perhaps once married he could discover the truth. Are they really very wealthy? Laughing internally he thought about his first encounter with Grace. How rude he had been on the journey to Wales, how he had been physically sick at the sight of the dead body taken to be Grace, of the octopus like encounter trying to extract himself from her body on their physical love making.

Only Hollis sitting in a car outside the house could be seen on their return. George had expected to see Police waiting to interview him. Beckoning George to his car window 'Hollis' barked quietly,

"Report to me at 10am at Head Office."

Then the car drove off.

As he entered the house Grace threw her arms around him whilst Natasha produced strong tea. With almost no questions about his ordeal he found himself pinching himself. Had it really happened? Conversation began about the wedding. Peter, about five minutes into the conversation, unusually entered the room saying he had broken four things, 'Sorry!' he then exited quickly to answer the phone before returning the Countess and saying that the Head of the Metropolitan Police wanted to speak to her.

Rising elegantly from her favourite chair, she addressed the caller by his Christian name, thanking him for the information, and then asking if Sylvia (his wife) would attend the next Bridge Party. The call ended.

In that matter of fact voice often used by the Countess, devoid of all emotion she spoke.

"They have those two nasty people Georgie. Their car hit a tree. They both sustained broken legs. I said no to a prosecution as long as the money is returned complete."

George wondered if he should make a connection between Peter saying four broken things with four broken legs plus no further action. His gut feeling was that he should.

In the Auction house there was disbelief in the rumour that both Jennifer and her brother were involved in a road accident, each sustaining two broken legs.

For the household there was a return to planning the wedding, normality after the explosive news when Natasha had noticed that George was missing. Wedding day preparation was now back to center stage, comings, goings, comings, wedding dress fittings, for George who would be best man? Would the sisters attend? As usual the Countess took the decision,

"Georgie have you a best man in mind?" Georgie was in thought, turning over in his mind the very few alternatives.

"No."

"Georgie would you kindly ask Peter?"

Relief from Georgie.

"Yes, a splendid idea. Will it be acceptable to Grace?"

"Of course Georgie, they are like brother and sister. You know that."

From each day to the next there was a regular visitor in the form of the assistant of the Archbishop of the Russian Orthodox Cathedral in London. He was the choirmaster. For George there was a rehearsal at home. Not being a man of religious persuasions he felt emotion or something during the on-going rehearsal. It was strange for George to notice that there were no bridesmaids. Perhaps if Peter had a sister she would have been the bridesmaid. He wondered if brides had bridesmaids in the Russian Orthodox Church. It was a question that went unanswered in his own mind. A question to Grace could provide the answer. He thought he should get his act together and visit his sisters.

Reporting to MI5 Head Office George reported directly to Hollis as Director. There was no waiting; he went directly in for a meeting. Hollis told him his assignment at Corsham was now terminated and his new appointment would be decided after his wedding. He would continue to monitor events in Cuba. Perhaps if his mind had been more 'work tuned' as opposed to concentrated on weddings and kidnaps, objections would have arisen. His dislike of the spy world at this time was not important. One of the Senior Staff had left on an extended trip to Beirut. George would use his office on the third floor.

An underling of Hollis escorted him to the temporary office, handing over a set of relevant keys, introducing George to a temporary secretary who provided instructions to those staff members George could call on for assistance. A glimpse around the office found his eyes alighting on a female face from his past. He thought it could be her. She caught him staring. No sign of recognition on her face. Time had moved on since the age of fifteen. Many female faces had come and gone since then. It was not difficult for him to establish if 'Heidi' had turned up out of the blueness of the past. Broken from his thoughts with the Secretary asking if he drank tea of coffee, how he liked it, then motherly enquiring how the wedding plans were progressing. Without thinking too deeply he requested a floor plan showing desks, staff name, area of work, with motherly protection the Secretary had it in his hands in moments.

He saw that Heidi was not the name of the person. That didn't surprise him. Many of the staff had different names in the service, although normally only the surname changed as it was easier to keep a Christian name. If Heidi did exist her name according to the floor plan had now become Heather. That amused him. They had rolled in heather more than once, an exaggeration, well, they'd rolled in heather at least once. His mind turned to his time in Switzerland on the school annual spring visit to Thun. He'd been young, free, with no responsibility, no spying.

The day had started slowly, but by 11am he had a list of appointment running through the new weeks until his holiday for the wedding. The Heidi/Heather conundrum was far away in the back burner of his mind. At 2pm (14:00) he was sharply ordered to attend another meeting, with Gray, Ward, Ivanov and the Soviet Deputy Ambassador to whom Ivanov deferred in total obedience. Moscow had a proposal to be sent to the Americans requesting that they remove missiles based in Europe pointing into the Union of Socialist Republics. A nonstarter thought George then again diplomacy moves strangely and slowly. With the world in near nuclear crisis, politicians playing at politics.

Much later in the day George found himself requesting a file from Registry. When there Charles came to ask how the wedding plans were progressing. Without too much though he asked to see the personnel file of Heather. Charles hesitated, not for such an important player in the team with that rumour mill suggesting that George would receive a very high posting after his honeymoon. George didn't take the file out of registry, made no notes, his memory would suffice. There was no mention whatsoever of Switzerland or the different name. Her references were impeccable.

Dinner at home. The indifferent food was normal for him now. There was constant chitter chatter with wedding plans. The Countess, Grace, Natasha, all now totally consumed in the forthcoming event.

"Georgie," he put the Times down, "I", (yes 'I') "have arranged for a fitting for your wedding clothes tomorrow after work at 6. Peter and his father will collect you. You will all be measured by Mr Tyreitt in Saville Row. He already has my instructions for what you three are to wear."

George must have pulled one of those man faces as she continued,

"Georgie, no funny faces. I want all my boys to look smart,"

On cue the bride to be giggled. Thankfully The Times was crammed full of information on the Cuban Crisis. He slid down his now usual armchair, as if hiding from those sisters long ago. Still reading he came to the letter page, one with the heading "American Aggressors to Invade Cuba." A letter sent from America apparently signed by a Lee Harvey Oswald, to paraphrase the letter, 'leave Cuba alone.' Thinking to make a mental note to see what information exists on this anti-American person. Head still in The Times, the telephone never stopped ringing, keeping a sort of mental score. Every ten incoming calls were Countess 7, Grace 2, Natasha 1, George nil. In fact Natasha would also have been nil except that she had taken on the role of organizing the multi-layered cake. Following, what over his time of living in the house, his routine of listening to the ten o'clock news on the radio, all three drifted off to bed, often, as this evening, George departed first for his night time ablutions.

Peck on the cheek for the Countess, more of lips for Grace, polite goodnight to Natasha. Settling into bed Grace blew him a kiss as she passed pulling the door closed in the process, little George safely in bed. In bed with a brain in overdrive thinking about the circumstances in which Heidi/Heather came to be employed by the Security Service, MI5, her references impeccable. Convinced beyond any doubt that Heather had first been Heidi, he ran over the meetings in Thun in his mind. During the third day of the school visit (they'd travelled by overnight train through France from the Channel Port) he went into a violent epileptic seizure. For the first night My Joyner, Mr Thomas, the designated teachers for his part of the school group, moved him out of the dormitory bedroom of six pupils into a downstairs lounge. During the night they took it in turns mopping the sweat pouring out of him. With morning light jumping in through Alpine flowered curtains, a group leader meeting decided the doctor should be called urgently. For the rest of the schoolboys the day was to continue as planned. The teachers were to keep a watchful eye to see if anyone else went down with the same symptoms. Mr Davis, who spoke French with a little German, would stay to deal with the doctors. By general agreement there was no need to inform the school or to contact the parents of George. On arrival the doctor looked more like a clock maker, with little beady eyes, round lensed glasses perched just on the end of his nose, his professional giveaway the black bag all doctors own.

He administered penicillin up to the permitted dosage, a telephone call for an ambulance. Before you could say 'cuckoo clock' George found himself in the sanatorium (hospital) of Thun set directly on the banks of the lake. George often recalled the first night of being delirious, constantly buffeted with giant enormous blue elephants, and then dancing on his chest. In saturated pajamas, saturated bed linen, a nurse dried him completely. Even safely in a comfortable bed in his new home, shudders of fear raced down his spine thinking of the loneliness, fear of an operation, dealing with the unknown, thinking I want to die back at home with my family, fear of communicating only by hand signals.

More penicillin, only liquid water, no food. Time lost all meaning. More penicillin, more elephants, now pink ones joining the blue, vague voices in the background, dark, light, dark again. Green elephants, no still blue, still pink, now with green tinkerbell lights dancing with the elephants. More penicillin.

After all the years he had forgotten about the green lights. On recollection they were identical to those when he first met Grace. Green tinkerbell light still dancing in front of eyes he vaguely made out the shape of a young lady.

In beautiful eloquent English,

"Hello George, my name is Heidi. My father is a doctor here. I have been asked to help you now that you are showing signs of recovery. Everyone has been concerned you might die or at best, have a paralysis. Then over the last hour you showed a dramatic recovery. The doctors have suggested I take you outside into the fresh air. You will need me to push you in a chair."

Dressed into a mixed concoction of clothes, George re-entered the world of the living. Fresh air can smell very special. Swiss fresh air tinged with that faint smell of flowers, even more special. In his own mind a welcoming song from birdworld at his revival. She chatted constantly, George listened, and he knew instantly that this would be everlasting love.

A path from the sanatorium went down towards the lakeside, some distance on, a stop by a wooden backed bench on went the brake on the wheelchair. How hot the sun burnt into his soft skin. He noticed she already had the first hint of a sun-browned complexion. Through the pine trees dancing white lights hitting the lake water coloured deep blue, well within sight one of those clinically clean white boats chuntering around from pier to pier, lake side to lake side. Heidi constantly chattering away in perfect English.

Little more than thirty minutes after the adventure into the real world began, George found himself returned to his prison now sitting at a table, the two of them consuming soup whilst downing a plateful of fresh bread. Why does continental bread taste better than English bread? As if to answer his own thought, he remembered that as a war measure (World War II) chalk would be mixed into bread, so do they still do it? Helped into bed by Heidi, a 'see you later' as she left, then a visit from two masters (teachers) now pleased that the 'will he live or will he die' discussion was now a decision of the past.

One of the conferences about George, in front of George, 'would he be well enough to travel?' Doctors were of the opinion with three days before the school was due to return that with special travel arrangements he might be alright. A long telephone conversation from Mr Thomas (a serious rugby player) to the headmaster giving up to date information for parents, then the travel insurance company for them to make travel arrangements for George to return to England. That night George still slept with elephants with those green dancing lights, next morning he actually felt hungry for breakfast. Another warm sunny blue sky, an early visit from Mr Thomas carrying a telegram sent from his parents wishing that George could be back with the family looking after him, love with kiss. George still had the telegram inside a bible given to him by his maternal grandmother when he first went away to boarding school. In his new home bed, tossing, turning, stretching, anything to get the thought of Heidi clear in his head. The paperwork at '5' clearly demonstrated a lady called Heather not Heidi. How could he resolve his belief?

Doctors came around, one introducing himself as the father of Heidi. She sent a message that she would come soon to take him out into the fresh air again. His accent a little different from the other staff. Must make polite inquiry as to where he originates from? More penicillin. Heidi arrived pushing a wheelchair; a nurse dressed him in warmer clothes for outside. Pushed downhill to the same bench, she chatted a little more with him than yesterday. He asked about her language proficiency, where her father originated from? She spoke fluent German, French, English, Russian; her father grew up in what is now East Germany.

The sun was hot on his face, that white ferry boat was further around the lake than yesterday in the very far distance, white sails stretched into fullness, more wind over there.

She stood up to point out an old fashioned paddle steamer far away in the other direction. She even knew the name of the steamer. All around, so idyllic, he hoped she noticed not his wandering eye, give or take a little, five feet nine inches, shoulder length blonde hair, no apparent makeup, skin the faintest of summer bronze, short sleeve dress, size eight definitely not ten and might even squeeze into a six. White ankle socks, summer shoes. She did notice him staring but ladylike, continued talking about rides on the old paddle steamer and then turning the tables, asking him about his family. He seemed tall for his age (George already six foot tall) the Doctors only think you have survived as a result of you being very fit (tall, lean, thin, athletic).

[The Watchers in Deep Earth could only agree. Barbara looking at Miss Moneylegs in disbelief. No one would ever describe their George in such a way. In sprang a Tony Computron thought, 'let's look at you two when you were fifteen.' Neither had a chance to think No! Before them their fifteen-year-old imagers were available for anyone to look at.]

Heidi continued.

"They've asked me to tell you that as a result of all the penicillin you may in the future have an allergic reaction."

Somewhat going over his head the after effects of reactions to penicillin were of very little concern. His interest fully focused on this young lady, perhaps five, six or seven years his elder. She did say the doctors would prepare a letter for him to give to his doctor. They had asked for her help in translating the letter into English.

Holding his hand as if taking a racing pulse she announced,

"You're getting cold, time to go back indoors."

The same routine as the day before, eating a meal together, back into bed, a visit from teacher Thomas. Good news the insurance company have arranged for you to travel back home with the rest of the school on the same train. You will travel in a sleeping carriage. Once at Victoria Station in London, a private car/taxi will get you back home. Commenting a good job the school insists on insurance on these continental holidays. Drifting off to sleep those elephants only came and went a couple of times, the green dancing tinkerbell lights brighter, dreamland full of visions of Heidi.

Waking slowly in the morning after dreamland he knew only one or two more days with Heidi. (Perhaps he should have thought hospital, well they both start with an 'h'.) Breakfast came, breakfast went, doctor's rounds came, doctor's rounds went, lunch arrived, and lunch went. Now time for Heidi. Up on the wall that cuckoo clock must have stopped, looking around the ward he noticed that one of the four beds in the ward, the one in the opposite corner was now empty. From memory the occupant had been a young lady, older than George, from Thun itself. Where had she gone? George had never communicated, though he couldn't remember seeing her awake, most of the time hospital screens were left in place around the bed. Where had Heidi gotten to? Didn't she understand he would be waiting? Why today had the hospital decided to be so quiet. He did not think Sunday had arrived. A quiet hospital can be very unnerving; the other two occupants within the ward were fast asleep. Come on cuckoo clock, do some cuckooing! Frustrated George decided to play Heidi and seek. Fortunately in exiting the bed he knocked over a chair, the crashing noise brought in a nurse quicker than on the double somewhere else in the world she might have been a matron, one look from the granite Alpen face and George was back in bed, also quicker than on the double. She spoke no English, often he thought back to that moment as the time he decided to learn foreign languages.

In Deep Earth, Tony Computron decided this to be another good time to pronounce on the stupidity of Earth Crust not having one universal language. How can it be possible for one such insignificant planet, one insignificant sun (star) two thirds of the way within the Milky Way, not have a common, one only Earth language? What existences from other planets would even attempt to communicate with so many, many, many languages, some 6500, yes 6500. That's just you humans, what about animals, birds, insects, fish and so on. Can you imagine how devastated humanity would be if an entity arrived from another part of the Universe and started to communicate directly with the fishes of the sea? Yet a world uniform language could be learned in a generation. No baby is born speaking a language so start all on only one language. Within one hundred of your years there would be a common language speaking Earth population. That wonderful organization should have been called United Nations separated by Un-united languages. It would have been such an easy language programme to achieve, one voice, one Earth. So everyone, particularly the political class, afraid to loose language and therefore political control, afraid one language could lead to a single political system. Listen all those vested interests screaming, 'No, we must keep our own language.' So what language did the first humans use? No one knows. What would become a world language, well Mandarin as some twenty percent of the population speak it already, so only eighty percent to convert. Coming to the end of his comments some of the younger Computrons arrived forming one of those American football hurdles around him. Emerging from within he explained that the young Computrons wanted to ask why money had overtaken all things to be the main religion, the basis on which money was created meant it had no value to support the face value on the bank notes. Why did people not understand that?

Heidi arrived later than the days before, she had obviously been crying, and wasn't her previous happy self. George, still in bed, took the initiative.

"What's happened?"

Pointing to the empty bed Heidi replied,

"The young lady who died, we had been at school together, at university together. The Doctors couldn't find what had caused her illness. Unlike you George, penicillin didn't save her. When someone your own age dies so young, you start thinking."

George could only say sorry though having unburdened her thoughts, Heidi brightened up. Continuing their routine, a nurse dressed him and Heidi produced the wheel chair. Her mother had sent some cakes for a minor picnic. They walked slightly further, another bench closer to the lake, still sky blue lake meeting blue sky, still the pristine white of the ferry boats, one closer to them than on any other day.

Today a fresh dress hinting of a traditional Alpine costume, her shoes cherry red, those ankle socks with bare legs. George now feeling happier, thankful his hospital ordeal was nearly over, excited to see his family again. This would be his last time alone with her. In his mind he had a plan. Helping him out of the wheelchair in clumsy schoolboy fashion he went to kiss her lips, reaching out to hold her waist, they both lost their balance, falling to the floor he held on tight to her as they rolled down the steep incline, both laughing at their predicament.

Perhaps fifty yards later the incline ceased and they came to a stop with Heidi lying on top of him. Embracing tighter, their lips met, her bare no lipstick lips. She broke into emotional crying. Not what the schoolboy expected from his forwardness. Sobbing out came the words she felt very sad that her friend Heather had died, she felt she should not be happily enjoying herself. George didn't know how to answer that question, his schoolboy education having never covered this type of conversation. So George held on more tightly to let her continue getting her sadness off that heaving chest. Did she feel that the male item at the point where his legs met had expanded, growing very hard? She did yes, moving her hand to touch from above them, no waterfall of flowing emotion, no doves flying overhead. For this time of peace, no animals' heads looking out of homes in the ground.

"No!" the booming voice of Mr Joyner.

"George what are you doing?"

Their faces now as red as those discarded cherry shoes. No explanation possible. Even 'Old Joyner' the Geography teacher could not but be impressed by the contour lines showing clearly through her somewhat misplaced clothing. For 'Old Joyner' the story, with a few embellishments would be a good one for the staff room.

He delivered his message that the bus for the train station would collect them at 10am the next morning, giving them plenty of time to get to Zurich and the night train. He left leaving them sitting properly, clean, tidy on the seat.

When 'Old Joyner' had travelled out of earshot they both burst into laugher of the 'caught being naughty, sensibility prevailed' type. They ate the picnic. Why does the food of a picnic taste better than the same food indoors? They chatted, promised to keep in touch, and exchanged addresses. She reminded him that there would be a letter for his doctor.

At last a quite night with no elephants, no dancing green lights. This hospital that had saved his life even provided a handsome Swiss picnic made for his journey.

Heidi, her father, mother and some of the nurses were waiting as the coach full of 'rowdies' arrived. Hugs and kisses all around from the hospital staff for George. Polite thanks from Thomas and Joyner to the hospital administrator. One of those life moments arrived as Heidi pushed the wheel chair to the coach steps. George, back in school uniform went back from young manhood to schoolboy. They embraced without kissing, wolf whistles from the usual culprits. A last minute request for him to also take another letter to her father's friend, Dr Wilby, who would be at Victoria Station to make sure he had travelled safely.

The two front seats of the bus had been removed for George and his wheelchair. The doors were closed, lots of waving, Heidi and her mother shed a tear. George swears he didn't, but if he didn't he was suddenly starting to perspire profusely. The school party leaders breathed a sigh of relief to be returning with all their charges in tact. The not so well George fell asleep to the disgust of his schoolmates who wanted the low down on life in the hospital. When he was awake he mainly talked about the girl who died in his little ward. He felt lucky to have survived the unidentified illness. For the others, time for that final shopping trip in Zurich with two hours left until the overnight train departed for Calais. Some had squeezed into a drinking establishment having a crafty fag (cigarette). Everything was so cheap with so many Swiss francs for every £1.00 (fags really cheap).

When the teachers gathered the flock together it was obvious that a number had been enticed into those inexpensive shorts, alcoholic spirits. The group, minus George and Mr Thomas, were sorted into the compartments for the journey, eight into each carriage, everyone soon found out who their best friends were, as with any group, loyalties had changed during the holiday.

In Deep Earth, Mason, Barbara, Miss Moneylegs watching George, were surprised by Esamia with her friends in tow. Traditionally that meant am important event in the life of George was about to happen. She had, surprisingly, not appeared during his near death experience, so why now? 'Now watch,' she instructed.

George arrived at the carriage door in his wheelchair. Mr Thomas knocked and more than one voice said enter. ('Watch, watch,' Esamia implored.) Inside the sleeping compartment a large number of girls, perhaps a year or so older then George from a famous girls public school were preparing in various states of undressedness to climb onto/into sleeping bunks. There were six bunks with George allocated the lowest, on the left hand side when going through the door.

'Thomas' enquired where he could find a teacher (he had previously been given the name Miss Bryant by the insurance company as the contact for the girls group.) Esamia and her friends were in fits of laugher, the three Earth Crusters not much further behind in the laughing game. So in a nutshell, George would try to sleep with two well-developed schoolgirls on top of him, with another three only an arms length away. Even George, only just back from near death, could only watch the getting into bunks gyrations. His groins did expand. Miss Bryant, Mr Thomas discussed the not to be encouraged sleeping arrangements with responsibility handed over to the senior girl of the group (prefect, hockey captain, member of the equestrian team) to report any George problems to Miss Bryant in the next compartment.

At that Miss Bryant and Mr Thomas went their separate ways. Esamia's gang went back to what they were doing.

Everyone in Deep Earth was still surrounded by the noise from those Founding Protectors.

With George having taken his prescribed medication, girls'

hands continually appeared to massage his insecurity with sweets, so many sweets. Such thin girls. Where do they put all those calories? The next few hours turned into a dormitory pop and sweet party, where should he place his eyes, no girl pajamas, just very short skimpy covernothing slips. George was living in a world of never ending legs.

Are they required to put on lipstick to go to bed? In adult life what stories could be made from this unexpected highlight of six pupils school continental holiday. George went to sleep with his face turned towards the metal wall. Sometime in the middle of the night an urgent feeling that he needed to pass water. How to get to the toilet which would be at the end of the carriage, he thought remembering they were somewhere in the middle so neither end would be closer. Hanging on was not an option. An urgent exit needed to happen.

In regulation school striped pajamas, he slipped bare feet into his shoes, stood up, immediately falling forward to land on Hilda who was asleep on the other bottom bunk. Screaming, pandemonium broke out. Miss Bryant arrived as if waiting for her expectation of trouble. Half drugged, half awake, George tried to explain his urgent need for a piss (then thought that's lavatory talk for boys not for teachers of the elder variety.)

All of the girls were now awake, Hilda and another (Henrietta) received instructions to go with him to the toilet, wait outside, and then help him back. Both girls received their first lesson in the length of time a man takes to 'piss' when his concentration is elsewhere. Why every time it started to pour out did the train find points so that his aim went everywhere? In desperation he decided to sit on the seat then immediately passed wind.

In exiting the convenience Hilda and Henrietta were shivering with that cold air which infests those early morning hours. Miss Bryant switched off the light again, saying the goodnight of the unwanted disturbed; Hilda and Henrietta wee so cold they decided to huddle together in the bottom bunk. George felt guilty.

When George awoke in the morning they were still huddled together in the bottom bunk. If getting changed for bed proved an expose what George witnessed getting dressed into day school uniforms could have made a combined St Trinians/Carry On Film. Even having older sisters did not prepare him for all those bits and pieces of female bodies flaunted in front of his eyes, had he worn glasses they would have steamed up.

It took great mental determination to turn his back on such gyrations; even a gentleman of discretion would sneak a peek.

Onto the cross-channel ferry, connection with trains to London, the five girls all came to say goodbye. The adventure over, would they ever meet again? Would they recognize one another? At Victoria Station a smart city gentleman approached the school party that had a schoolboy in a wheelchair. Approaching George he held out a hand to shake his own,

"Hello George, I am Dr Wilby. Heidi's father has sent me a letter."

Without a second thought George handed over the letter and continued to sit in the wheelchair. Mr Thomas came to introduce himself to Dr Wilby, who rather curtly commented,

"I'm supposed to take the wheelchair back to the hospital on my next visit."

Fate intervened with the simultaneous arrival of families to collect their precious children. Sprinting towards the front were the two sisters of George, with his mother a few feet behind. Miraculously George no longer needed his wheelchair support and so the international communications spat was nipped in the bud.

Dr Wilby with no emotion wheeled the empty chair away before anyone had a chance to say thank-you for your time. If it had been a foggy London day the shroud of fogginess would have engulfed him. George did not make it straight home, his mother had arranged for him to visit the family doctor. George handed over his letter from the hospital. He had to make visits to the doctor every day for the next fourteen days and he could never be treated with penicillin again as he'd have an allergic reaction for ever more.

George's dreamland was abruptly shattered by an urgent, desperate call to get into the office quicker than quickly. Racing to shave, no breakfast, he timed himself arriving in the MI5 headquarters thirty-six minutes after waking. '5' has staff on duty for twenty-four hours everyday including Christmas Day. Most of the time it was spent in sheer monotonous boredom of routine. No James Bond lifestyle, every day employed work. First call was to Registry to order and sign for the file on Dr Wilby. He knew the face immediately. A number of pictures no doubt about him, matter now involving that sister agency the Intelligence Service, MI6. For MI5 what to do about 'Heidi'? As if to make greater urgency, Gray called for an urgent meeting about Cuba. From Ivanov they'd received information that the missile carrying cargo ships were within a few days of Cuba. With tension rising President Kennedy would be receiving hourly updates accompanied by increasing pressure from the military to take first strike actions. The vested interests within the American military are very persuasive; fortunes can be made from a good war, by those nowhere near danger or action. It was always good to have a Senator or Congressman as a director or even more secretive consultant, creative accounting hiding all sorts in consultancy fees. Governments manage exactly the same, many a politicians partner receiving consultancy fees from Government departments, perhaps even those organizations seeking to obtain lucrative government contracts. Gray presented options as to what procedure to take with the Ivanov information. Play safe, only tell the Prime Minister.

CHAPTER THIRTY

Around the same time George arrived in the office, two of the most important trade union leaders were boarding a flight to Moscow. Some twenty-four hours before they had received an invitation from Moscow to attend a meeting to help resolve the Cuba Crisis. From Embassy staff of the Soviet Union, special visas were delivered to their London offices, together with first class air tickets, along with further instructions that their Soviet hosts had arranged hotels (bound to be the National Hotel on Red Square) all their meals, all their transport would be provided.

Long before the days of credit cards or ATM machines their respective accounting staff provided a large cash float for any expenses. Self-educated, self-centered, self-motivated, each believed they had the ordained ability to resolve the crisis. On the flight of less than four hours they were the only passengers in first class and therefore felt more comfortable to speak openly. Expert communication specialists regularly connected the first class cabin to listening devices situated under the floor. Microphones permanently placed in any available nook or crannies were easily pressed into service at the request of the Lords and Masters of the K.G.B. In earlier days the problem of shoes constantly moving (obviously on legs) caused difficulty in listening. This problem had been overcome by providing comfy slippers in the in-flight travel bag. Many a trade unionist had a nice collection of these from numerous comings, goings to Moscow.

So the two sat chattering away putting the none socialist world to rights. On arrival at Moscow, always a long drawn out ordeal for the normal traveller whom it was normal to allow three hours to get through passport control, and hence the rush to get from the plane to be the first to present documents at the border control booth.

There were armed military everywhere, not least preventing multiple access to the plane side conveniences. For the normal traveller the border control booth is always the first taste of Soviet bureaucracy. Unnerving the unsuspecting arrivals at the open booth window, passports were handed over, along with plane tickets, visa, and invitations from the Soviet organization. Once in the hands of the border officer, the window is promptly closed. Now the arrival is in no-mans land, no proof of identity, nothing, naked in front of Soviet paperwork. Within the booths light's start to flash, the sound of something like a machine working. Nothing after that. No-mans land as a captive, no forward, no backward, locked in by gates front, and back. Time passes, ten, twenty, thirty minutes, normal time lapses. Who? Where? Is looking at the precious 'get me back home documents'. Relief when the locked window opens, the officer now looking at the incomers face. Instructions to the incomer to remove hat, scarf, turn coat collars down, remove spectacles, unnerved the unseasoned traveller, now desperate to go back home on the next available plane.

Now the open window smartly closed bang shut. Shuffling from behind with the lengthy line of newcomers wondering what this person must have done in the past to be held up for so long, not realizing their torture was yet to come.

Now the experienced travellers looking to see if another booth would be opened up to speed through the waiting incomers, sadly that is not the way. Those poor unexpected at the back of the single line could be waiting longer than the four-hour flight time from London.

For the two trade union officials, they came straight through the diplomatic booth in the care of some official expected to have them exited through the airport to the waiting Zill limousine. Before one could say, 'Comrade Jones.' Even the favoured getting immediately into the open door of the 'Zill' could not help other than to choke on the diesel exhaust fumes of the multifarious official cars from the humblest to the grandest, sitting with engines running to keep the car warm for their important guests. Once inside their shared 'Zill' the trade unionists were swept at ever increasing speed on that special car lane reserved for the 'most equal of equals'. Traffic lights were no obstruction to these 'most equal of equals'. With traffic stopped at any crossroad or junction to let them straight through.

A favoured interpreter would be happily sitting in the back of the 'Zill' facing the guests with his back to the driver. Every driver had an assistant (why does the KGB go around in cars in threes? One to drive, one to direct the way, the third to watch what the other two are doing.)

Arriving at Red Square straight past the international hotels (only foreigners allowed to stay) into the holy of holies, the Kremlin itself. Alighting from the 'Zill' these two proud men of importance with chests puffed out, could hear from somewhere the patriotic music of the Soviet national anthem. If ever a solid trade union leader felt emotion this had to be the moment, hairs standing up on the back of the neck, a tear forming in the eye, the sounds that meant equality for all, common sharing of wealth for the common man. If only the Russian Revolution could come to their capitalistic homeland.

Smartly passed guards into a central building into a lift, four of them now less the driver, down it went, further down, polite nervous chitchat from the visitors wondering where they were going. Abruptly the Soviet made lift comes to a halt, exiting out they were in bright light. Like one of those brilliant blue sky spring days. What a contrast to the arrival hall at Moscow airport where the lights were so dim it looked like twilight. Perhaps one of the unexpected benefits of communism was that people could see better in the dark.

From an adjacent lift their bags arrived, the bags departed in one direction to their bedrooms (no doubt being debriefed, desocked, deshirted), they themselves entered a chandelier lighted conference hall. The escorts take them over to well? Who but very attractive females, who took them to what obviously was the top table, introducing them to many friends they already knew, then sitting with, beside them attractive interpreters. No doubt interpreters would be available for other services, the first of which consisted of bringing large platefuls of food from an extensive, expensive buffet. Tucking into caviar, drinking ice-cold vodka, the Unionists were given a timetable of events that started at mid-day the next day, which would give ample time to get a sauna and massage so as to get too much vodka out of the system. As they ate earlier arrivals came over to them, backslapping, hard hand shaking, it soon became very obvious that every European (western) country had trade union or communist party leaders present. This looked liked the largest meeting of the great and good that they had witnessed before. (Did Western intelligence services know about this meeting or this underground place beneath the Kremlin? If they did they could not listen to conversations.)

General conversation from the assembled elite centered on where under the Earth they were, over the loudspeaker came an announcement that coaches would be leaving in ten minutes for an escorted tour of where they were. Coaches, underground! About to see another fantastic achievement of socialism at work. The two Union men made a mental note to make a visual record to pass on to those back in England who would be interested in such information like the Intelligence Service or the Security Service. Going off into the unknown underground most expected a thirty minute cruise, when they returned two hours later everyone looked goggle-eyed, gob-smacked, far too much to start to remember. Whatever else to remember the extraordinary hyper activity everywhere, preparation very obviously in hand expecting the worst from the Cuban Missile crisis.

Somewhere a figure of 30000 people working underground

had been mentioned. 30000 now on nuclear war alert. The missile crisis now understood by the visitors as a deliberate and planned attack to provoke America into a full blown nuclear war. They were privileged to witness this state of 'we will win', enough people down here to run a socialist (communist) controlled world.

There was more drinking when the coaches returned, much excitement at capitalist America coming under attack. With drink flowing, for the unsuspecting to get very drunk on strong quality vodka. Interpreters were on heightened alert for any useful intelligence provided by the drunkards. Like all good Soviet parties with foreigners involved a good intermingling of professional K.G.B employees, often more linguistic than spy, still however report makers.

With a two or three hour time difference most guests from Western Europe who arrived that day were still drinking hard at 2am the next morning and some slept with interpreters hardly understanding their conquest would be filmed for use in the future. Some spent the night puking up drink with a generous portion of the previous evening's meal, some tried to ring back home to inform loved ones that they had arrived and were safe. As good socialists they understood all telephone calls had to be censored/monitored. For each and every country a limited number of lines were available, perhaps to the United Kingdom ten in total, so it was usual to book telephone calls days in advance.

For international phone calls an independent telephone exchange had been created in what had been a small rural village somewhere southeast of Moscow. Womaned by strong babushkas each had their own country of responsibility, working shifts, twenty-four hours a day, three hundred and sixty five days of the year. Fully trained to be evasive, knowing every conversation would be recorded here and wherever, such is the way of the Cold War.

Many delegates missed that meal called breakfast, many headed immediately to the sauna and the steam rooms, all wanted to look un-drunk for the midday opening formal session. For a congress room think of a room in a luxury ocean cruiser, no expense spared for this encounter with opulence, rather like the mystical amber halls in the St Petersburg (Leningrad) Palace, all the halls there amber from top to bottom. A stage built from length upon length of pristine mahogany, as was the large table set on top. Where the delegates were going to sit a gentle incline attempting to give all seated a view of the stage. In sharp unedifying contrast the delegates chairs row upon row of little more than wooden oversize school chairs.

A hush, clapping, standing up. From behind side curtains on the stage walked all the members of the Politburo. Standing behind respective chairs looking back at where they came from, they started to clap as the First Secretary of the Soviet Communist Party, also Prime Minister, Nikita Sergeyevich Khrushchev, walked over to the lectern. He tested again the microphone and started to speak.

In walking onto the stage, he started speaking, an impolite disturbance when none-Russian guests hurriedly placed their earphones on to listen to one of the many interpreters providing simultaneous translation. Not quite true as each translator would have received a copy of Khrushchev's speech in advance so they could practice becoming word perfect. All wary that Khrushchev had an annoying habit of going off text if something important came to mind as he spoke. For the visitors a reasonably short diatribe of only just over the hour. He finished, waited for the regulation five minutes of clapping, left the stage, followed by all the other members of the stage party who had said nothing other than nodded their heads, clapped hands, where they'd been previously instructed to do so.

With the last of the stage party exiting behind the curtains a new group walked onto the stage to take up the vacant seats. Each one carried a large file of papers; these were Government Department Head's come to give details of how what Khrushchev had spoken of in principal would happen on the ground. Succinctly, the delegates had been told they were to stay here in the underground bunkers, safe whilst the expected nuclear war took place. The Cuban Missile Crisis was a highly developed plan to provoke such a war. The real objective for the Soviet Union was to take over Western Europe, leaving America with a sphere of influence only over the Americans. Soviet Union short and medium range missiles were ready for firing into non-Eastern European Block countries. President Kennedy could retaliate (he would, losses had been estimated) but when understanding the Soviet Union only wanted to expand its borders to the Atlantic and Mediterranean he (Kennedy) would not risk a full blown nuclear war between the Super Powers when neither could win.

Cuba existed as a disposable piece on a chessboard. Those delegates here would be returned to their own countries to take them over to run them as Socialist (communist) Republics. Khrushchev had expressed sorrow for those who would lose families in the cause of the greater good. Unfortunately all telephone calls to outside the Soviet Union were no longer possible due to a major failure at the international telephone exchange. The delegates were now 'captives for communism'. Emotions ranged from thoughts of becoming Presidents, Prime Ministers, Kings (all guests were male) of their European country, to what money could they make (high ranking Communists always had plenty), to what about their families or loved ones (not necessarily the same people), to who they would appoint to senior positions in their new country, what about changing the name of the country?

A break for the best coffee. During the coffee break the country delegates were joined by those specialists from Moscow who would go through the detailed planning. Underneath Moscow a new Western Europe would take shape, missiles would be targeted at government, the main centers of population, any missile sites. It would all take place whilst America slept. The Soviets had some unknown 'sputniks' in space that would be effective at minimizing American retaliation.

No one slept; intense planning went on unbroken for the next twenty-four hours. Not one Soviet Embassy anywhere in the world knew of the plan. Such people were expendable in the march of socialism (communism). If they were told somewhere there would be a leak, or more likely someone with a grudge would attempt to sell such highly prized information to a spy network like Mossad.

CHAPTER THIRTY-ONE

Deep, deep down within Deep Earth humanity more and more specialists were brought into the research groups. All activity and all research was concentrated on the George Double W effect, the sound of the Founding Protectors as loud as ever, with millions of them passing through the Earth every second the cumulative total of them on just this one small insignificant planet Earth could not be calculated. Where would a scientist start trying to calculate the numbers that pass through the Solar System, through the Milky Way? Some scientists were considering they were really that matter which hold the Universe together, generally referred to as black matter. They passed through the Earth, everything that lived they also passed through. How could anything of such smallness pass through everything? Where did the power to travel at such high speeds come from? Was it possible to postulate that what was accepted as solid was not solid in any universal sense? Stop, think, millions pass through the human body. Can you feel them? Can you touch them? What in the name of the Universe are they doing?

Humanity is so clever it knows nothing. Does humanity exist for them or is humanity insignificant on a much greater journey? If humanity is so important, if nothing like humanity exists in any other place, why do they not stop to look at humanity, or did they look, not like what they saw and so continued onwards forever and ever?

On direction of the Elder Elders a further scientific study group found itself situated under the Artic Ice. Not at magnetic north, rather a point that had been calculated to be the point where maximum continuous monitoring could be undertaken to see most of the Universe at the same instantaneous time. Much of the work undertaken by Computrons who apparently feel neither the cold or the heat, some way they either reflect or ingest heat or cold. This group made a discovery similar to that of George just before he died. His discovery of the Wind Wave Anomaly was perhaps the most magnificent finding since mankind first existed.

For the Arctic Scientists the initial discovery produced a feeling best described as professional shame. How had it been missed? Could it be that so much energy had been spent on the George Double W anomaly? This was not the time for recriminations; Elder Elder came exceptionally quickly to see the confirmation. Only one explanation, a second George Double W anomaly had appeared. Then the questions. Were they connected? Would other sides appear for example were they seeing North, South? Would East and West join them, something akin to being encircled? Some of the scientists now proposed an idea that the Universe would be squeezed, squeezed until little more than an atom and would then explode, another big bang.

For the Elder Elder the decision to fortify Deep Earth humanity was more justified than before. Extra effort was placed on the creation of a protected environment for Deep Earth Humanity. Within Deep Earth Humanity protracted conversations continued about what they should do. What were the Founding Protectors? An overall consensus that everything within the Universe existed for a purpose, much of it, perhaps ninety nine percent, not understood by mere mortals whether Earth Crust or Deep Earth Humanity. Certainly one idea that had been presented openly was that they were the creative element there at the moment of conception. To many an interesting intellectual thought would support the idea that when passing through they existed or created the fact of conception. Obviously no proof. Then the thought that they were there at the moment of bodily function cessation. Did one stop for the length of a lifetime and then move onwards on their apparent never-ending journey through the Universe. Do they die? Do they live forever? Do they multiply? Have they been a constant totality from the instant of the Big Bang? Do they have intelligence? Surely they must have. Do they eat, drink, and defecate? Are humanities brains so pathetic to think in such terms? Is humanity so pathetic that they pass through, keep going, onwards forever?

CHAPTER THIRTY-TWO

On Friday October 26th 1962, the Cuban Missile Crisis ended with the Soviet ships turning around to head back to Soviet ports. Within a very short period of time these events led to the establishment of the 'Hot Line' between the two Super Powers, although the world never knew at the time that America removed missile sites in Turkey. The Soviet Union received an undertaking from America that America would not invade Cuba. The Soviets therefore had a permanent base not far from the Florida coast. That strange anomaly in Cuba called Guantanamo, the American naval base, remained. History is full of the question why did Khrushchev take the world to the brink of nuclear war and then stop? Which story of the two sides do you believe Capitalist America, Communist Russian, perhaps both tell part of the same story.

For George the cessation of hostilities came only one day before the wedding to Grace, a wedding that had quickly entered into the social calendar. After the wedding his new posting, rumour rife in both the Foreign Office and the Security Services as to what it would be. A very strong rumour that he would be the next ambassador for the Soviet Union. One of the closest buildings to the Kremlin wall, the British Embassy was literally a thorn in the side of the heart of Communism. Within the Capitalist world many an enquiry as to why Khrushchev came back from the brink, Russian staff at the British Embassy spoke of a rumour circulating in Moscow that Khrushchev with his Politburo mates had been drinking heavily on the night of October 25th when some awoke they complained of such a severe hangover all they could see around them were green flashing lights. Only when they took a collective decision to recall the ships on route to Cuba did the flashing green lights cease. Not a political military reason for bringing the crisis to an end, no one believed the joke story to be true, but then fiction can be truer than fact. A more interesting question, why did Castro and Khrushchev allow the Americans to keep Guantanamo Bay?

Saturday October 27th 1962, George sat down to breakfast first, the usual food was served. Sometimes he longed for bacon, sausage, and egg with fried bread. Next came the Countess followed shortly by Grace. It felt like the calm before the storm. The activity level would soon be heightened with the arrival of the long time hairdresser with an assistant. Many a man just like George wondering what on Earth he could do for the next hours before he and Peter were the first to depart for the Church. A quick word from Natasha to the Countess saying she would leave in five minutes to ensure the flowers were in the Church, Peter and Grigory would be with her to oversee the seating arrangement, to ensure the service sheets were delivered.

The choir had a ten o'clock practice. The Church Elders would then take over receiving guests. To ensure the Church would be safe for the high profile guests, there had been a policeman on duty overnight who would be replaced with four officers for the rest of the day. She had received a message that there would be a military guard of honour for the couple as they exited the Church. George thought every now and again that this wedding had been totally organized, in the sense of doing the actual work, by Natasha.

Having heard all the details again (for the umpteenth time) George remained, still at a loose end as to what could occupy him. Without thought he wondered back into the Library, with a naughty cup of tea. The Countess would not approve. Taking down the first old book to catch his eye, in beautiful limp velum he looked on the spine to see the hand written title in brown ink, 'Virgilius Maro (Publis) Opera Cum Decem Commentis 1529'. Holding a four hundred year old book, one of many such books in the private library. His old Cambridge College would be more than thankful to receive such a handsome library. It could not be his to donate, Grace and the Countess having told him, not asked his opinion, that it would pass to Grace on the death of the Countess, and then from George and Grace to their children and on and on. He mused 'their children' never a thought he had until he met Grace. George knew the countess expected early results for a first grandchild.

Carefully replacing the book he took down another, 'Livius (Titus) and Lucius Florus. Von Ankunnfft und Urspung Des Roemischen Reichs, 1574'. Nearly four hundred years old, the mortal words of those departed to another, little is left of any human, other than those objects of material, buildings, statues, books (now to be added photographs, records, films) not much to show for a lifetime, for the great majority of mankind, nothing, absolutely nothing. They came, they went, and they are no more. So fragile, yet humanity convinces itself that it is the blueprint for life in the Universe, life must have water, must have oxygen. Why do the feeble brains not understand that limitation contradicts the very Universe, an existence of perpetual change? Would mankind live as long as a light year? It normally doesn't even see out one hundred years. So what do you look for within the Universe to find humanity? Stupid question thought George. Start the other way round that there is life in the Universe, however Earth Humanity has no idea what to look for. Then he got stuck on the first fundamental, what existed before the universe. Light is a life form that we never see, were our eyes created that we are unable to see light? Is it the similar phenomenon that we are unable to stare at the sun for any length of time without damaging them? Why can't humanity see at night in the dark? Many other forms of life can see wonderfully at night. Does too much night-light damage our eyes?

George continued his thinking. Grace and I can expect to be alive together for fifty years. Neither of us met our great grand-parents, neither of us is likely to see our great grandchildren.

Grace, in full hair do looked around the door, laughing she giggled.

"The Countess wants to know if Georgee is alright?"

"I am using my thinking powers to think," then a pause. "Am I supposed to give a thank you speech?"

But she'd gone before he'd finished asking his question. George had a thank you speech ready in case the Countess let him speak, but she would no doubt give a thank you speech. Laughing to himself, 'such is the way of mother-in-law.' That really answered his own question about human frailty. For him no mother, or father, both gone. Perhaps a tear at the moment of their thought, eventually the sisters agreed to attend when friends of the Countess agreed to give them commissioned works that would last a year or two. He suspected the Countess would be paying the bills herself through her friends. Anyway, thankfully his two sisters agreed to support him, new suitable wedding clothing had been provided. A friend of Peter would chauffeur them around for the day. Moving around the shelves with the Russian books he pulled out a long thin book, trying to remember if the size would be called elephant or folio. It contained black and white photographic plates of the Russian royal family with some official state engagements, mainly though family photos of holidays between 1906 and 1914. A small note on the title page written in a handwriting all to familiar with the words, 'page 36, myself playing with Anastasia.' George missed page 36 on the first attempt almost as if it had been lost between pages 34 and 38. Second time he found it but out of place next to page 54, with two circles over two heads, one saying me, one saying Anastasia. Looking almost like twins, there was no mistaking the Countess; if the other name had been Natasha he would not have been surprised as there was a striking likeness. Who was Anastasia? Which of the Russian Royals might she be related to? Continuing to look through the photographs, he found no more of the Countess. Anastasia appeared another three times. From the pictures he could conclude that Anastasia would have been much closer to the Royal Family than the Countess. [Note: Grand Duchess Anastasia Nikolaigvna Romanova 1901-1918?, the youngest daughter of Tsar Nicholas II of Russian, believed to have perished when the Romanov family were executed by the Bolsheviks in 1918.]

Since that time George knew that a number of ladies had claimed to be Anastasia, the latest claimant was Mrs Anna Anderson Manahan. Continuing to look at the many photos, Natasha walked in to say a light lunch had started without him. Looking at his watch three hours had been spent in the library. Staring at her face, the resemblance to the little girls after all these years was absolutely remarkable.

"George you're staring," she commented.

Thinking quickly George responded, "I thought how nice your hair looks."

Like a good dog he followed her, the main dining room opened up for once. Hopelessly outnumbered by females, he dutifully sat next to the not yet blushing bride. Quick introductions from the Countess, hairdresser and assistant, dress maker with assistant, manicurist with assistant. Four girls from Grace's hospital who would carry the long wedding dress train. On the male side the Cathedral organist was receiving last minute instructions from the Countess. Then Grigory, already half in his wedding clothes, Peter fresh from the bathroom. Chatter, chatter, tittle, tattle, chatter, chatter. When Grigory spoke, most unusual as he rarely spoke other than instructions in the big house.

"George, thank goodness the Cuban affair is over. No worry about missile attacks during the wedding." Natasha wasn't impressed by the comment.

"I don't expect Khrushchev or Kennedy to remain in power for very long," he continued forcing Natasha to intervene.

"No politics on a wedding day."

Hardly had George sat down than people started to disappear, getting the main players into Prima Donna status. George felt sure that he had eaten something but it was already a passing memory. Then some caterers appeared to clean up and take away whatever was left. He did remember no alcoholic drinks as normal. All over the house a general hub of noisy activity. George knew the 'make me look beautiful professional's each occupied a separate room. He knew his place now, to be in his bedroom, only to move at 2pm on the instructions of Peter.

In the cathedral the familiar music, 'Here comes the bride' started playing on the organ, the choirboys stood, George with Peter moved to the steps, beyond the choir stalls, directly in front of the altar. There were flowers everywhere, each guest received a posy for the ladies and a buttonhole for the gentlemen, when they arrived. Now the smell of flowers enriched the wafting smoke as the two choir seniors swung the incense in front of the priest, his golden red robes glinting in the late October sunshine piercing through stained glass windows. He led the Countess, holding the arm of Grigory. She was radiant, he with a long row of military medals. George could see the Victoria Cross, the Purple Heart. Grigory had never spoken about his wartime heroics. He was so tall when not bending over his spade or shovel in the garden.

'Here comes the bride' slowed a little to allow the guests to see Grace closely. George turned just enough to catch the full view of her. Guests were clapping. Such a sight. The wedding dress and the train stretching far behind her, he had never seen such a black, black colour the blackest black he had ever, ever seen. No veil. Her eyes covered by a masquerade mask. No bouquet. On her shoulders each carried an AK47 assault rifle, within each hand a grenade minus the pins. She reached the steps, next to George, holding out skeleton fingers still hanging onto decaying flesh. George squeezed the outstretched hand tightly, what had happened to that grenade? Was it with the choir boys, tossing it to each other in a game of catch? Daring not to drop it they burst into song with the organist increasing the tempo making the catch game more exciting. So the priest threw off his cloak joining the ever-increasing mumbo tempo as he cartwheeled up the church. George could see under the wedding dress. He could now see the baby she carried. Grace wore the same clothes she had in Wales under her dress when he left her for dead.

Peter knocked George's bedroom door. Walking in Peter found him in hysterical laugher. Twenty minutes later they arrived by car at the cathedral. Before, when exiting the house as a single man, the Countess gave her Georgee a kiss, as did Natasha to an embarrassed Peter. To the casual observer these elegant beautiful ladies looked like twins, not dressed the same, their physical appearance. George wondered why he had never noticed the truly twin like looks before. (The house worker scrubs up very nicely – Cinderella like).

CHAPTER THIRTY-THREE

With George arriving in church, Esamia's teacher came to collect Mason, Barbara (Tony Computron close by) Miss Moneylegs, and Bruce with tail waging vigorously raced ahead. At school parents and teachers mingled together, outside the main building not yet allowed in to see what the excited children had been preparing for days. Ringing church bells heralded the opening of the doors for all to enter with instant admiration for the transformation to look like the Earth Crust cathedral. Amazement from those Earth Crusters as ushers took them to their seats. In front of them all around the room vast screens showed the real wedding on Earth Crust.

All the girls wore very beautiful wedding dresses, each accompanied by a boy who looked like George. Barbara was of the opinion she could hear a general buzz of excitement. How could that be possible for those who only communicated through the mind (telepathy) if any one down here might be deaf it made no difference whatsoever. Esamia stood on a little platform to explain that everyone in Deep Earth had met George and that today, many Earth Crust years ago, he had married Grace. For the class it had been educational to study the strange marriage customs of Earth Crust humanity and with child-like innocence claiming that the Founding Protectors were showing wedding interest as their noise level had reduced in volume. There was polite applause as she sat down, thinking on with the wedding. Then a surprise Barbara had, with no ones help, produced a sort of wedding cake which several of Tony Computron's friends carried in. It wasn't edible, but it looked real.

Watching the wedding, one of the most excited of all turned out to be Miss Moneylegs. Her journalist background pointing out anyone of any importance as the famous and infamous arrived to sit in waiting for the ceremony to begin. She exclaimed in disbelief every now and again as a really important guest arrived. The media were there, newspaper photographers, television news reporters. She knew not one of them. Such is the way of the media world, here today, sacked tomorrow, those poor radio broadcasters only voices never a face, one would pass them in the street never knowing who they were unless of course they spoke. Then they looked nothing like the picture in your mind when hearing them speak on the radio. As for television reporters, why do they look smaller in the flesh than on the television screen? So Deep Earth humanity watched as the wedding of the year commenced.

Those Naval Officers were already seated at the back of the Church ready to make up the honour guard. When sending out invitations in great politeness the Countess had indicated which side of the church guests should sit. Bride side invitations in pink, grooms side invitations in blue. Not to make life easy for the ushers, rather that the only people who would normally sit on the grooms side were the two sisters with half a dozen work colleagues, not friends. Hollis should out of politeness to the Countess, as well as George, must honour his invitation to the wedding. But! But! But! Work first. Having reviewed the Heather case file, particularly the matter that George flagged that one of her references was that Dr Wilby who met George at Victoria Station on his ill-fated school trip to Switzerland.

The Security Service now knew that had been another name used by one of the Cambridge Spies. Hollis issued a warrant for Heather/Heidi to be arrested. As the wedding ceremony began a team were on route to her London home. Hollis looked again for the umpteenth time at the Countess file he had requested weeks ago. A copy of the same photograph George had looked at only a few hours ago, like George he remained intrigued by the captions over the two little girls, one saying 'me' the other saying 'Anastasia', a page number 36 at the bottom, he thought he would like to have the rest of the book. Could that have been one of the items that Miss Merchant had removed?

Folding the copy pictures in his pocket he though during the wedding reception he could ask the Countess about it. She might be more forthcoming in the expected jovial atmosphere. Calling his driver, looking at his watch, he might just make the end of the Church service. The Countess would not be able to complain he had been rude to George.

After that formal part of 'Man and Wife' exchanging of rings, two chairs were brought forward for the now husband and wife to sot on whilst the Bishop gave his formal speech. Grace knew George would be bored out of his mind, she moved her hand to hold his, then moved both of them to rest on her lap, their golden wedding rings glinting in the candle light. As usual, she was right. George, his mind wondering here there and every-where, not in disrespect, just not his cup of tea. Wandering backwards in time he though about the wheelchair journey from Switzerland. In his mind he now had no doubt that some-where in the wheelchair frame an item from the spying word, particularly as he now knew who Dr Wilby really was. No won-der he had been adamant about George not keeping the chair. Grace squeezed his hand to pay attention as from the pulpit the name of the Countess entered the talk/speech, thanking her for the financial support over so many years in keeping the Russian Community with a place to worship, particularly during the dark days of World War II. To commemorate this happy event and to thank her for such support the current community had raised the funds for a flagstone close to the altar. A church elder escorted a happily surprised Countess to walk her up to the flagstone, George took the initiative and held Grace around the waist and followed the Countess. A blessing was made over the flagstone and it was sprinkled with holy water. Applause from the guests. The simple inscription, 'With thanks to the Countess (no surname) on the happy event of the wedding of her daughter Grace to George, 26th October 1962.'

The Countess was escorted back and George and Grace returned to their place with the chairs now removed. Standing again, thankfully George knew the end of the service was now in sight. Thinking when he boarded that train to Wales he little realized how his world would be turned upside down by beautiful Grace, now a few months later his wife. He knew his Corsham days were over. That very negative existence planning for a nuclear war. Neither he nor Grace were convinced that the rumoured position in Moscow would be of interest to their married plans. Now the strange truth that neither of them needed to work to receive income to live (survive) on. When George had turned around to walk back from the flagstone he could not help but see that of all people, Grigory had a pristine white handkerchief wiping away a team, the exact same scene as seen in marriage ceremonies all over everywhere when a father sees a precious daughter saying, 'I do.' For George, to see solid, safe, sensible Grigory in tears was more than a surprise. If it had been the Count he wouldn't have been surprised, but Grigory!!

George in the same glance around noticed that on returning from the flagstone the Countess and Natasha were holding hands, that picture again (me, Anastasia, like twins.) At last the music from Swan Lake filled the church. It was now time to exit. In turning around Grace whispered,

"You are now the Count."

George whispered back, "Is it time for bed time yet?"

Grace giggled.

Exiting the aisle seemed to take much longer than when he

entered, and not arm in arm, but rather Grace clutching his arm with both hands. Everyone wanted to speak to Grace. George's sisters did manage a smile when he walked past them, followed quickly by the Countess. She smiled at Hollis.

Out through the wide double twelve foot high doors made from best English oak, into daylight, under the archway of Naval formal dress swords; five on each side, camera flashlights all around.

Behind the happy couple, guests poured out chitchatting over the wonderful service, what a wonderful idea about the flagstone for the Countess. Carefully inconspicuous as ever, Hollis mingled, seeing on the outside one face he recognized, a second he had a faint memory off. Without hurry he walked some eighty yards down the road, his driver opened a rear door. Hollis spoke, on the car phone,

"All plain clothes security service staff to the Russian Cathedral. I am sitting outside in my car."

A second call. "All plain clothes police officers in the vicinity of the Russian Cathedral report to me immediately, no sirens, no marked police cards. I am outside the Cathedral notice board. Speed is of the essence."

Dispatching his driver to a point back beyond the Cathedral, conveniently on the other side of the road into a red telephone box. Driver was not an accurate word for the trained marksman. The 'driver' now knew exactly which person Hollis wanted under surveillance. Would time be of the essence? Probably not. No one would be hurrying away with all the photographs being taken, certainly not prior to the bride and groom leaving for the reception.

Having only recently featured on the 'wanted list' the target was unaware of the interest of the Security Service. With photography now progressing this group, that group, always the bride, not always the groom, the Naval guard had taken their places inside the exit gate leading to the wedding cars. Whenever many photographs are taken guests start to fidget wondering what to do unless of course they smoke then it's round a corner for a quick drag within a smoking friendship group. Todays more than experienced photographers, three of them, sense time had arrived for the huge photographs of all the guests. This, as always, is the nightmare moment for photographers. So many people, many more than usual. A substantial cross-section of important guests, every one of them expecting to see their own faces when the photographs appeared for viewing. Good photographers examine the area for this momentous task at the cathedral, enough steps from ground level into the church doors to give ample scope for moving people from here to there, then somewhere else. During the photographers organization, a nightmare as the Countess kept moving from one guest to another, many more guests engaged in private conversations; eventually they had a possible composure. On the third step up the wedding party reading from right to left; sister, sister, George, Grace, Countess, Natasha, Grigory, Peter, then in horseshoe fashion guests behind to the left, to the right, starting on the fourth step. So the wedding party cocooned around by guests. A shout from the cameraman, 'this is a trial don't blink at the flash' everyone blinked at the bright flash. 'No good,' he shouted, 'you all blinked'. Laughter. Flash, flash. He caught them all laughing, not blinking. On the second flash, the voice of Heidi/Heather shouted, 'Romanov', the ten naval officers fired two gun shots each, twenty shots, a moments pause, ten more shots, following instantly two more shots.

(In Deep Earth screens went blank with the Elder Elder turning the off switch. He did not want the children to see anymore. Mason, Barbara, Miss Moneylegs, motionless, statuesque. Bruce made the first noise, whining as only a dog can whine. Everyone erupted into crying.)

George caught Grace falling forward, blood pouring through the white bridal dress, that part of her head above her eyes spread over the guests behind. George held her in his arms as she fell to the floor; he fell with her, with that decapitated head resting in his lap. Now blood red the contents of which spilled over George, now awash in her blood, with spatter of part of the Countess mingling over George with that of Grace. The sisters pulled off their clothing to make blood-absorbing bandages. Hollis, with the first of the plain clothes police moved on the sound of the first shot so before guests could even think of the death horror they were rounded up like sheep to be penned back inside the Church. A sister wiped blood from the face of George. They were strong in this moment of terror. Blood and brains were everywhere, in the moment; the Countess and Natasha fell together, hand in hand. Grigory and Peter slumped as if string puppets when a moment before they had been strong, tall, handsome, now heaped the puppet strings cut.

Perhaps sixty seconds had lapsed and there were plainclothes policemen and Security Service personnel everywhere. It was not what they were expecting to find when they received the urgent call from Hollis. Within minutes the area was flooded with uniformed police and the first of the ambulances arrived. George sat motionless, the sisters behind him holding tightly to any part of his frozen body. From nowhere the two Syds were kneeling in front of George, trying to assist him preventing Grace from sliding into blood on the cold stone steps. Of that small group only George could not cry. The sisters, the Syds, tears torrenting down their faces. Time stood still. That group of the living five felt ice cold. Late October sun rays faded into a slate grey sky. George heard silence, his grip on Grace so tight they were entering rigormortis together.

Ambulance crews stood helpless, not really knowing which corpse to deal with first. With a Metropolitan Police Commander arriving, Hollis exited, going directly to inform the Prime Minister. Meeting him on the steps of Number 10, the Attorney General informed Hollis that a 'D Notice' had already been used to broadcasters, to newspaper proprietors, no lurid story, bare facts only, no pictures. Better no story at all. On arrival the head of the Intelligence Service received instructions to appoint a team to examine what secrets Heather/Heidi could have given to her Soviet masters. At much the same time, the Soviet State Broadcasters read a statement issued by the Kremlin that twelve brave protectors of Soviet Socialist Communism had this day received posthumous awards of Heroes of the Soviet Union. They would receive a group funeral.

Around the table at Number 10, an investigation into the Naval guard of honour best fell to the Security Service itself. They continuing to investigate the arrival of those Soviet illegals several months ago.

[In Deep Earth one of the Elder Elders came to explain why viewing the wedding tragedy had been terminated. George remains alive. Obviously many of you met him after this event. Grace, her mother, Natasha, Grigory, Peter were dead. Twelve people committed suicide. Ten men dressed as Naval Officers, two ladies. Those twelve belonged by belief to the principals of Soviet Communism. What you witnessed is how on Earth Crust politics and religions cause people to kill one another. It remains to us a problem as to how their brains are polluted to have no regard for each other's right to exist peacefully. To us the events cannot be comprehended. That is why no action was taken to help those with such a lack of understanding of the sanctity of life. They deserved the termination brought about by the Whale Anomaly.]

Department 13 arrived to deal with bodies only. Police were left to deal with all other matters. Department 13 took the decision to remove the twelve criminals to Northolt Base. Time passed, having loaded the criminals into a large blacked out van, who could attempt to remove Grace? Moving Grace meant extricating George from his vice-lock holding of Grace, Joy, a terrible name for a sister in this time of despair, from deep inside kissed George's bloody cheeky saying,

"George, in this moment of horror, Grace needs dignity, not to be outside here."

George moved enough for the two Syd's to ease a stretcher under the bloodied corpse. They each carried one end. Joy and Heather, the other end. George stumbled alongside the stretcher holding one of Grace's hands, both covered in red blood.

Into a normal everyday ambulance, none of the splendor of that first ambulance journey to Wales, the same four people with the two Syd's sitting side by side. No emergency sirens or bells. A slow, dignified journey to the hospital mortuary, that same hospital where Grace had first brought George back to life. Joy with Heather, a female police counselor in a following ambulance. Department 13 delicately prepared the Countess, Natasha, Grigory, Peter for the journey to Northolt to make them as presentable as possible for their burial.

George went with Grace into the ice, cold stainless steel clad mortuary. Colleagues from the hospital lined the inside walkway from the ambulance bay to the mortuary, only the odd hardened specialist refrained from sobbing tears of grief. Those two Syd's led him away into a private part of emergency admissions where in total silence the three men were washed down, Joy and Heather enduring the same process a few cubicles away. Their clothes were placed into forensic bags; each one of the five was dressed into laundry fresh replacements. Within time all five were driven together to the house which had been home for him and Grace for eternity. Staff from the Security Service were in residence long before the five returned to do whatever was necessary for George.

The five continued in this way for the next few days. One Syd was on night duty, the other during the day. A member of the Security Service prepared meals. George spoke virtually nothing. Anything he did say was reported back to Hollis. Only two people visited, Sir Peter with the banks legal advisor. On the very first visit Sir Peter only to show George where the numerous safes were hidden in the house, opening them and resetting the combination when George directed. George was now one of the richest men in 1960's England. Sir Peter first broached funeral matters. George had obviously given this a great deal of thought.

"It will be quiet, as early in the morning as convention allows. Five side-by-side but individual graves, that cemetery within walking distance from here. No advance notice other than perhaps yourself, two or three of those close friends of the Countess, my sisters, the two Syds. I will walk there alone. I will return alone. No wake, no mourning. Each grave is to have a simple grave stone, the cemetery staff to be paid to keep the graves tidy, placing seasonal flowers every week. After a few days following the 'goodbye' I would like a meeting to explain what I intend to do but with your agreement it will involve the establishment of 'The Grace Foundation'."

In true blue city style, Sir Peter left having made notes of the instructions with one of those beautiful pens such men have. For once in his life George thanked whoever it might have been in providing a November morning fog, dense enough to keep away spectators with the small group standing alongside five earthen holes, sides precisely manicured to receive shiny polished wooden coffins. On entry into the ground a prayer was said over each coffin, a sprinkling of holy water, a handful of Earth. George had decided how the five would be laid forever, guardians at each end in Grigory and Peter, Countess next to Peter, Natasha next to Grigory, Grace in the middle, family to keep her safe forever, for eternity.

Alone George walked back to his home, all now empty except for the Security Service housekeeper. George placed a small advert in The Times personal column for a housekeeper who would be responsible for running a large London house with others, a live in position, very suitable for a widow.

Two days elapsed from the foggy funeral with George arriving to meet Sir Peter. George had written down in precise detail how 'The Grace Foundation' would be funded, the purpose, 'to

extend understanding of the universe from original thought.'
George had a detailed statement of which funds would go into
the 'Foundation', what funds would be left for him, then on his
death the remainder would go to the 'Foundation' as well. Each
of his sisters was to receive income only, on their death the capital sum returning to the 'Foundation'. Each of the two Syd's to
be purchased, as a gift, a motor vehicle of their own, to keep. Sir
Peter was to sit as a paid trustee of 'The Grace Foundation' with
two others to be chosen. On the first day of Spring 1963 a me-
morial service was to be held for the five of them.

With that George immersed himself into a life of scientific research, scientists came, scientists went, thankful for the opportunity to explore original thinking. Early research discovered
the first galaxy which received the name 'Ecarg' then in the
same area of the Universe, a second galaxy which the international community named A15ATSANA. George knew they
were out there looking out for him.

George dreaming, Peter waiting in the hallway, he inserted his blood red rose into his buttonhole, George cursed those damn green lights. If only Grace lived with me here in Deep Earth Humanity.

Esamia knew what he thought. She thought, 'George, Grace is always with you; never will you be without her. She is part of you, you always part of her. There is no beginning, no end only an onward neutrinos journey, there at inception, there at death, carrying the human spirit into eternity.'

Printed in Poland
by Amazon Fulfillment
Poland Sp. z o.o., Wrocław

50098017R00157